Campaign Pictures of the War in South Africa (1899-1900)

A. G. Hales

Contents

Dedication. 7

Australia's Appeal to England. 8

AUSTRALIA ON THE MARCH. 11

WITH THE AUSTRALIANS. 14

A PRISONER OF WAR. 19

"STOPPING A FEW." 27

AUSTRALIA AT THE WAR. 32

AUSTRALIA ON THE MOVE. 38

SLINGERSFONTEIN. 45

THE WEST AUSTRALIANS. 50

IN A BOER TOWN. 53

BEHIND THE SCENES. 58

A BOER FIGHTING LAAGER. 62

THROUGH BOER GLASSES. 70

LIFE IN THE BOER CAMPS. 76

BATTLE OF CONSTANTIA FARM. 82

WITH RUNDLE IN THE FREE STATE. 94

RED WAR WITH RUNDLE. 100

THE FREE STATERS' LAST STAND. 108

CHARACTER SKETCHES IN CAMP. 119

CHARACTER SKETCHES IN CAMP. 122

CHARACTER SKETCHES IN CAMP. 127

PRESIDENT STEYN. 130

LOUIS BOTHA, ...133

WHITE FLAG TREACHERY. 136

THE BATTLE OF MAGERSFONTEIN. 139

SCOUTS AND SCOUTING. 146

DRISCOLL, KING OF SCOUTS. 146

HUNTING AND HUNTED. 152

WITH THE BASUTOS. 158

MAGERSFONTEIN AVENGED. 166

THE CONDUCT OF THE WAR. 171

HOME AGAIN. 177

CAMPAIGN PICTURES OF
THE WAR IN
SOUTH AFRICA
(1899-1900)

BY

A. G. Hales

Dedication.

This book, such as it is, is dedicated to the man whose kindliness of heart and generous journalistic instincts lifted me from the unknown, and placed me where I had a chance to battle with the best men in my profession. He was the man who found Archibald Forbes, the most brilliant, accurate, and entertaining of all war correspondents. What he did for that splendid genius let Forbes' memoirs tell; what he did for me I will tell myself. He gave me the chance I had looked for for twenty years, and the dearest name in my memory to-day is the name of

SIR JOHN ROBINSON,
Manager of the *Daily News*, London.

Australia's Appeal to England.

We grow weary waiting, England,
For the summons that never comes--
For the blast of the British bugles
And the throb of the British drums.
Our hearts grow sore and sullen
As year by year rolls by,
And your cold, contemptuous actions
Give your fervent words the lie.

Are we only an English market,
Held dear for the sake of trade?
Or are we a part of the Empire,
Close welded as hilt and blade?
If we are to cleave together
As mother and son through life,
Give us our share of the burden,
Let us stand with you in the strife.

If we are to share your glory,
Let the sons whom the South has bred
Lie side by side on your battlefields
With England's heroes dead.
A nation is never a nation
Worthy of pride or place

Till the mothers have sent their firstborn
To look death on the field in the face.

Are we only an English market,
Held dear for the sake of trade?
Or are we a part of the Empire
Close welded as hilt and blade?
If so, let us share your dangers,
Let the glory we boast be real,
Let the boys of the South fight with you,
Let our children taste cold steel.

Do you think we are chicken-hearted?
Do you count us devoid of pride?
Just try us in deadly earnest,
And see how our boys can ride.
We are sick of your empty praises!
If the mother is proud of her son,
Let him do some deed on a hard-fought field,
Then boast what he has done.

A nation is never a nation
Worthy of pride or place
Till the mothers have sent their firstborn
To look death on the field in the face.
Australia is calling to England,
Let England answer the call;
There are smiles for those who come back to us,
And tears for those who may fall.

Bridle to bridle our sons will ride
With the best that Britain has bred,
And all we ask is an open field

And a soldier's grave for our dead.
I have decided to enclose these verses in my book because some critics
have pronounced me anti-English in my sentiments. Heaven alone
knows why; yet the above poem was written and published by me in
Australia just before war was declared between England and the
Republics, at a time when all Australia considered it very
probable that we should have to fight one of the big European
Powers as well as the Boers.

A. G. HALES.

AUSTRALIA ON THE MARCH.

BELMONT BATTLEFIELD.

At two o'clock on the morning of Wednesday, the 6th of the month, the reveille sounded, and the Australians commenced their preparations for the march to join Methuen's army. By 4 a.m. the mounted rifles led the way out of camp, and the toilsome march over rough and rocky ground commenced. The country was terribly rough as we drove the transports up and over the Orange River, and rougher still in the low kopjes on the other side. The heat was simply blistering, but the Australians did not seem to mind it to any great extent; they were simply feverish to get on to the front, but they had to hang back and guard the transports.

At last the hilly country faded behind us. We counted upon pushing on rapidly, but the African mules were a sorry lot, and could make but little headway in the sandy tracks. Still, there was no rest for the men, because at intervals one of Remington's scouts would turn up at a flying gallop, springing apparently from nowhere, out of the womb of the wilderness, to inform us that flying squads of Boers were hanging round us. But so carefully watchful were the Remingtons that the Boers had no chance of surprising us. No sooner did the scouts inform us of their approach in any direction than our rifles swung forward ready to give them a hearty Australian reception. This made the march long and toilsome, though we never had a chance to fire a shot. At 5.30 we marched with all our transports into Witteput, the wretched little mules being the only distressed portion of the contingent.

At Witteput the news reached us that a large party of the enemy had managed to pass between General Methuen's men and ourselves, and had invested Belmont, out of which place the British troops had driven them a few weeks previously. We had no authentic news concerning this movement. Our contingent spread out on the hot sand at Witteput, panting for a drop of rain from the lowering clouds that hung heavily overhead. Yet hot, tired, and thirsty as we were, we yet found time to look with wonder at the sky above us. The men from the land of the Southern Cross are used to gorgeous sunsets, but never had we looked upon anything like this. Great masses of coal-black clouds frowned down upon us, flanked by fiery crimson cloud banks, that looked as if they would rain blood, whilst the atmosphere was dense enough to half-stifle one. Now and again the thunder rolled out majestically, and the lightning flashed from the black clouds into the red, like bayonets through smoke banks.

Yet we had not long to wait and watch, for within half an hour after our arrival the Colonel galloped down into our midst just as the evening ration was being given out. He held a telegram aloft, and the stillness that fell over the camp was so deep that each man could hear his neighbour's heart beat. Then the Colonel's voice cut the stillness like a bugle call. "Men, we are needed at Belmont; the Boers are there in force, and we have been sent for to relieve the place. I'll want you in less than two hours." It was then the men showed their mettle. Up to their feet they leapt like one man, and they gave the Colonel a cheer that made the sullen, halting mules kick in their harness. "We are ready now, Colonel, we'll eat as we march," and the "old man" smiled, and gave the order to fall in, and they fell in, and as darkness closed upon the land they marched out of Witteput to the music of the falling rain and the thunder of heaven's artillery.

All night long it was march, halt, and "Bear a hand, men," for those thrice accursed mules failed us at every pinch. In vain the niggers plied the whips of green hide, vain their shouts of encouragement, or painfully shrill anathemas; the mules had the whip hand of us, and they kept it. But, in spite of it all, in the chilly dawn of the African morning, our fellows, with their shoulders well back, and heads held high, marched into Belmont, with every man safe and sound, and every waggon complete.

Then the Gordons turned out and gave us a cheer, for they had passed us in the train as we crossed the line above Witteput, and they knew, those veterans from Indian wars, what our raw Volunteers had done; they had been on their feet from two o'clock on Wednesday morning until five o'clock of the following day, with the heat at 122 in the shade, and bitter was their wrath when they learnt that the Boer spies, who swarm all over the country, had heralded their coming, so that the enemy had only waited to plant a few shells into Belmont before disappearing into the hills beyond. That was the cruel part of it. They did not mind the fatigue, they did not worry about the thirst or the hunger, but to be robbed of a chance to show the world what they could do in the teeth of the enemy was gall and wormwood to them, and the curses they sent after the discreet Boer were weird, quaint, picturesque, and painfully prolific.

We are lying with the Gordons now, waiting for the Boers to come along and try to take Belmont, and our fellows and the "Scotties" are particularly good chums, and it is the cordial wish of both that they may some day give the enemy a taste of the bayonet together.

WITH THE AUSTRALIANS.

BELMONT.

Australia has had her first taste of war, not a very great or very important performance, but we have buried our dead, and that at least binds us more closely to the Motherland than ever before. The Queenslanders, the wild riders, and the bushmen of the north-eastern portion of the continent have been the first to pay their tribute to nationhood with the life blood of her sons, two of whom--Victor James and McLeod--were buried by their comrades on the scene of action a couple of days ago, whilst half a dozen others, including Lieutenant Aide, fell more or less seriously wounded. The story of the fight is simply told; there is no necessity for any wild vapouring in regard to Australian courage, no need for hysterical praise. Our fellows simply did what they were told to do in a quiet and workmanlike manner, just as we who know them expected that they would; we are all proud of them, and doubly proud that the men in the fight with them were our cousins from Canada.

The most noteworthy fact about the engagement is to be gleaned by noting that the Australians adopted Boer tactics, and so escaped the slaughter that has so often fallen to the lot of the British troops when attacking similar positions. Before describing the fight it may be as well to give some slight idea of the disposition of the opposing forces. Our troops held the railway line all the way from Cape Town to Modder River. At given distances, or at points of strategic importance, strong bodies of men are posted to keep the Boers from raiding, or from interfering with the railway or telegraph lines. Such a force, consisting of Munster Fusiliers, two guns of R.H. Artillery, the Canadians, and the Queenslanders, were posted at Belmont under Colonel Pilcher. The enemy had no fixed camping ground. Mounted on hardy Basuto ponies, carrying no provisions but a few mealies and a little bil-tong, armed only with rifles, they sweep incessantly from place to place, and are an everlasting source of annoyance to us. At one moment they may be hovering in the kopjes around us at Enslin, waiting to get a chance to sneak into the kopjes that immediately overlook our camp, but thanks to the magnificent scouting qualities of the Victorian Mounted Rifles, they have never been able to do so. During the night they disperse, and take up their abode on surrounding farms as peaceful tillers of the soil. In a day or so they organise again, and swoop down on some other place, such as Belmont. Their armies, under men like Cronje or Joubert, seldom move from strongly-entrenched positions.

The people I am referring to as reivers are farmers recruited by local leaders, and are a particularly dangerous class of people to deal with, as they know every inch of this most deceptive country. As soon as they are whipped they make off to wives and home, and meet the scouts with a bland smile and outstretched hand. It is no use trying to get any information out of them, for no man living can look so much like an unmitigated fool when he wants to as the ordinary, every-day farmer of the veldt. I know Chinamen exceptionally well, I have had an education in the ways of the children of Confucius; but no Chinaman that I have come in con-tact with could ever imitate the half-idiotic smile, the patient, ox-like placidity of countenance, the meek, religious look of holy resignation to the will of Providence which comes naturally to the ordinary Boer farmer. It is this faculty which made our very clever Army Intelligence people rank the farmer of the veldt as a fool. Yet, if I am any judge, and I have known men in many lands, our friend of the veldt is as clever and as crafty as any Oriental I have yet mixed with.

Now for the Australian fight. On the day before Christmas, Colonel Pilcher, at Belmont, got wind of the assemblage of a considerable Boer force at a place 30 miles away, called Sunnyside Farm, and he determined to try to attack it before the enemy could get wind of his intention. To this end he secured every nigger for some miles around--which proved his good sense, as the niggers are all in the pay of the Boers, no matter how loyal they may pretend to be to the British, a fact which the British would do well to take heed of, for it has cost them pretty dearly already. On Christmas Eve he started out, taking two guns of the Royal Navy Artillery, a couple of Maxims, all the Queenslanders, and a few hundred Canadians. Colonel Pilcher's force numbered in all about 600 men. He marched swiftly all night, and got to Sunnyside Farm in good time Christmas Day. The Boers had not a ghost of an idea that our men were near them, and were completely beaten at their own game, the surprise party being complete. The enemy were found in a laager in a strong position in some rather steep kopjes, and it was at once evident that they were expecting strong reinforcements from surrounding farms. Colonel Pilcher at once extended his forces so as to try to surround the kopjes. Whilst this was going on, Lieutenant Aide, with four Queensland troopers, was sent to the far left of what was supposed to be the Boer position. His orders were to give notice of any attempt at retreat on the part of the enemy. He did his work well. Getting close to the kopje, he saw a number of the enemy slinking off, and at once challenged them. As he did so a dozen Boers dashed out of the kopje, and Aide opened fire on them, which caused the Boers to fire a volley at him. Lieutenant Aide fell from his horse with two bullets in his body; one went through the fleshy part of his stomach, entering his body sideways, the other went into his thigh. A trooper named McLeod was shot through the heart, and fell dead. Both the other troopers were wounded. Trooper Rose caught a horse, and hoisted his lieutenant into the saddle, and sent him out of danger.

Meantime the R.H. Battery, taking range from Lieutenant Aide's fire, opened out on the enemy. Their guns put a great fear into the Boers, and a general bolt set in. The Boers fired as they cleared, and if our fellows had been formed up in the style usual to the British army in action, we should have suffered heavily; but the Queensland bushmen had dropped behind cover, and soon had complete possession of the kopjes; another trooper named Victor Jones was shot through the brain, and fourteen others were more or less badly wounded. The Boers then surrendered. We took 40 prisoners, and found about 14 dead Boers on the ground, besides a dozen wounded. They were all Cape Dutch, no Transvaalers being found in their ranks. We secured 40,000 rounds of their ammunition, 300 Martini rifles, and only one Mauser rifle, which was in the possession of the Boer commander. After destroying all that we took, we moved on, and had a look at some of the farms near by, as from some of the documents found in camp it was certain that the whole district was a perfect nest of rebellion. Quite a little store of arms and ammunition was discovered by this means, and the occupants of the farms were therefore transported to Belmont. Our fellows carried the little children and babies in their arms all the way, and marched into Belmont singing, with the little ones on their shoulders. Every respect was shown to the women, old and young, and to the old men, but the young fellows were closely guarded all the time. The Canadians did not lose a single man, neither did any of the others except the Queenslanders.

Another Boer commando, about 1,000 strong, with two batteries of artillery, is now hovering in the ranges away to the north-west of Enslin, but Colonel Hoad is not likely to be tempted out to meet them, since his orders are to hold Enslin against attack. However, should they venture to make a dash for Enslin, they will get a pretty bad time, as the Australians there are keen for a fight.

Concerning farming, it is an unknown quantity here, as we in Australia understand it. These people simply squat down wherever they can find a natural catchment for water. There is no clearing to be done, as the land is quite devoid of timber. They put nigger labour on, and build a farmhouse. These farmhouses are much better built than those which the average pioneer farmer in Australia owns. They make no attempt at adornment, but build plain, substantial houses, containing mostly about six rooms. The roofs are mostly flat, and the frontages plain to ugliness. They do no fencing, except where they go in for ostrich breeding. When they farm for feathers they fence with wire about six feet in height. This kind of farming is very popular with the better class of Boers, as it entails very little labour, and no outlay beyond the initial expense. They raise just enough meal to keep themselves, but do not farm for the market. They breed horses and cattle; the horses are a poor-looking lot, as the Boers do not believe much in blood. They never ride or work mares, but use them as brood stock. This is a bad plan, as young and immature mares breed early on the veldt, and throw weedy stock. Their cattle, however, are attended to on much better lines, and most of the beef that I have seen would do credit to any station in Australia, or any American ranch. They mostly raise a few sheep and goats; the sheep are a poor lot, the wool is of a very inferior class, and the mutton poor. I don't know much about goats, so will pass them, though I very much doubt if any Australian squatter would give them grass room.

On most of the farms a small orchard is found enclosed in stone walls. Here again the ignorance of the Boers is very marked; the fruit is of poor quality, though the variety is large. Thus, one finds in these orchards pears, apples, grapes, plums, pomegranates, peaches, quinces, apricots, and almonds. The fruit is harsh, small, and flavourless, owing to bad pruning, want of proper manure, and good husbandry generally. The Boer seems to think that he has done all that is required of him when he has planted a tree; all that follows he leaves to nature, and he would much rather sit down and pray for a beautiful harvest than get up and work for it. He is a great believer in the power of prayer. He prays for a good crop of fruit; if it comes he exalts himself and takes all the credit; if the crop fails he folds his hands and remarks that it was God's will that things should so come to pass. He knocks all the work he can out of his niggers, but does precious little himself. In stature he is mostly tall, thin, and active. He moves with a quick, shuffling gait, which is almost noiseless. Some of his women folk are beautiful, while others are fat and clumsy, and are never likely to have their portraits hung on the walls of the Royal Academy.

A PRISONER OF WAR.

BLOEMFONTEIN HOSPITAL.

I little fancied when I sat at my ease in my tent in the British camp that my next epistle would be written from a hospital as a prisoner, but such is the case, and, after all, I am far more inclined to be thankful than to growl at my luck. Let me tell the story, for it is typical of this peculiar country, and still more peculiar war. I had been writing far into the night, and had left the letter ready for post next day. Then, with a clear conscience, I threw myself on my blankets, satisfied that I was ready for what might happen next. Things were going to happen, but though the night was big with fate there was no warning to me in the whispering wind. Some men would have heard all sorts of sounds on such a night, but I am not built that way I suppose. Anyway, I heard nothing until, half an hour before dawn, a voice jarred my ear with the news that "there was something on, and I'd better fly round pretty sharp if I did not mean to miss it."

By the light of my lantern I saddled my horse, and snatched a hasty cup of coffee and a mouthful of biscuit, and as the little band of Tasmanians moved from Rensburg I rode with them. Where they were going, or what their mission, I did not know, but I guessed it was to be no picnic. The quiet, resolute manner of the officers, the hushed voices, the set, stern faces of the young soldiers, none of whom had ever been under fire before, all told me that there was blood in the air, so I asked no questions, and sat tight in my saddle. As the daylight broke over the far-stretching veldt, I saw that two other correspondents were with the party, viz., Reay, of the Melbourne *Herald*, and Lambie, poor, ill-fated Lambie, of the *Melbourne Age*. For a couple of hours we trotted along without incident of any kind, then we halted at a farmhouse, the name of which I have forgotten. There we found Captain Cameron encamped with the rest of the Tasmanians, and after a short respite the troops moved outward again, Captain Cameron in command; we had about eighty men, all of whom were mounted.

As we rode off I heard the order given for every man to "sit tight and keep his eyes open." Then our scouts put spurs to their horses and dashed away on either wing, skirting the kopjes and screening the main body, and so for another hour we moved without seeing or hearing anything to cause us trouble. By this time we had got into a kind of huge basin, the kopjes were all round us, but the veldt was some miles in extent. I knew at a glance that if the Boers were in force our little band was in for a bad time, as an enemy hidden in those hills could watch our every movement on the plain, note just where we intended to try and pass through the chain of hills, and attack us with unerring certainty and suddenness. All at once one of our scouts, who had been riding far out on our left flank, came flying in with the news that the enemy was in the kopjes in front of us, and he further added that he thought they intended to surround our party if possible. Captain Cameron ordered the men to split into two parties, one to move towards the kopjes on our right; the other to fall back and protect our retreat, if such a move became necessary. Mr. Lambie and I decided to move on with the advance party, and at a hard gallop we moved away towards a line of kopjes that seemed higher than any of the others in the belt. As we neared those hills it seemed to us that there were no Boers in possession, and that nothing would come of the ride after all, and we drew bridle and started to discuss the situation. At that time we were not far from the edge of some kopjes, which, though lying low, were covered with rocky boulders and low scrub.

We had drifted a few hundred yards behind the advance party, but were a good distance in front of the rearguard, when a number of horsemen made a dash from the kopjes which we were skirting, and the rifles began to speak. There was no time for poetry; it was a case of "sit tight and ride hard," or surrender and be made prisoners. Lambie shouted to me: "Let's make a dash, Hales," and we made it. The Boers were very close to us before we knew anything concerning their presence. Some of them were behind us, and some extended along the edge of the kopjes by which we had to pass to get to the British line in front, all of them were galloping in on us, shooting as they rode, and shouting to us to surrender, and, had we been wise men, we would have thrown up our hands, for it was almost hopeless to try and ride through the rain of lead that whistled around us. It was no wonder we were hit; the wonder to me is that we were not filled with lead, for some of the bullets came so close to me that I think I should know them again if I met them in a shop-window. We were racing by this time, Lambie's big chestnut mare had gained a length on my little veldt pony, and we were not more than a hundred yards away from the Mauser rifles that had closed in on us from the kopjes. A voice called in good English: "Throw up your hands, you d---- fools." But the galloping fever was on us both, and we only crouched lower on our horses' backs, and rode all the harder, for even a barn-yard fowl loves liberty.

All at once I saw my comrade throw his hands up with a spasmodic gesture. He rose in his stirrups, and fairly bounded high out of his saddle, and as he spun round in the air I saw the red blood on the white face, and I knew that death had come to him sudden and sharp. Again the rifles spoke, and the lead was closer to me than ever a friend sticks in time of trouble, and I knew in my heart that the next few strides would settle things. The black pony was galloping gamely under my weight. Would he carry me safely out of that line of fire, or would he fail me? Suddenly something touched me on the right temple; it was not like a blow; it was not a shock; for half a second I was conscious. I knew I was hit; knew that the reins had fallen from my nerveless hands, knew that I was lying down upon my horse's back, with my head hanging below his throat. Then all the world went out in one mad whirl. Earth and heaven seemed to meet as if by magic. My horse seemed to rise with me, not to fall, and then--chaos.

When next I knew I was still on this planet I found myself in the saddle again, riding between two Boers, who were supporting me in the saddle as I swayed from side to side. There was a halt; a man with a kindly face took my head in the hollow of his arm, whilst another poured water down my throat. Then they carried me to a shady spot beneath some shrubbery, and laid me gently down. One man bent over me and washed the blood that had dried on my face, and then carefully bound up my wounded temple. I began to see things more plainly--a blue sky above me; a group of rough, hardy men, all armed with rifles, around me. I saw that I was a prisoner, and when I tried to move I soon knew I was damaged.

The same good-looking young fellow with the curly beard bent over me again. "Feel any better now, old fellow?" I stared hard at the speaker, for he spoke like an

Englishman, and a well-educated one, too. "Yes, I'm better. I'm a prisoner, ain't I?" "Yes." "Are you an Englishman?" I asked. He laughed. "Not I," he said, "I'm a Boer born and bred, and I am the man who bowled you over. What on earth made you do such a fool's trick as to try and ride from our rifles at that distance?" "Didn't think I was welcome in these parts." "Don't make a jest of it, man," the Boer said gravely; "rather thank God you are a living man this moment. It was His hand that saved you; nothing else could have done so." He spoke reverently; there was no cant in the sentiment he uttered--his face was too open, too manly, too fearless for hypocrisy. "How long is it since I was knocked over?" "About three hours." "Is my comrade dead?" "Quite dead," the Boer replied; "death came instantly to him. He was shot through the brain." "Poor beggar!" I muttered, "and he'll have to rot on the open veldt, I suppose?"

The Boer leader's face flushed angrily. "Do you take us for savages?" he said. "Rest easy. Your friend will get decent burial. What was his rank?" "War correspondent." "And your own?" "War correspondent also. My papers are in my pocket somewhere." "Sir," said the Boer leader, "you dress exactly like two British officers; you ride out with a fighting party, you try to ride off at a gallop under the very muzzles of our rifles when we tell you to surrender. You can blame no one but yourselves for this day's work." "I blame no man; I played the game, and am paying the penalty." Then they told me how poor Lambie's horse had swerved between myself and them after Lambie had fallen, then they saw me fall forward in the saddle, and they knew I was hit. A few strides later one of them had sent a bullet through my horse's head, and he had rolled on top of me. Yet, with it all, I had escaped with a graze over the right temple and a badly knocked-up shoulder. Truly, as the Boer said, the hand of God must have shielded me.

For a day and a half I lay at that laager whilst our wounded men were brought in, and here I should like to say a word to the people of England. Our men, when wounded, are treated by the Boers with manly gentleness and kind consideration. When we left the laager in an open trolly, we, some half-dozen Australians, and about as many Boers, all wounded, were driven for some hours to a small hospital, the name of which I do not know. It was simply a farmhouse turned into a place for the wounded. On the road thither we called at many farms, and at every one men, women, and children came out to see us. Not one taunting word was uttered in our hearing, not one braggart sentence passed their lips. Men brought us cooling drinks, or moved us into more comfortable positions on the trolly. Women, with gentle fingers, shifted bandages, or washed wounds, or gave us little dainties that come so pleasant in such a time; whilst the little children crowded round us with tears running down their cheeks as they looked upon the bloodstained khaki clothing of the wounded British. Let no man or woman in all the British Empire whose son or husband lies wounded in the hands of the Boers fear for his welfare, for it is a foul slander to say that the Boers do not treat their wounded well. England does not treat her own men better than the Boers treat the wounded British, and I am writing of that which I have seen and know beyond the shadow of a doubt.

From the little farmhouse hospital I was sent on in an ambulance train to the hospital at Springfontein, where all the nurses and medical staff are foreigners, all of them trained and skilful. Even the nurses had a soldierly air about them. Here everything was as clean as human industry could make it, and the hospital was worked like a piece of military mechanism. I only had a day or two here, and then I was sent by train in an ambulance carriage to the capital of the Orange Free State, and here I am in Bloemfontein Hospital. There are a lot of our wounded here, both officers and men, some of whom have been here for months.

I have made it my business to get about amongst the private soldiers, to question them concerning the treatment they have received since the moment the Mauser rifles tumbled them over, and I say emphatically that in every solitary instance, without one single exception, our countrymen declare that they have been grandly treated. Not by the hospital nurses only, not by the officials alone, but by the very men whom they were fighting. Our "Tommies" are not the men to waste praise on any men unless it is well deserved, but this is just about how "Tommy" sums up the situation:

"The Boer is a rough-looking beggar in the field, 'e don't wear no uniform, 'nd 'e don't know enough about soldiers' drill to keep himself warm, but 'e can fight in 'is own bloomin' style, which ain't our style. If 'e'd come out on the veldt, 'nd fight us our way, we'd lick 'im every time, but when it comes to fightin' in the kopjes, why, the Boer is a dandy, 'nd if the rest of Europe don't think so, only let 'em have a try at 'im 'nd see. But when 'e has shot you he acts like a blessed Christian, 'nd bears no malice. 'E's like a bloomin' South Sea cocoanut, not much to look at outside, but white 'nd sweet inside when yer know 'im, 'nd it's when you're wounded 'nd a prisoner that you get a chance to know 'im, see." And "Tommy" is about correct in his judgment.

The Boers have made most excellent provision for the treatment of wounded after battle. All that science can do is done. Their medical men fight as hard to save a British life or a British limb as medical men in England would battle to save life or limb of a private person. At the Bloemfontein Hospital everything is as near perfection, from a medical and surgical point, as any sane man can hope to see. It is an extensive institution. One end is set apart for the Boer wounded, the other for the British. No difference is made between the two in regard to accommodation--food, medical attendance, nursing, or visiting. Ministers of religion come and go daily--almost hourly--at both ends. Our men, when able to walk, are allowed to roam around the grounds, but, of course, are not allowed to go beyond the gates, being prisoners of war. Concerning our matron (Miss M.M. Young) and nurses, all I can say is that they are gentlewomen of the highest type, of whom any nation in the world might well be proud.

I have met one or two old friends since I came here, notably Lieutenant Bowling, of the Australian Horse, who is now able to get about, and is cheerful and jolly. Lieutenant Bowling has his right thumb shot off, and had a terribly close call for his life, a Mauser bullet going into his head alongside his right eye, and coming out just in front of the right ear. His friends need not be anxious concerning him; he is quite out of danger, and he and I have killed a few tedious hours blowing tobacco smoke skywards, and chatting about life in far off Australia. Another familiar face was that of an English private, named Charles Laxen, of the Northumberlands, who was wounded at Stormberg. I am told that he displayed excellent pluck before he was laid out, firstly by a piece of shell on the side of the head, and, later, by a Mauser bullet through the left knee. He is getting along O.K., but will never see service as a soldier again on account of the wounded leg.

I had written to the President of the Orange Free State, asking him to grant me my liberty on the ground that I was a non-combatant. Yesterday Mr. Steyn courteously sent his private secretary and carriage to the hospital with an intimation that I should be granted an interview. I was accordingly driven down to what I believe was the Stadt House. In Australia we should term it the Town Hall. The President met me, and treated me very courteously, and, after chatting over my capture and the death of my friend, he informed me that I might have my liberty as soon as I considered myself sufficiently recovered to travel. He offered me a pass *via* Lourenco Marques, but I pointed out that if I were sent that way I should be so far away from my work as to be practically useless to my paper. The President explained to me that it was not his wish nor the desire of his colleagues to hamper me in any way in regard to my work. "What we want more than anything else," remarked the President, "is that the world shall know the truth, and nothing but the truth, in reference to this most unhappy war, and we will not needlessly place obstruction in your way in your search for facts; if we can by any means place you in the British lines we will do so. If we find it impossible to do that you must understand that there is some potent reason for it." So I let that question drop, feeling satisfied that everything that a sensible man has a right to ask would be done on my behalf.

President Steyn is a man of a notable type. He is a big man physically, tall and broad, a man of immense strength, but very gentle in his manner, as so many exceptionally strong men are. He has a typical Dutch face, calm, strong, and passionless. A man not easily swayed by outside agencies; one of those persons who think long and earnestly before embarking upon a venture, but, when once started, no human agency would turn him back from the line of conduct he had mapped out for himself. He is no ignorant back-block politician, but a refined, cultured gentleman, who knows the full strength of the British Empire; and, knowing it, he has defied it in all its might, and will follow his convictions to the bitter end, no matter what that end may be. He introduced me to a couple of gentlemen whose names are very dear to the Free Staters, viz., Messrs. Fraser and Fischer, and whilst the interview lasted nothing was talked of but the war, and it struck me very forcibly that not one of those men had any hatred in their hearts towards the British people. "This," said the President, "is not a war between us and the British people on any question of principle; it is a war forced upon us by a band of capitalistic adventurers, who have hoodwinked the British public and dragged them into an unholy, an unjust struggle with a people whose only desire was to live at peace with all men. We do not hate your nation; we do not hate your soldiers, though they fight against us; but we do hate and despise the men who have brought a cruel war upon us for their own evil ends, whilst they try to cloak their designs in a mantle of righteousness and liberty." I may not have given the exact words of the President, as I am writing from memory, but I think I have given his exact sentiments; and, if I am any judge of human nature, the love of his country is the love of his life.

"STOPPING A FEW."

I saw him first, years ago upon a station in New South Wales; a neat, smart figure less than nine stone in weight, but it was nine stone of fencing wire full of the electricity of life. He was in the stockyard when I first saw him, working like any ordinary station hand, for it was the busy portion of the year, and at such times the squatters' sons work like any hired hand, only a lot harder, if they are worth their salt, and have not been bitten by the mania for dudeism during their college course in the cities. There was nothing of the dandy about this fellow. From head to heel he was a man's son, full of the vim of living, strong with the lust of life. The sweat ran down his face, dirty with the dust kicked up by the cattle in the stockyard. His clothes were not guiltless of mire, for he had been knocked over more than once that morning, and there was an edge upon his voice as he rapped out his orders to the stockmen who were working with him. He did not look in the least degree pretty, and there was not enough poetry about him just then to make an obituary jingle on a tombstone. I little thought that day that a time would come when he would prove the glory of his Australian breeding in the teeth of an enemy's guns on African soil.

I saw him again--under silk this time--as a gentleman rider. He was the same quiet, cool little fellow, grey-eyed, steel-lipped, stout-hearted, with "hands" that Archer might have envied. He rode at his fences that day as the Australian amateurs can ride, with a rip and a rattle, with the long, loose leg, the hands well down, and head up and back, and "Over or Through" was his motto. I did not know him to speak to in those old days. We were to shake hands under peculiar circumstances away in a foreign land, in a foreign hospital, both of us prisoners of war, both of us wounded. That was where and how I spoke to little Dowling, lieutenant in the First Australian Horse, as game a sample of humanity as ever threw leg over saddle or loosed a rifle at a foe. He came to my bedside the morning after I entered the hospital, and standing over me with a green shade over one eye, and one hand in a sling, said laconically:

"Australian ain't you?"

"Yes, by gad, and I know you." He reached out his left hand, and placed it in mine.

"Been 'stopping one'?" he remarked.

"Only a graze, thank God," I replied.

Then the matron and the German doctor, as fine a gentleman as ever drew breath, came along to have a look at me, and he was turned out; but we chummed, as Australians have a knack of doing in time of trouble, and I tried hard to get him to talk of his adventures, but he was a mummy on that subject. He would not yarn about his own doings on the fateful day when he was laid out, though he was eloquent enough concerning the doings of his comrades. All I could get out of him in regard to his own part in the fray was that his men and he had been ambushed, and that he had "stopped one" with his head, and one with his hand, and another with his leg, his horse had been killed, and he knew mighty little more about it until he found himself in the hands of the Boers, who had treated him well and kindly. I asked the matron about his wounds, and she told me that a bullet had entered the corner of his right eye, coming out by the right ear, ruining the sight for ever. Another had carried away his right thumb, and a couple had passed through his right leg, one just below the groin, another 'just above the knee. That was what he modestly termed "stopping a few."

After I had been in hospital a little while, the matron gave me leave to prowl about to pick up "copy," and my feet soon led me into the ward where the wounded Dutchmen were lying, and there I met a couple of burghers who had been in the *melee* when Dowling was gathered in. One of them was a handsome Swede, with a long blonde moustache, that fell with a glorious sweep on to his chest, as the Viking's did of old. He was an adventurer, who knew how to take his gruel like a man. He had joined the Boers because he thought they were the weaker side, and had done his best for them. He saw Dowling talking to me one day, and asked me if I knew the "little devil." "Yes," I replied, "we are countrymen." "Americans?" he asked. "No, Australians." He raised himself on his elbow, whilst I propped his shoulders up with pillows, and as he remained thus he gazed admiringly at the slight, boyish figure which limped lazily through the ward. "What a little tiger cat he is," muttered the recumbent giant. "I thought we'd have to kill him before we got him, and that would have been a shame, for I hate to kill brave men when they have no chance." "Tell me about it," I said. "He won't give me any information himself, only tells me he 'stopped a few.'" The big, handsome Swede laughed a mighty laugh under his great blonde moustache.

"Stopped a few, did he? If all your fellows fought it out to the bitter end as he did, we should run short of ammunition before the war was very old."

A Boer nurse came over and asked us "what nonsense we made one with the other, that we did laugh to ourselves like two hens clucking over one egg." The blonde giant turned his joyous blue eyes upon her, and paid her a compliment which caused her to bridle, whilst the blood swept like a race-horse in its stride over neck, and cheek, and brow, causing her dainty, girlish face to look prettier than ever. "Ah, little Eckhardt," he whispered, and then murmured something in Dutch. I did not understand the words, but there was something in the sound of the adventurer's voice which conjured up a moonlit garden, a rose-crowned gate swinging on one hinge, a girl on one side and a fool on the other. The nurse tossed her pretty head with its wealth of jet black hair, and as she smoothed his pillows with infinite care she murmured: "Fighting and making love, making love and fighting--it is all one to you, Karl. I know you, you big pirate; you are as a hen that lays away from home." And with that round of shrapnel she left us.

Karl got rid of a fourteen-pound sigh, which sounded like the bursting of a lyddite shell. Then he slipped his hand under his pillow and drew forth a flask of "Dop." "Drink to her," he said. "To whom?" I asked, falling in with the humour of the man. "To the girl I love," he muttered like a schoolboy. "Which one, Karl?" I asked, and I laughed as I spoke. He snatched the brandy from my hand, lifted the flask to his lips, and drank deeply. Then again his mighty laugh ran through the hospital ward. "Which one?" he said; "why, all of them, God bless them. But the maid that is nearest is always the dearest." "Shut up, you Goth," I said, "and tell me about Dowling, for some day I shall write the story, and I would like to hear it from the lips of one of his enemies." The Swede lay back upon his pillow, stroking the golden horns of hair that fell each side of his mouth, and I noticed that the lips which a little time before had been smiling into the face of the nurse were now hard set and stern. So I could have imagined him standing by the side of his gun, or rushing headlong on to our ranks. A man with a mouth like that could not flinch in the hour of peril if he tried, for his jaw had the Kitchener grip, the antithesis of the parrot pout of the dandy, or the flabby fulness of the fool.

"It was in the fore part of the day," he said at length. "We had been posted snugly overnight on both sides of two ranges of kopjes, for we knew that your fellows were going to attempt a reconnaissance next day. How did we know? you ask. Well, comrade, ask no questions of that kind, and I'll tell you no lies. The truth I won't tell you."

But we knew, and we were ready. We were disappointed when we saw the force, for we had expected something much bigger, and had made arrangements for a larger capture. It was only a troop of Australian Horse that came our way, and 'the little devil' was riding at their head. We bided our time, hoping that he might be followed by more men, and, above all, we expected and wanted some guns; but they did not put in an appearance, so we loosed upon the little troop. They were fairly ambushed; they did not know that a rifle was within miles of them until the bullets were singing through their ranks. Horses plunged suddenly forward, reared, lurched now to the near side, now to the off, then blundered forward on their heads, for many of our men fired at the chargers instead of at the riders. Dowling's horse went down with a bullet between the flap of the saddle and the crease of the shoulder, and the little chap went spinning over his head amongst the rocks. But a good many saddles were empty. He was up in a moment, yelling to his men to ride for their lives, and they rode. We charged from cover, and rode down on the men who had fallen, and as we closed in on them your countryman lifted his rifle and loosed on us.

"One of our fellows took a flying shot at him at close quarters, for his rifle was talking the language of death, and that is a tongue no man likes to listen to. The bit of lead took him in the eye and came out by his ear, and down he went. But he climbed up in a moment, and his rifle was going to his shoulder again, when I fired to break his arm, and carried his thumb away--the thumb of the right hand, I think. The rifle clattered on to the rocks, but as we drew round him he pulled his revolver with his one good hand, and started to pot us. He looked a gamecock as he stood there in the sunlight, his face all bathed in blood, and his shattered hand hanging numbed beside him. So we gave him a couple in the legs to steady him, and down by his dead horse he went; but even then he was as eager for fight as a grass widow is for compliments, and it was not until Jan Viljoens jammed the butt of his rifle on the crown of his head that he stretched himself out and took no further part in that circus. We carried him into our lines, and handed him over to our medical man, though even as we gathered him up our scouts came galloping in to tell us that a big body of British troops were advancing to cut us off from our main body. But we knew that if we left him until your ambulance people found him, it was a million to one that he would bleed to death amongst the rocks, and he was too good a fighter and too brave a fellow to be left to a fate like that. Had he shown the white feather we might have left him to the asvogels."

"And so," said I, "that is how little Dowling, son of Australia, came, as he said, 'to stop a few' for the sake of his breeding. If I live, the men out in the sunny South-land shall hear how he did it, and his name shall be known round the gold-hunters' camp fires, and be mentioned with pride where the cattle drovers foregather to talk of the African war and the men who fought and fell there."

AUSTRALIA AT THE WAR.

ENSLIN CAMP.

Lately I have been over a very considerable tract of country in the saddle. I might remain at one spot and glean the information from various sources, but do not care to do my business in that manner, simply because one is then at the mercy of one's informants. I find it quite hard enough to get at the truth even when it is personally sought for. It is really astounding how lies increase and multiply as they spread from camp to camp. At one spot a fellow ventilates an opinion that a big battle will be fought next day at a certain spot; some other person catches a portion of the conversation, and promptly tells his neighbour that a big battle has taken place at the spot mentioned. A little later a passing train pulls up at that camp, and a party possessing a picturesque and vivid imagination at once informs the guard that a fearful fight has occurred, in which a General, a Colonel, twelve subs., and six hundred men have been killed on our side, with fourteen hundred wounded and nine hundred prisoners. The Boer losses are generally estimated at something like five times that number.

The guard tells the tale later on to some traveller, who embellishes it, and passes it along as a fact. He goes into details, tells harrowing stories concerning hair-raising escapes from shot and shell. He splashes the surrounding rocks with gouts of blood, and then shudders dismally at the sight his fancy has conjured up. When the thrilled listener has refreshed the tale-teller from his whisky flask, the romancist takes up the thread of his narrative once more, and tells how the Lancers thundered over the shivering veldts in pursuit of flying hordes of foemen, and for awhile, like some graveyard ghoul, he revels in the moans of the dying and the blood of the slain. Another pull at the flask sets him going again like clockwork, and he makes a vivid picture out of the thunder of the guns as our gallant (they are always gallant) fellows bombarded the enemy from the heights.

Then he switches off from the artillery, and tells a blood-curdling tale of Boer treachery and cowardice. He tells how the enemy held out the white flag to coax our men to stop firing. Then, in awe-inspiring tones, he sobs forth a tale of dark and dismal war, how our soldiers respected the white flag and rested on their arms, only to be mowed down by a withering rifle fire from the canaille who represent the enemy in the field. Having got so far, he does not feel justified in stopping until he has thrown in some flowery language concerning a Boer cannonade upon British ambulance waggons, full of wounded; from that he drifts by easy and natural stages to Dum-Dum bullets, and the robbing of the wounded, and insults to the slain. And that is very often the person who is quoted in newspaper interviews--as a gentleman who was an eye-witness, and etc., etc., etc.

And yet, for some reason which I have been unable to gauge, the military authorities talk of sending all correspondents away from the front. It seems to me that it would be far better to give **bona fide** newspaper men every reasonable opportunity of discovering the truth instead of hampering them in any way. I fail to see why Great Britain and her Colonies should be kept in the dark concerning the progress of the war, for all the foreign Powers will be well supplied with information from the Boer lines; and, if we are blocked, some at least of the British newspapers will most assuredly go to foreign sources for news, if they are not allowed to obtain it for themselves. Others will content themselves with news gathered haphazard, and the last state of the Army, as far as the public mind is concerned, will be far worse than the first.

Colonel Hoad, who commands the Australians at Enslin, has offered the seven hundred and sixteen men, who up to date have acted as infantry, to the authorities as mounted infantry, and the offer has been accepted, much to the delight of the men, all of whom are very eager to get into the saddle, as they imagine that when their mounts arrive they will get a chance to go into action. They have been practising horsemanship during the day, and did fairly well, as many of them are expert riders, many more are fair; but a few of them are more at home on a sand-heap than in a saddle. There are not many of the latter kind, however. They will soon knock into shape, for Colonel Hoad hates the sight of a slovenly horseman as badly as a duck hates a dust storm. He is an untiring rider himself, and will work the beggars who cannot ride until they can.

After the arrival in Capetown of the two celebrated soldiers, Lords Roberts and Kitchener, I made it my business to converse with as many Boers as possible in regard to the two Generals, and was astonished to find how much they knew concerning them. How, and from whom, they get information passes my comprehension, but the fact remains that they knew all over the country as soon, if not sooner, than we did that our great leaders had arrived. They do not seem to fear them, though they invariably speak of them as wonderful soldiers. "God and Oom Paul Kruger will look after us," is their creed. Their faith in President Kruger is simply boundless. Not only do they fancy that he is a man of dauntless courage, great sagacity, and indomitable will, but they really seem to think that he has God's special blessing concerning this war.

He is to the Boers what Mahomet was to the wild tribesmen of Arabia, and it is as impossible to shake their faith in him as it would be to shake their faith in the story of Mount Calvary. It is all very well for a certain class of writers to attempt to cast unbounded ridicule upon these men and their leader, but it is not by ridicule that they can be conquered. It is not by contemptuous utterances or by untrue reports that they can be overcome. It is not by belittling them that we can raise ourselves in the eyes of the men of to-day or ennoble ourselves upon the pages of history. It would be conduct more in accordance with the traditions of a great nation if we gave them credit for the virtues they possess and the courage they display.

It is hard to drag any sort of information from a Boer, whether bond or free, but from what I can pick up they are perfectly satisfied with what they have done up to date. They think that President Kruger has astonished the world, and they wag their heads, and give one to understand that the same old gentleman has a good many more surprises in store for us. It is impossible to get a direct statement of any kind from them, but by patching fragments together I incline to the opinion that they really count on Cape Colony rising when Kruger wants a rising. Personally, from my own limited observations, I would not give a fig of tobacco for the alleged loyalty of the Cape Colony. If I am correct, this "surprise" will give the enemy an additional force of 45,000 men, most of whom will be found able to ride well and shoot straight.

It is nonsense to say that they will only form a mob destitute of discipline and unprovided with officers. They will not be a mob, they will be guerilla soldiers of the same type that the North and South in America provided, and they will take a lot of whipping at their own peculiar tactics. As for officers--well, up to date, they have not gone short of them. It is true they do not bear the hallmark of any modern university, but they know how to lead men into battle, all the same. They wear no uniforms, neither do they adorn themselves with any of the stylish trappings of war, but they are brainy, resourceful men, highly useful if not ornamental. Like Oliver Cromwell's hard-faced "Roundheads," they are the children of a great emergency, not much to look at, but full of a "get there" quality, which many school-bred soldiers lack entirely.

I rode down to Belmont a couple of days ago, and had a look at the Canadians and Queenslanders, who are quartered there. They are all in excellent health and spirits, and seem to be just about hungry for a fight. The Munsters, who are quartered there, are simply spoiling for a brush with the enemy, and seem to be as full of ginger as any men I have ever seen.

And every one of them with whom I conversed--and I chatted with a good many of the burly young Irishmen--expressed a keen desire to meet in open fight the Irish brigade now fighting on the side of the Boers. Should it ever come to pass during the progress of the war, I devoutly hope that I may be handy to witness the struggle. It will not be a long-range fight if I am any judge of men and things; it will be settled at close quarters, and the "baynit and the butt" will play a prominent part in the *melee*.

A few of our New Zealand fellows got to close quarters with the enemy recently up Colesberg way, and they did just as we knew they would when it came to the crossing of steel. The Boers stormed the position, and the New Zealanders joined in the bayonet charge which drove them back. Our men had a couple killed and one or two wounded. The enemy left a goodish number of dead on the field when they retired, about thirty of whom met their fate at the bayonet's point. The British losses were small. There was nothing remarkable about the behaviour of the New Zealanders in action; they simply did coolly and well what they were ordered to do, and proved that they are quite as good fighting material as anything the Old Country can produce. The gravest misfortune which has yet befallen any of the

Australians happened at the same locality, when eighteen New South Welshmen allowed themselves to be pinned in a tight place. Eight escaped, but the others are either prisoners or killed. We do not like the surrender business, and would rather see our men do as their fathers and grandfathers used to do--bite the motto, "No surrender," into the butts of their rifles with their teeth, and fight their way out of a hot corner. There has been a good deal too much of this throwing up of arms during the present campaign, and I hope that we shall hear less of it in the future.

We had a nasty night here at Enslin. Word reached our headquarters that three thousand mounted Boers were on the move towards our camp, which, for strategic purposes, is the most important between Methuen's column and De Aar. If the enemy could take Enslin they could make things very awkward for General Methuen, because they would then have him between two fires. As soon as the news came our fellows, with the Gordons, were ordered to occupy the surrounding heights. All night long, and well on into the day, we held them until we learned that the enemy had decided not to attack us. Had they done so they would have paid bitterly for their rashness, for the place is practically impregnable. A thousand resolute and skilful men, who knew how to use both rifle and bayonet, could hold the place against 20,000 of the finest troops in the world, providing the defenders were not hopelessly crushed by an immense artillery force.

General Hector Macdonald went through here the other day to take the command of the Highland Brigade, in the place of the late General Wauchope. The "Scots" who were with us lined up and gave the General a thrilling welcome, whilst our fellows, who are not usually demonstrative, crowded around the railway line to get a look at the brilliant soldier who, by sheer merit, dauntless pluck, and iron resolution, forced his way from the ranks to the high place he holds. The Australians had expected to see a gaunt, prematurely aged man, war-worn and battle-broken, and were surprised to see a dashing, gallant-looking man, who might in appearance comfortably have passed for five-and-thirty. The grey-clad men, in soft slouch hats, from the land of the Southern Cross, lounging about with pipes in their teeth, did not break into hysterical cheering--they are not built that way; they simply looked at the man whose full history every one of them knew as well as he knew the way into the front door of a "pub." But their flashing eyes and clenched hands told in language more eloquent than a salvo of cheers that this was their ideal man, the man they would follow rifle in hand up the brimstone heights of hell itself, if need be; aye, and stand sentry there until the day of judgment, if Hector Macdonald gave the order.

AUSTRALIA ON THE MOVE.

RENSBURG.

A complete change has come to the Australians who are in Africa under Colonel Hoad. We have left General Methuen's column, and joined that of General French. Formerly we were at Enslin, within sound of the guns that were fired daily at Magersfontein; now we are two hundred and twenty miles away, and are within easy patrolling distance of Colesberg.

Before we left Methuen's column we had one small night affair, which, however, did not amount to a great deal, though it has been very much exaggerated in local newspaper circles, and will, I fear, be unduly boomed in some of the Australian journals. The whole affair simply amounted to this. One hundred of the Victorian Mounted Rifles went out to make a demonstration towards Sunnyside, in Cape Colony, where a number of rebels were known to congregate. A hundred Queenslanders and Canadians were with them, when a corporal and a trooper of the Victorians saw an unarmed Boer and a nigger riding towards them in the twilight. The Boer, as soon as he was challenged, wheeled his horse and rode off at a gallop; our men rode after the runaway, but would not fire upon the white man because they thought he was simply a farmer who had got rather a bad scare at meeting armed men.

The Boer, however, played a deep game; he rode for a bit of a rise composed of broken ground, where, unknown to our scouts, a party of rebels lay concealed. As soon as the flying rebel was in safety the Boers opened fire, shooting Peter Falla, the trooper, twice through the arm, one bullet entering a few inches below the shoulder, the other shattering the bone a little way above the elbow. The corporal got away safely, taking his wounded comrade with him. Our fellows rode out and swept the veldt for miles, but saw no more of the enemy. So ended what has grandiloquently been termed "an Australian engagement," which, I may add, is just the kind of flapdoodle our troopers do not want. What they most desire on earth at present is an opportunity to show what they are made of. They don't want cheap newspaper puffs, nor laudatory speeches from generals. They want to get into grip with the enemy, and, as an Australian, let me say now that Imperial federation will get a greater shock by keeping these fine fellows out of action than by anything else that could happen under heaven. They did not come here on a picnic party, they did not come for a circus; they don't want a lot of maudlin sentiment wasted on them whilst they stay out of the firing line to mind the jam, or give the African girls a treat.

Mr. Chamberlain has made a good many mistakes in regard to the war, mistakes that will live in history when his very name is forgotten, but he need not add to them by alienating Australian sentiment by coddling men who came across the Indian Ocean to prove to the whole world that on the field of battle they are as good as their sires. Our fellows have got hold of a rumour (the prophets only could tell whence camp rumours originate) that instructions have been received from England that they are to be kept out of danger, and a madder lot of men you could not find anywhere between here and Tophet. They wanted to send a petition to Lord Roberts asking to be allowed to face the enemy, but though the officers are quite as sore as the men, they could not permit such a breach of discipline. So now the men ease their feelings by jeering at each other.

"What are we here fer, Bill?"

"Oh, get yer head felt; any fool knows why we are here. There's a blessed marmalade factory somewhere about, and we are going to mind it whilst the British Tommy does the fighting."

"Marmalade be d----!" chirruped a voice down the lines. "Think they'd trust us to look after anything so important?"

"Oh, you're a blessed prophet, you are," snarls the little bugler. "P'raps you'll tell us what our game is."

"Easy enough, little 'un. Our officers 've got to practise making mud maps in the dust with a stick, and we've got to fool around and keep the flies away."

"I suppose they'll keep us at this till the war's over, and then send us to England, 'nd give us a bloomin' medal, 'nd tell us then we are gory, crimson heroes. Ugh!" grunts a big West Australian with a face like a nightmare, and a voice that comes out of his chest with a sound like a steam saw coming through a wet log.

"Don't know about England 'nd the medal, 'Beauty,'" chirrups a Sydney gunner, "but I know what they'll give us in Australia if we go back without a fight."

"P'raps it'll be a mansion, or a sheep station, or a stud of racehorses," meekly suggests a tired-looking South Australian, with a derisive twist of his under lip.

"No, they won't present us with a racing stud," lisps the gunner, "but, by G----, they'll shy chaff enough at us to keep all the bloomin' horses between 'ere and 'ell, and the girls will send us a kid's feedin' bottle, as a mark of feelin' and esteem, every Valentine's Day for ten years to come, because of the glorious name we made for Australia on the bloody fields of war in Africa."

"Fields o' war--fields o' whisky 'nd watermelons! Oh, d---- it! I'm going ter stop writing ter my girl before she writes ter tell me that a white feather don't suit a girl's complexion in Australia."

He lifts his bugle, and sounds "Feed up" so savagely that the horses strain on their leg ropes and kick themselves into a lather as hot as their riders' tempers, the long, loose-limbed troopers move off, cursing artistically in their beards at the very thought of the roasting they will get from the witty-tongued, red-lipped girls of Australia, when--

> They cross the rolling ocean,
> Back from the fields of war,
> To show the British medal
> They got for guarding a store.
>
> To show the British medal
> On stations, towns, and farms,
> They got for guarding the marmalade,
> Far away from war's alarms.
>
> To show the British medal,
> With a blush of angry shame,

For which they went to risk their lives
In young Australia's name.

To show the British medal,
With a sneer that's half a sob,
Ere they pawn it to their uncle,
And go and drink the "bob."

When we received notice to move away from Enslin down the line through Graspan, Belmont, Orange River, to De Aar, our fellows were naturally very wrathful; they had done splendid work for many weeks up that way; they had dug trenches, sunk wells, drilled unceasingly; they had watched the kopjes and scoured the veldt, and all that they were told to do they did like soldiers--readily and un-complainingly. The cold nights and the scorching days, the monotonous drudgery, found them always ready and willing, because they believed that when the order came for a great battle at Magersfontein, or an onward march to Kimberley, they would be in the thick of it. But for some reason, known only to those who gave the order, they were sent away from the front, and they felt it keenly. From De Aar they were sent on to Naauwpoort, and from this latter place they were forwarded on to Rensburg.

At Naauwpoort nearly all the Australians were mounted, and now acted as mounted infantry. The horses supplied are Indian ponies, formerly used by the Madras Cavalry. They are a first-class lot of cattle, well suited to the work that lies before them, and have evidently been selected by someone who knows his business a good deal better than a great number of his colleagues. General French inspected the men at Rensburg during the first day or two, and seemed fairly well satisfied with them, though, of course, they did not make a first-class show in their initial efforts on horseback. A great number of them rode well, but very few of them had ever gone through a course of mounted drill, and it will take a week or two to knock them into shape for this work; though, when once out of the saddle, they are not in any way inferior to the best British regiments I have seen. But they are keen to learn, and very willing, so that I expect to see them make wonderfully rapid strides towards efficiency as mounted men. They seem to feel that their only chance to get a fight is to become high grade soldiers, and to that end they will stand all the work that can be crowded into them. I have no idea what their future movements will be, nor do I think anyone else connected with the regiment has; but one thing seems certain, that sooner or later they will fall foul of the enemy in small skirmishing parties, as the kopjes for a length of twenty miles are infested by little bands of Boers, who have a knack of disappearing as soon as a British force draws near them, only, however, to crop up again in a fresh place, a short distance away.

For the Boer is a past master in this kind of warfare, and knows how to play his own game to perfection. What the Goorkha is in Indian warfare, so the Boer is in Africa. He does not fight in our style, but that does not say that he cannot fight, neither does it argue that he is devoid of courage. As a matter of fact, the more I have seen of this country, and note what the Boers have done in opposition to all the might of Great Britain, the more I am impressed with the idea that our alleged Intelligence Department wants cutting down and burning root and branch, for it must have been absolutely rotten, or unquestionably corrupt. We were led by members of this Department to believe that the Boer was a cowardly kind of veldt pariah, a degenerate offshoot of a fine old parent stock. Well, the Boer is nothing of the kind. He is not in any way degenerate. He is a good fighting man, according to his lights. He does not wear a stand-up collar, nor an eyeglass, nor spats to his veldtschoon. He does not talk with a silly lisp or an inane drawl. Therefore, the useless fellows whom Britain trusted with the important task of watching him and sizing him up counted him as a boor as well as a Boer--a mere country clod. But now, from the rocky hills, these clods, these sons of semi-white savages, laugh at us derisively, and answer our jeers with rifles that know how to speak in a language that even the bravest of our troops have learnt to understand--and respect.

I have a keen recollection of the last Franco-Prussian War. I remember how the English newspapers ridiculed the French military authorities because, whilst the Germans had accurate maps of every province within the French borders, the French themselves were grossly ignorant of their own territory. Now we can eat our own sarcasms and enjoy the bitter fruit of our own irony, for, thanks to the Intelligence Department connected with the War Office in Great Britain, we to-day stand precisely in the same position towards our African enemy as France did towards Prussia. A glance at the country through which I have recently passed shows only too clearly that, whilst Paul Kruger and his advisers knew our full strength to a man, we, on our part, knew nothing about him or the men, money, or ordnance at his command. We knew nothing of the country which had been patiently fortified by the best skilled military engineers in Europe. We know nothing of his rocky, well-fortified country, which lies behind that which we have already attacked. Our generals, instead of being supplied with maps covering every inch of country within the enemy's borders, have to gather information at the bayonet's point at a loss to the Empire in men, money, and in prestige. If our commanders blunder, who is to blame but the criminally negligent officials who have supplied them with false or foolish data to work upon? The Empire has been betrayed, either wilfully or through crass idleness upon the part of men who have dipped deeply into the Empire's coffers, and the nation should demand their impeachment, apart from their position, place, or power, and punishment of the most drastic kind should follow speedily in the footsteps of impeachment.

The failure of General Buller to relieve Ladysmith was not due to any want of sagacity on the part of that General. It was not due to any want of bravery on the part of his troops. The General is worthy of his rank, and worthy of the confidence of the nation, and his troops are as good as the men who, under the same flag, taught the Russians to respect the power of Britain. The cause of the failure lay mainly in the want of knowledge on our part concerning the strength of the country the Boers held, and the strength of the country they had to fall back upon when hard pressed.

That information the "Intelligence" Department ought to have been able to place in the hands of General Buller before he moved forward to the relief of the beleaguered garrison in Ladysmith. But they could not give what they had never possessed.

Right up to the present moment, when the Boers have been forced to meet our troops at close quarters, they have been found to possess no other arms than the rifle. This has given truth to the belief that the enemy as an attacking force is next door to useless, as no men, no matter how brave and determined, could do very much damage to first-class troops armed with the bayonet.

However, there is a whisper in the air that the Boers are not deficient in side-arms; it is rumoured that the President of the Boer Republic has immense supplies of offensive as well as defensive weapons safely placed away until they may be required Right up to date his war policy has been to remain passive, excepting in a few isolated positions, allowing the British to attack his generals in almost impregnable positions, and by so doing put heart into the burghers, and dishearten our forces. But should the tide of war continue to roll onward in his favour he may attempt to put in force the oft-told Boer threat, and try to sweep the British into the sea. Should that day dawn, it is rumoured that the enemy will be found well supplied with side-arms and with mercenaries trained to their use in one of the best schools that modern times have known. Where do these rumours come from? Well, a Boer prisoner, taunted perhaps by a guard, loses his temper and drops a hint, or a Boer farmer, exultant over the latest news of his countrymen's success, lifts the veil a little, and a jealously-guarded secret drops out; or, again, a Boer's wife or daughter, flinging a taunt at a cursed "Rooinek," allows her temper to run away with her discretion. There are a hundred ways in which such things get about; only straws, perhaps, but a straw can point the way windward. A talkative Kaffir who has been reared on a Dutch farm will at times give things away that would cost him his life if the length of his tongue was known to his master; especially will the nigger talk if his mouth be judiciously moistened with Cape smoke brandy.

Information that comes to a war correspondent's hand is of many colours, shapes, and sizes, but if he is born to the business he pieces the whole together and picks out what seemeth good to his own soul at the finish. Sometimes, at the end of a week's hard work, he finds himself possessed of a patchwork of information like unto Joseph's coat of many colours, but it is hard fortune indeed if he cannot find something in the lot to repay him for his earnest endeavours.

SLINGERSFONTEIN.

RENSBURG.

Scarcely had I returned from posting my last letter when the camp was in a commotion, caused by the news that the West Australians were in action at Slingersfontein, distant about twelve miles from Rensburg. To saddle up and get out as fast as horseflesh would carry a man was but the work of a very short period of time, for the gallop across the open veldt was not a very laborious undertaking. I soon found that the stalwart sons of the great gold colony were in it, and enjoying it.

Slingersfontein is an important position on the right flank of French's column. It is not only an important but a very hard position to hold on account of the nature of the country. Here there is but very little open veldt; mile after mile is covered by small kopjes that rise in countless numbers, until the whole country looks as if it were covered with a veritable forest of hills. Once inside that labyrinth of rocky excrescences, an army might easily be lost, unless every individual man and officer knew the place thoroughly. The Boers know the lay of the land, and, consequently, shift from post to post by paths that are unknown to anyone else with marvellous dexterity and incredible swiftness. Our forces hold a small plain, which is like the palm of a giant's hand, with the surrounding kopjes representing the digits. We hold those kopjes also. The shape of the camp is in the form of a horseshoe, all around the little basin great hills rise, and from those hills England's watch-dogs keep a sharp look-out on the movements of the foe; and well they need to, for, in ground which suits him, the African farmer is as 'cute and cunning as a Red Indian. Behind our position, or, rather, outside of it, there is another small tract of open country, but beyond that, lapping around our stronghold like a crescent, is rough, hilly ground.

None of those hills is worth dignifying with the title of mountain, but all of them are big enough to shelter a hundred or two of the enemy, and it is there that they play their game of hide and seek, which is so trying to the nerves of young troops. The Boers hold that rough country entirely, and the outer edge of their semi-circle is not, at any given point, more than four miles from our centre at Slingersfontein.

The outer line of kopjes which skirt their stalking ground are bigger than the hills on the inner side, so that they have an excellent opportunity to conceal their movements from the observation of our most astute pickets, and the only way in which our commanding officer can locate the enemy with any degree of certainty is by making a reconnaissance in force, and, if possible, drawing their fire. If the Boers fall into this trap they invariably pay dearly for the slight advantage they gain over the investigating force, for our guns soon make any known position untenable. The Boer leaders know this, however, and are very loth to allow temptation to overcome discretion; but at times, either through the impetuosity of their troops or through errors in generalship, they give themselves away entirely, and that is precisely what they did upon this occasion.

By means only known to those high up in authority, our people had become acquainted with the fact that the enemy intended to try to extend their line on our right flank, and so threaten us not only upon the left flank, the direct front, and right flank, but also in the rear. Could they succeed in doing this they would have us in a peculiarly tight place, as, once posted in force well down on our right flank, they would then at least be able to harass us badly in our communications with Rensburg, which is our main base of operations. It is there that the General has his headquarters; it is from there that we keep in touch, per medium of the railway and telegraph lines, with the rest of the British Army in South Africa. It is from there that we draw all our supplies of fodder and ammunition. It is from there we should draw all our additional force if we needed reinforcements in case of a general assault by the enemy upon our position at Slingersfontein, and it is from there that we should be strengthened should we decide to make a forward move on the Boers' position. Therefore it behoved us to keep that line of communication intact, no matter what the cost. All these things were as well known to the Boer leader as to us, and that is why they were as keen to get the position as we were, and why we are keen to stop them from accomplishing their object.

It was for the purpose of ascertaining just what the enemy intended to do, and how many men they had to do it with, that Major Ethoran ordered out the West Australian Mounted Infantry, consisting of about 75 men, under Captain Moor, an Imperial soldier in the pay of the West Australian Government, and a small body of Inniskilling Dragoons and Lancers, with a section of the Royal Horse Artillery and two guns. The men moved out of Slingersfontein on Tuesday about midday, and at once proceeded towards a farmhouse located right under the very jowl of an ugly-looking kopje.

This farm was known as Pottsberg, and was well known as a regular haunt of the most daring and dangerous rebels in the whole district. The farm consisted of the usual white stone farmhouse of five or six rooms, a small orchard, surrounded by rough stone walls from three feet six to four feet in height, and about two feet thick, a small cluster of native huts, and a kraal for cattle, made of rough, heavy stones, topped by cakes of sun-baked manure, stored by the farmers for fuel. Some little distance from the back of the farmhouse a stout stone wall ran down from the kopjes on to the plain. This wall was between four and five feet in height and half a yard across in its weakest place--an ugly barricade in itself--behind which a few resolute men with quick-firing rifles, which they know how to use, could make a good stand against vastly superior numbers advancing upon them from the open veldt.

When our fellows trotted out from camp, Captain Moor received orders to distribute his men in small bodies all along the edge of the kopjes between Pottsberg farmhouse and Kruger's Hill, a small kopje lying almost in a line with our camp, on the right. The men were ordered to go as close as possible to the enemy's position, to see as much as they could possibly see in regard to the numbers of troops in the hills held by the enemy. If they succeeded in discovering the rebels in large bodies they were to draw their fire and immediately retreat at full speed. In the meantime the two guns belonging to the Royal Horse Artillery were beautifully placed in a dip in the veldt, where they could play upon the Boers should they attempt to rush the West Australians at any given point. The Lancers and Dragoons were placed in charge of some kopjes behind the guns, in order to protect them should a concerted onslaught be made upon them by the mounted Boers, who were shrewdly suspected to be in hiding in strong force behind the first row of hills, which screened the enemy's position.

The Australians rode out steadily, and took up their positions with an amount of coolness that startled older soldiers. This was absolutely their first trial on real fighting service, and everybody connected with them was anxious to see how they would comport themselves in the face of the enemy. Not only was it their first fighting effort, but it was their debut in the saddle, as until a week previous they had been simply infantrymen, and not a dozen of them had ever been in the hands of a mounted drill instructor. It was a big task to set such green men, but they proved before the day was out that they were worthy of the confidence reposed in them. Captain Moor, Lieutenant Darling, and Lieutenant Parker each took a small section into action; the others were under the immediate control of their sergeants. They split up into small parties, and swept the very edge of the kopjes, peering into gullies, climbing the outer hills, working along the ravines with a courage and thoroughness that would have done credit to the oldest scouts in all the Empire. Yet nothing came of their investigations for quite a long time. The enemy did not mean to be drawn, and remained passive, so that the West Australians at last became a little bit reckless, and were consequently not so guarded as they might have been. All at once a body of scouts ran upon a large body of the enemy near Pottsberg Farm, in a deep and shady ravine. The enemy were trying to evade notice, but that was now impossible. In a moment rifles were ringing on the air, and after that first volley the little band of Australians wheeled and galloped for the open country. To have remained there would have meant certain death to every one of the half-dozen who comprised the picket, so they did their duty--they fired and rode for the veldt. In a few seconds Boers were dashing out of the kopjes on all sides, trying to cut the small band of Australians off or shoot them down. But the Australians knew their game; they opened out, so that each man was practically riding alone.

The Boers could do little with them. Those who stood by the guns noticed that very large numbers of men in the Boer ranks were either niggers or half-castes, and it was also very noticeable that they knew but little about the use of the rifle. They fired high and wide, and notwithstanding the fact that they poured their ammunition away in wholesale fashion, they did little harm worth mentioning, although many of them fired at little more than pistol range. They were simply crazed with excitement, and did not succeed in cutting off a single member of that adventurous band. Whenever an Australian found himself in a tight place he simply dug his spurs into his horse's flanks, lifted his rifle, and blazed into the ranks of the foe. If his horse was shot dead under him he coo-eed to his mates, and kept his rifle busy, and every time the coo-ee rang out over the whispering veldt the Australians turned in their saddles, and riding as the men from the South-land can ride, they dashed to the rescue, and did not leave a single man in the hands of the enemy. Many a gallant deed was done that day by officers and men. Captain Moor gave one fellow his horse, and made a dash for liberty on foot, but he would have failed in his effort had not Lieutenant Darling, a West Australian boy, ridden to his aid, and together the two officers on the one horse got back to the shelter of the guns. The enemy still blazed away in the wildest and most farcical fashion. Had they been Boer hunters or marksmen very few of the West Australians would ever have got across that strip of veldt alive. As it was, only two of them got wounded, none were killed, one or two horses were shot dead, and then the big guns got to work in grim earnest.

A party of Boers, however, got round one of the kopjes, where some of the Lancers were posted, and now half a dozen of those brave fellows are missing, and I fear they are to be counted amongst those who will never return again. Sergeant Watson, of the R.H., was killed, and several of his men and a few of the Lancers were wounded, but the R.H. guns soon swept the plain clear of the enemy, and they retired, carrying their dead and wounded with them. The work for the day was done, and well done, for the enemy had shown his hand. We knew his position and his strength, and next day we went out in force to have a word with him, but the wily Boers kept strictly under cover, and refused on any terms to be drawn again.

THE WEST AUSTRALIANS.

BETHANY.

I was feeling miserable as I sat in the hospital garden, and I rather fancy I looked pretty much as I felt, for a cheery-faced Boer nurse, with her black hair, blacker eyes, and rose-blossom lips, came up to where I sat, bringing with her two or three slightly wounded Boers. "I have brought some Boers who know something of your countrymen, Mr. Australian," she said. "I thought you would be glad to hear all about them." "By Jove! yes, nurse. If I were not a married man, I should try to thank you gracefully." "Oh, yees; oh, yees," she answered, tossing back her head; "that is all right. You say those pretty things; then, when you go away from here, you tell your wife, and you write in your papers we Boer girls are fat old things, who never use soap and water. All the Rooibaatjes do that." And off she went, laughing merrily, whilst my friends the enemy grinned and enjoyed the little comedy. So we fell to talking, and half a dozen wounded "Tommies" gathered round and chipped into the conversation, which by degrees worked round to a deed which the West Australians did; and as I listened to the tale so simply told by those rough farmer men, I felt my face flush with pride, and my shoulders fell back square and solid once more, whilst every drop of blood in my veins seemed to run warm and strong, like the red wine they grow on the hillside in my own sunny land; for the story concerned men whom I knew well, men who were bred with the scent of the wattle in the first breath they drew, men who grew from childhood to manhood where the silver sentinel stars form the cross in the rich blue midnight sky. My countrymen--Australians--men with whom I had hunted for silver in the desolate backblocks of New South Wales; men with whom I had scoured the interior of West Australia seeking for gold; men who had been with me on the tin fields and opal fields. I had never doubted that they would keep their country's name unsullied when they met the foe on the field of war, yet when I heard the tale the enemy told I felt my eyes fill as they have seldom filled since childhood, for I was proud of the western diggers, proud of my blood; and at that moment, with British "Tommies" sprawling on the grass at my feet, and the Boer farmers grouped amongst them, I would sooner have called myself an Australian commoner than the son of any peer in any other land under high heaven.

I will take the story from the Boer's mouth and tell it to you, as I hope to tell it round a hundred camp fires when the war is over, and I go back to the Australian bush once more. "It happened round Colesberg way," he said; "we thought we had the British beaten, and our commandant gave us the word to press on and cut them to pieces. Our big guns had been grandly handled, and our rifle fire had told its tale. We saw the British falling back from the kopjes they had held, and we thought that there was nothing between us and victory; but there was, and we found it out before we were many minutes older. There was one big kopje that was the very key of the position. Our spies had told us that this was held by an Australian force. We looked at it very anxiously, for it was a hard position to take, but even as we watched we saw that nearly all the Australians were leaving it. They, too, were falling back with the British troops. If we once got that kopje there was nothing on earth could stop us. We could pass on and sweep around the retiring foe, and wipe them off the earth, as a child wipes dirt from its hands, and we laughed when we saw that only about twenty Australians had been left to guard the kopje.

"There were about four hundred of us, all picked men, and when the commandant called to us to go and take the kopje, we sprang up eagerly, and dashed down over some hills, meaning to cross the gully and charge up the kopje where those twenty men were waiting for us. But we did not know the Australians--then. We know them now. Scarcely had we risen to our feet when they loosed their rifles on us, and not a shot was wasted. They did not fire, as regular soldiers nearly always do, volley after volley, straight in front of them, but every one picked his man, and shot to kill. They fired like lightning, too, never dwelling on the trigger, yet never wildly wasting lead, and all around us our best and boldest dropped, until we dared not face them. We dropped to cover, and tried to pick them off, but they were cool and watchful, throwing no chance away. We tried to crawl from rock to rock to hem them in, but they, holding their fire until our burghers moved, plugged us with lead, until we dared not stir a step ahead; and all the time the British troops, with all their convoy, were slowly, but safely, falling back through the kopjes, where we had hoped to hem them in. We gnawed our beards and cursed those fellows who played our game as we had thought no living men could play it Then, once again, we tried to rush the hill, and once again they drove us back, though our guns were playing on the heights they held. We could not face their fire. To move upright to cross a dozen yards meant certain death, and many a Boer wife was widowed and many a child left fatherless by those silent men who held the heights above us. They did not cheer as we came onward. They did not play wild music, they only clung close as climbing weeds to the rocks, and shot as we never saw men shoot before, and never hope to see men shoot again.

"Then we got ready to sweep the hill with guns, but our commandant, admiring those brave few who would not budge before us in spite of our numbers, sent an officer to them to ask them to surrender, promising them all the honours of war. But they sent us word to come and take them if we could. And then our officer asked them three times if they would hold up their hands, and at the third time a grim sergeant rose and answered him: 'Aye, we will hold up our hands, but when we do, by God, you'll find a bayonet in 'em. Go back and tell your commandant that Australia's here to stay.' And there they stayed, and fought us hour by hour, holding us back, when but for them victory would have been with us. We shelled them all along their scattered line, and tried to rush them under cover of the artillery fire; but they only held their posts with stouter hearts, and shot the straighter when the fire was hottest, and we could do nothing but lie there and swear at them, though we admired them for their stubborn pluck. They held the hill till all their men were safe, and then, dashing down the other side, they jumped into their saddles and made off, carrying their wounded with them. They were but twenty men, and we four hundred"

A "Tommy" sitting at the speaker's feet looked up and said: "What are yer makin' sich a song abart it far? Lumme, them Horstraliars are as Hinglish has hi ham!"

IN A BOER TOWN.

BETHANY.

A Boer town is not laid out on systematic lines, as one sees towns in America, or Canada, or Australia. The streets seem to run much as they please, or as the exigencies of traffic have caused them to run. I doubt if the plan of a town is ever drawn in this country. People arrive and settle down in a happy-go-lucky manner, and straightway build themselves a home. Their homes are places to live in; not to look at. There is an almost utter absence of architectural adornment everywhere. My eyes range over a large number of dwellings. They are nearly all alike--plain, square structures, plastered snow white. There is a double door in the centre of the front, and a window at each side of the door. A stoep, about six feet wide, rises a foot from the pathway, and there is nothing else to be seen from the outside front. These houses look bare and bald, and are as expressionless as a blind baby. To me most houses have an expression of their own. In an English town a quiet walk in the dawning, making a survey of the dwelling-places, always leaves the impression that I have gleaned an insight into the character of the dwellers therein. The cheeky-looking villa, with its superabundance of ornament, is a monument in masonry to the successful mining jobber on a small scale. The solemn-looking, solid dwelling, standing in its own grounds, where every flower bush has its individual prop, where the lawn is trimmed with mathematical exactitude, and not one vagrant leaf is allowed to stray, speaks with a kind of brick-and-mortar eloquence of virtue that has never grasped the sublime fulness of the Scriptural text which saith: "The way of transgressors is hard!" That is the home of the middle-aged Churchman, whose feet from infancy have fallen amidst roses. He has never erred, because he has never known enough of human sympathy and human toil and struggle to feel temptation. The coy little cottage further on, sur-rounded by climbing roses and sweet-smelling herbs, where the gate is left just a little bit open, as if inviting a welcome, seems to advertise itself as the home of two maiden sisters, who, though past the giddy girlhood stage, still have hopes of being somebody's darling by-and-by.

But in a Boer town most of the piety is knocked out of a man. You stare at the houses, and they stare back at you dumbly. There is nothing pretentious or rakish about any of them; no matter how riotous a man's imagination might be, he could never conjure up a "wink" from a Boer house, though I have seen houses in other parts of the world that seemed to "cock an eye" at a passing traveller and invite him to try the door.

They have only two styles of roofing their dwellings--either the old-fashioned gable roof, or the still older kind of "lean-to," the latter being nothing but a flat top, high at the front and running lower towards the back, in order that the rain water may carry off rapidly. They paint their doors and windows a sober reddish brown, for your true Boer has an utter contempt for anything gaudy or gay. He leaves that sort of thing to his nigger servants, who make up for their master's lack of apprecia-tion in the matter of colour by rigging themselves out in anything that is startling in the way of contrasts, for if the white master is a Puritan in such things, the nigger servant, male and female, is a perfect sybarite.

Right opposite where I am sitting a family group, or all that is left of the family, is sitting, as the custom is at evening, out on the stoep. On the side nearest me is a young widow. I have made inquiries concerning her. Her husband was killed fight-ing against our troops at Graspan. She, poor thing, is dressed in deepest mourning. Her dress is made of some heavy black material, and has no touch of white or any colour anywhere to relieve its sombre shades. On her head she wears a jet black cap, which rises high and wide, and falls around her neck and shoulders. The cap is fashioned much after the style of the sun bonnets worn by the peasant women of Normandy, but hers is black, black as the grave. She has rather a nice face, a good woman's face, pale and refined by suffering. No one looking at her can doubt that she has suffered, and suffered as only such women can, through this brutal, bloody war. I thought of the widows away in our own land as I looked at her sitting there, so silently and sadly, with her thin white hands clasped on the black folds of her lap. On one hand I plainly saw the gold circle shining, which a few months ago had meant so much to her; now, alas! only the outward and visible sign of all she had been and of all that she had lost. Behind her the snow-white wall of the house, sparkling in the red rays of the setting sun; at her feet only the white slate of the stoep. And well enough I knew that under the proud Empire flag many a widow as young and as heart-broken as this Dutch girl would watch the sun go down as hopelessly as she, and I could not help the thought which sprang to my soul--God's bitter curse rest on the head of the man, be he Boer or Briton, who brought about this cruel war.

On the street in front of the house where the widow sat I noticed a group of niggers. Some of them were merely local "boys," who worked for the townspeople. They were dressed in the usual nigger fashion, in old store clothing, patched or ventilated according to the wearer's taste. One fellow had on a pair of pants that had at some former stage belonged to a man about four times his size. The portion of those pants which is usually hidden when a man is sitting in the saddle had been worn into a huge hole, which the nigger had picturesquely filled by tacking on a scarlet shawl. As the pants were made of navy blue serge the effect was unquestionably artistic, especially as the amateur tailor had done his sewing with string, most of the stitches running from an inch to an inch and a half in length. Still, he was only one of many in similar case, so that he did not feel in the least degree lonely. There were other niggers there--"boys" belonging to the mule-drivers of the army. These "boys" nearly all sported a military jacket and some sort of field service cap, which they had picked up somehow in camp. The "side" these niggers put on when they get inside odds and ends of military wearing apparel is something appalling. They swagger around amongst the civilian niggers, and treat them as beings of a very inferior mould, whilst the lies they tell concerning their individual acts of heroism would set the author of "Deadwood Dick" blushing out of simple envy.

The nigger girls cluster round these black veterans like flies around a western water hole in midsummer, and their shrill laughter makes the air fairly vibrate as they bandy jests with the cheeky herds. The girls are rather pleasing in appearance, though far from being pretty. As a rule, they wear clean print dresses and white aprons; they never wear hats of any kind, but coil a showy kerchief around their heads in coquettish fashion. They are not particular as to colour, red, blue, yellow, or pink, anything will do as long as it is brilliant. The skins of the girls are almost as varied as the headgear. The Kaffir girl is very dark, almost black. The bushman's daughter is dirty yellow, like river water in flood time. Some of the other tribes are as black as the record of a first-class burglar, but they have bright black eyes, which they roll about as a kitten rolls a ball of wool in playtime.

But whether they are black, brown, or coffee-coloured, they are all alike in one respect--every daughter of them has a mouth that is as boundless as a mother's blessing, and as limitless as the imagination of a spring poet in love. When they are vexed they purse that mouth up into a bunch until it looks like a crumpled saddle-flap hanging on a hedge. When they are pleased the mouth opens and expands like an indiarubber portmanteau ready for packing; that is when they smile, but when they laugh their ears have to shift to give the mouth a chance to get comfortably to its destination. They have beautiful teeth, the white ivory showing against the black foreground like fresh tombstones in an old cemetery on a dark night. It is amusing to watch them flirting with the soldier niggers. They try to look coy, but soon fall victims to the skilful blandishments of the vain-glorious warriors, and after a little manoeuvring they put out their lips to be kissed, a sight which might well make even a Scotch Covenanter grin. They suck their lips in with a sharp hissing breath; then push them out suddenly, ready for the osculatory seance, the lips moving as if they were pushed from the inside by a pole. The "boys" enjoy the picnic immensely. As a matter of fact, these "boys" always seem to me to be doing one of four things. They are either eating, smoking, sleeping, or making love; and they do enough love-making in twenty-four hours to last an ordinary everyday sort of white man four months, even if he puts in a little overtime. One of the most charming things noticeable about a Boer town is the plenitude of trees in the streets. They are often ornamental, always useful for purposes of shade. There is no regularity about their distribution; they seem to have been planted spasmodically at odd times and at odd positions. There is little about them to lead one to the belief that they receive over much care after they have been put into the soil. I have found a very creditable library in pretty nearly every Boer town that I have visited, and it is a noteworthy fact that all of our most cherished authors find a place on their book-shelves. One other thing I have also noticed, which, though a small thing in itself, is yet very significant. In nearly every hotel, and in many of the public places, portraits of our

Queen and members of the Royal Family have been hanging side by side with portraits of notable men, such as Mr. Gladstone, Lord Salisbury, Mr. Chamberlain, and Mr. Rhodes. During the course of the war all kinds and conditions of Boers have had free access to the rooms where those portraits were to be seen, but now I find that no damage has been done to any of those pictures, excepting those of Mr. Rhodes and Mr. Chamberlain. This has not been an oversight on the part of the Boers, for I defy any person to find a solitary picture of the two last-named gentlemen that has not been hacked with knives. But the Queen and Royal Family photos have in every case been treated with respect.

BEHIND THE SCENES.

STORMBERG.

I am writing this from Stormberg, a tremendously important military position, which was taken on Monday, the 5th, by General Gatacre, without a blow, the enemy falling back cowed by the British general's tactics. Had they remained here another twenty-four hours Gatacre would have had them in a ring of iron, but the Boer general is no fool. He saw his danger, and, like a wise man, he dodged it. Gatacre's generalship was simply superb. Let the idiotic band of critics who sit in safety in England howl to their heart's content; Gatacre deserves well of his country. Had he dashed recklessly into this hornet's nest he would have sacrificed four-fifths of his gallant officers and a host of his men. Had I to write his military epitaph to-day I should say that "he won with brains what most generals would have won with blood."

Strangely enough, I was a prisoner in the very room where I am penning this epistle only last Saturday night. I left here in the centre of a Boer commando, with a bandage over my eyes, on Sunday morning, and returned to the spot surrounded by British "Tommies" a few days later.

All the glory of this bloodless victory does not rest with the general who commands the column. To Captain Tennant no small meed of praise is due. This officer was here on secret service before hostilities commenced, and he did his work so thoroughly that the country is as familiar to him as paint to a barmaid. He is one of those men, unfortunately so rare in the British Army, combining dash and dauntless pluck with a cool, level head. If he gets his opportunity, England will hear more of this officer. I have been intensely struck by the class of officers by whom General Gatacre is surrounded. They all look like soldiers. I have not seen a single dude, not one of those wretched fops of whom I have seen only too many in South Africa. They speak like soldiers too. No idiotic drawl, no effeminate lisp, no bullying, ill-bred, coarseness of tongue; they are neither drawing-room dandies nor camp swashbucklers, but officers and gentlemen--and, I can assure you, the terms are not always synonymous, even under the Queen's cloth. I have seen mere lads in this country leading men into action who in point of brains were not fit to lead a mule to water, and others who, in regard to manners, were scarcely fit to follow the mule. But, thank God, the Boers have taught our nation this, if they have taught us nought else--that it needs something more than an eye-glass, a lisp, a pair of kid gloves, and an insolent, overbearing manner to make a successful soldier.

But let me get amongst the Boers. I was only a prisoner in their hands for about a month, yet every moment of that time was so fraught with interest that I fancy I picked up more of the real nature of the Boers than I should have done under ordinary circumstances in a couple of years. I was moved from laager to laager along their fighting line, saw them at work with their rifles, saw them come in from more than one tough skirmish, bringing their dead and wounded with them, saw them when they had triumphed, and saw them when they had been whipped; saw them going to their farms, to be welcomed by wife and children; saw them leaving home with a wife's sobs in their ears, and children's loving kisses on their lips. I saw some of these old greyheads shattered by our shells, dying grimly, with knitted brows and fiercely clenched jaws; saw some of their beardless boys sobbing their souls out as the life blood dyed the African heath. I saw some passing over the border line which divides life and death, with a ring of stern-browed comrades round them, leaning upon their rifles, whilst a brother or a father knelt and pressed the hand of him whose feet were on the very threshold of the land beyond the shadows. I saw others smiling up into the faces of women--the poor, pain-drawn faces of the dying looking less haggard and worn than the anguish-stricken features of their womanhood who knelt to comfort them in that last awful hour--in the hour which divides time from eternity, the sunlight of lusty life from the shadows of unsearchable death. Those things I have seen, and in the ears of English men and English women, let me say, as one who knows, and fain would speak the plain, ungilded truth concerning friend and foe, that, not alone beneath the British flag are heroes found. Not alone at the breasts of British matrons are brave men suckled; for, as my soul liveth--whether their cause be just or unjust, whether the right or the wrong of this war be with them, whether the blood of the hundreds who have fallen since the first rifle spoke defiance shall speak for or against them at the day of judgment--they at least know how to die; and when a man has given his life for the cause he believes in he is proven worthy even of his worst enemy's respect. And it seems to me that the British nation, with its long roll of heroic deeds, wrought the whole world over, from Africa to Iceland, can well afford to honour the splendid bravery and self-sacrifice of these rude, untutored tillers of the soil. I have seen them die.

Once, as I lay a prisoner in a rocky ravine all through the hot afternoon, I heard the rifles snapping like hounds around a cornered beast. I watched the Boers as they moved from cover to cover, one here, one there, a little farther on a couple in a place of vantage, again, in a natural fortress, a group of eight; so they were placed as far as my eye could reach. The British force I could not see at all; they were out on the veldt, and the kopjes hid them from me; but I could hear the regular roll and ripple of their disciplined volleys, and in course of time, by watching the actions of the Boers, I could anticipate the sound. They watched our officers, and when the signal to fire was given they dropped behind cover with such speed and certainty that seldom a man was hit. Then, when the leaden hail had ceased to fall upon the rocks, they sprang out again, and gave our fellows lead for lead. After a while our gunners seemed to locate them, and the shells came through the air, snarling savagely, as leopards snarl before they spring, and the flying shrapnel reached many of the Boers, wounding, maiming, or killing them; yet they held their position with indomitable pluck, those who were not hit leaping out, regardless of personal danger, to pick up those who were wounded. They were a strange, motley-looking crowd, dressed in all kinds of common farming apparel, just such a crowd as one is apt to see in a far inland shearing shed in Australia, but no man with a man's heart in his body could help admiring their devotion to one another or their loyalty to the cause they were risking their lives for.

One sight I saw which will stay with me whilst memory lasts. They had placed me under a waggon under a mass of overhanging rock for safety, and there they brought two wounded men. One was a man of fifty, a hard old veteran, with a complexion as dark as a New Zealand Maori; the beard that framed the rugged face was three-fourths grey, his hands were as rough and knotted by open air toil as the hoofs of a working steer.

He looked what he was--a Boer of mixed Dutch and French lineage. Later on I got into conversation with him, and he told me a good deal of his life. His father was descended from one of the old Dutch families who had emigrated to South Africa in search of religious liberty in the old days, when the country was a wilderness. His mother had come in an unbroken line from one of the noble families of France who fled from home in the days of the terrible persecution of the Huguenots. He himself had been many things--hunter, trader, farmer, fighting man. He had fought against the natives, and he had fought against our people. The younger man was his son, a tall, fair fellow, scarcely more than a stripling, and I had no need to be a prophet or a prophet's son to tell that his very hours were numbered. Both the father and the lad had been wounded by one of our shells, and it was pitiful to watch them as they lay side by side, the elder man holding the hand of the younger in a loving clasp, whilst with his other hand he stroked the boyish face with gestures that were infinitely pathetic. Just as the stars were coming out that night between the clouds that floated over us the Boer boy sobbed his young life out, and all through the long watches of that mournful darkness the father lay with his dead laddie's hand in his. The pain of his own wounds must have been dreadful, but I heard no moan of anguish from his lips. When, at the dawning, they came to take the dead boy from the living man, the stern old warrior simply pressed his grizzled lips to the cold face, and then turned his grey beard to the hard earth and made no further sign; but I knew well that, had the sacrifice been possible, he would gladly have given his life to save the young one's.

A BOER FIGHTING LAAGER.

Many and wonderful are the stories written and published concerning the Boer and his habits when on the war-path. Most of these stories are written by men who take good care never to get within a hundred miles of the fighting line, but content themselves with an easy chair, a cigar, a bottle of whisky, and carpet slippers on the stoep of some good hotel in a pretty little Boer town. To scribes of this calibre flock a certain class of British resident, who is always full to the very ears of his own dauntless courage, his death-less loyalty to the Queen and Empire, his love for the soldier, and his hatred of the Boer. This gallant class of British resident has half a million excuses ready to his hand to explain why he did not take a rifle and fight when the war summons rang clarion-like through the land. Then he grits his teeth, knits his eyebrows, clenches his hands in spasmodic wrath, throws out his chest, and tells his auditors, in a voice husky with concentrated wrath and whisky, what he intends to do the next time the damnable Boer rises to fight. The old British pioneer may have whelped a few million good fighting stock in his time, but this class of animal is no lion's whelp; it is a thing all mouth and no manners, a shallow-brained, cowardly creature, always howling about the Boer, but too discreet to go out and fight him, though ready at all times to malign him, to ridicule him as a farmer or a fighter, and it is a perfect bear's feast to this hybrid animal to get hold of a gullible newspaper correspondent to tell him gruesome tales relative to Boer fighting laagers.

I had one of this peculiar species at me the other day in Burghersdorp, and he painted a Boer laager so vividly, between nips at my flask, that if I had not seen a few laagers myself I should have felt bad over the matter. He pictured the smell of that laager in language so intense, with gestures so graphic, that some of his auditors had to hold their nostrils with handkerchiefs, whilst they stirred the circumambient atmosphere with cardboard fans, and I could not help wondering, if the portrait of the smell was so awful, what the thing itself must be like. Flushed with success, the narrator pursued his subject to the bitter extremity. He conjured up scenes of half-buried men lying amongst the rocks surrounding the laager: here a leg, there an arm, further on a ghastly human head protruding from amidst the scattered boulders, until I had only to close my eyes to fancy I was in a charnel-house, where Goths and Huns were holding devilish revelry. The B.R. paused, and dropped his voice two octaves lower, and the crowd on the balcony craned their heads further forward, so that they might not miss a single word. He told of the women in the laagers, the wild, unholy mirth of women, who moved from camp fire to camp fire, with dishevelled hair streaming down their backs, with tossing arms, bare to the shoulders, and blood besmeared, not the blood of goats or kine, but the blood of soldiers--our soldiers. Thomas Atkins defunct, and done for by the she-furies.

He waded in again when the shudder which shook the crowd had died away, and hinted, as that class of shallow-souled creature loves to hint, of orgies under the dim light of the stars, or between the flickering light of smoking camp fires, until the sins of Sodom and Gomorrah seemed to be crowding all around us in a peculiarly beastly and uncomfortable fashion. Then he lay back in his chair and sighed; but anon he sprang upright, and, with flashing eyes and extended arms, wanted to know what the ---- Roberts meant by offering peace with honour to such a people. "Mow them down!" he yelled. "Shoot them on sight--no quarter for such devils! Kill 'em off! kill 'em off! kill 'em off!" and he half sobbed, half sighed himself into silence, whilst the audience gazed on him as on one who knew what war, wild, red, carmine war, was. I broke in on his stillness, as newspaper men who know the game are apt to do, for I wanted data, I wanted facts, and I had not swallowed his yarn as freely as he had swallowed my whisky.

"Born in this country?" I asked.

"Yorkshire," he answered laconically.

"Been in Africa long?"

"'Bout five years."

"Where did you put in most of your time before the war?"

"Johannesburg."

"Mines?"

"No."

"Merchant?"

"No."

"Hotel-keeper, perhaps?"

"No."

"Shopkeeper?"

"No."

"What was your calling, or profession, or business, or means of livelihood?"

"General agent, sharebroker, correspondent for some local papers."

H'm; I knew the class of animal well--general jackal; do the dirty work of any trade, and master of none.

"Where were you when the war broke out?"

He scowled savagely: "Johannesburg."

"Have the same hatred for the Boers before the war as you have now?"

"Yes."

"Why didn't you pick up a rifle and have a hand in the fighting?"

"I'm not a blessed 'Tommy,' sir! Do you take me for a d---- 'Tommy,' sir?"

"No; oh, no, I assure you I did nothing of the kind. But--er, have you been in the hands of the Boers since the war started?"

"Yes, until our troops marched in here a day or two ago."

"H'm. Did they rob you?"

"No."

"Did they ill-treat you--knock you about, and that sort of thing?"

"No."

"Why do you hate them so bitterly, then?"

"Oh, I can't stand a cursed Boer at any price. Thinks he's as good as a Britisher all the time, and puts on side; and he's a cursed tyrant in his heart, and would rub us out if he could."

"Yes, the Boer thought himself as good a man as the Britishers he met out this way," I replied, "and he backed his opinion with his life and his rifle. Why didn't you do the same if you reckoned yourself a better man?"

"Why should I; don't we pay 'Tommy' to do that for us?"

"Perhaps we do; but, concerning those Boer laagers you have been telling us about: where, when, and how did you see them; what was the name of the place; who was the Boer general in command, or the field cornet, or landdrost? I did not know the Boers gave British refugees the free run of their war laagers, and I'm interested in the matter, being a scribe myself and a man of peace. Just give me a few names and dates and facts, will you?"

"No, I won't," he snarled. "You seem to doubt my word, you do, and I'm as good a Britisher as you are any day, and you think you can come along and pump information out of me for nothing; but I'm too fly for that--they don't breed fools in Yorkshire."

"Well, sir, as it seems to suit your temper," I said as sweetly as I could, "I'll make it a business proposition. I'll bet you fifty pounds to five you have never put your head inside a Boer laager in war time in your life. If you have, just name it and give me a few facts."

The B.R. rose wrathfully and muttered something about it being a d---- good job for me that I was a wounded man and had one arm in a sling, or he'd show me a heap of things in the fistic line which I should remember for the rest of my life; but as I only laughed he slouched off, and now, when we meet in the street, we pass without speaking. But I got his history, all the same, from one of the Cape Police, who told me the beggar had refused to join a volunteer regiment when the war broke out, and had remained the whole time in a quiet little Boer village as a British refugee, and had not seen the outside, let alone the inside, of a Boer fighting laager in all his lying life. Yet such cravens at times help to make history--of a kind.

Possibly it may interest Englishmen--and women, too, for that matter--to know what a fighting laager is like, and as I have seen half a dozen of them from the enemies' side of the wall, a rough pen and ink sketch may not be amiss. In war time the Boer never, under any circumstances, makes his laager in the open country if there are any kopjes about. No matter how secure he may fancy himself from attack, no matter if there is not a foe within fifty miles of him, the Boer commander always pitches his laager in a place of safety between two parallel lines of hills, so that no attack can be made upon him, either front or rear, without giving him an immense advantage over the attacking force, even if the enemy is ten times as strong in numbers. By this means the Boers make their laagers almost impregnable. If they have a choice of ground, they pick a narrow ravine, or gully, with a line of hills front and rear, covered with small rocky boulders and bushes. They drive their waggons along the ravine, and make a sort of rude breastwork across the gully with the waggons. In between these waggons the women are placed for safety, for it is a noticeable fact that very large numbers of women have followed their husbands and fathers to the war, not to act as viragoes, not to play the wanton, not to unsex themselves, not to handle the rifle, but to nurse the wounded, to comfort the dying, and to lay out the dead. I have heard them singing round the camp fires in the star-light, but it was hymns that they sang, not ribald songs. I have seen them kneeling by the side of men in the moonlight, not in wantonness, but in mercy, and many a man who wears the British uniform to-day can bear me witness that I speak the truth.

The Boer never, if he can help it, allows himself to be separated from his horse; and these hardy little animals, mostly about fifteen hands high, and very lightly framed, are picketed close to the spot where the rider deposits his rifle and blankets. If they allow them to graze on the hillsides during the day, they run a rope through the halter near the horse's muzzle, and tie it close above the knee-joint of the near fore-leg. By this means the horse can graze in comfort, but cannot move away at any pace beyond a slow walk, and so are easily caught and saddled if required in a hurry. The oxen and sheep to be used for slaughtering purposes are driven up close to the camp; a waggon or two is drawn across the ravine above and below them, and they cannot then stampede if frightened by anything, unless they climb the rocky heights on either side of them, which they have small chance of doing, as the Kaffir herdsmen sleep on the hills above them. Having pitched his laager, the commander sends out his scouts; some amble off on horseback at a pace they call a "tripple"--a gait which all the Boers educate their nags to adopt. It is not exactly an amble, but a cousin to it, marvellously easy to the rider, whilst it enables the nag to get over a wonderful lot of ground without knocking up. It also allows the horse to pick his way amongst rocky ground, and so save his legs, where an English, Indian, or Australian horse would be apt to cripple himself in very short order. As soon as the mounted scouts set off on their journey, holding the reins carelessly in the left hand, their handy little Mauser rifles in their right, swaying carelessly in the saddle after the fashion of all bush-riders the world over, the foot scouts take up their positions amongst the rocks and shrubs on the hills in front and rear of the laager. Each scout has his rifle in his hand, his pipe in his teeth, his bandolier full of cartridges over his shoulder, and his scanty blanket under his left arm. No fear of his sleeping at his post. He is fighting for honour, not for pay; for home, not for glory; and he knows that on his acuteness the lives of all may depend. He knows that his comrades and the women trust him, and he values the trust as dearly as British soldier ever did. No matter how tired he may be, no matter how famished, the Boer sentinel is never faithless to his orders.

When the scouts are out the laager is fixed for the night--not a very exhaustive proceeding, as the Boers do not go in for luxuries of any kind. Here a tarpaulin is stretched over a kind of temporary ridge pole, blankets are tossed down on the hard earth, saddles are used for pillows, and the couch is complete. A little way farther down the line a rude canvas screen is thrown over the wheels of a waggon, and a family, or rather husband and wife, make themselves at home under the waggon; whilst the single men simply throw themselves at full length on the ground, wrap their one thin, small blanket round them, and smoke and jest merrily enough, whilst the Kaffirs light the fires and make the coffee. There is scarcely any timber in this part of Africa, and the fuel used is the dried manure of cattle pressed into slabs about fifteen inches long, eight inches wide, and three inches thick. The smoke from the fires is very dense, and soon fills the air with a pungent odour, which is not unpleasant in the open, but would be simply intolerable in a building. The coffee is soon made, and the simple meal begins; it consists of "rusks," a kind of bread baked until it becomes crisp and hard, and plenty of steaming hot coffee. I never saw any people so fond of this beverage as the Boers are. The Australian bushman and digger loves tea, and can almost exist upon it; but these Boers cling to coffee. They live, when out in laager, like Spartans, they dress anyhow, sleep anyhow, and eat just rusks and precious little else. Talk about "Tommy" and his hard times, why a private soldier at the front sleeps better, dresses better, and eats better than a Boer general; yet never once did I hear a Boer complain of hardships. After tea the Boers sit about and clean their rifles; the women move from one little group to another, chatting cheerfully, but I saw nothing in their conduct, or in the conduct of any man towards one of them, that would cause the most chaste matron in Great

Britain to blush or droop her eyes. There is in the laager an utter absence of what we term soldierly discipline; men moved about, went and came in a free and easy fashion, just as I have seen them do a thousand times in diggers' camps. There was no saluting of officers, no stiffness, no starch anywhere. The general lounges about with hands in pockets and pipe in mouth; no one pays him any special deference. He talks to the men, the striplings, and the women, and they talk back to him in a manner which seems strange to a Britisher familiar to the ways of military camps. After the chatting, the pridikant, or parson, if there is one in the laager, raises his hands, and all listen with reverent faces whilst the man of God utters a few words in a solemn, earnest tone; then all kneel, and a prayer floats up towards the skies, and a few moments later the whole camp is wrapped in sleep, nothing is heard but the neighing of horses, the lowing of cattle, the bleating of sheep, and the occasional barking of a dog. There is no clatter of arms, no ringing of bugles, no deep-toned challenge of sentries, no footfall of changing pickets.

At regular intervals men rise silently from the ranks of the sleepers, pick up their rifles noiselessly, and silently, like ghosts, slip out into the deep shadows of the kopjes, and other men, equally silent, glide in from posts they have been guarding, and stretch themselves out to snatch slumber whilst they may. At dawn the men toss their blankets aside, and spring up ready dressed, and move amongst their horses; the Kaffirs attend to the morning meal, the everlasting rusks and coffee are served up, horses are saddled, cattle are yoked to waggons, and in the twinkling of an eye the camp is broken up, and the irregular army is on the march again, with scouts guarding every pass in front, scouts watching (themselves unseen) on every height. They travel fast, because they travel light; they use very little water, because they find it impossible to move it from place to place. Many critics charge them with habits of personal uncleanliness. It is true that in their laagers one does not see as much soap and water used as in our camps, but this is possibly due to want of opportunity as much as to want of inclination. In sanitary matters they are neglectful. I did not see a single latrine in any of their laagers, nor do I think they are in the habit of making them, and to this cause and to no other I attribute the large amount of fever in their ranks. They do not seem to understand the first principles of the laws of sanitation, and had this season been a wet, instead of a peculiarly dry one, I venture to assert that typhoid fever would have wrought far more havoc amongst them than our rifles.

I saw no literature in laager except Bibles. I witnessed no sports of any kind, and the only sport I heard them talk about was horse-racing. I saw no gambling, heard no blasphemy, noticed no quarrelling or bickering, and can only say, from my slight acquaintance with life in Boer laager in war time, that it may be rough, it may be irksome, it may not be so fastidiously clean as a feather-bed soldier might like it, but I have been in many tougher, rougher places, and never heard anyone cry about it.

THROUGH BOER GLASSES.

I had a good many opportunities of chatting with Boers during the time which elapsed between my capture and liberation, and had a long talk with the President of the Orange Free State, Mr. Steyn; also with several of his ministerial colleagues. Their ministers of religion, whom they call pridikants, also chatted to me freely, as occasion offered. I had more than one interview with their fighting generals. Medical men in their service I found very much akin to medical men the world over. They patched up the wounded and asked no questions concerning nationality, just as our own medicos do. Personally, I must say that I found the Boers first-class subjects for Press interviews. They did not know much about journalists and the ways of journalism. Possibly had they had more experience in regard to "interviews," I should not have found them quite so easy to manage, but it never seemed to enter their heads that a man might make good "copy" out of a quiet chat over pipes and tobacco. One of their stock subjects of conversation was their great General, the man of Magersfontein--General Cronje.

"What do you Britishers and Australians think of Cronje?" was a stock question with them. "Do you think him a good fighter?"

"Well, yes, unquestionably he is a good fighting man."

"Do you think him as good as Lord Roberts?"

"No. We men of British blood don't think there are many men on earth as good as the hero of Candahar."

"Do you think him as good a man as Lord Kitchener?"

"No. Very many of us consider the conqueror of the Soudan to be one who, if he lives, will make as great a mark in history as Wellington."

At this a joyous smile would illuminate the face of the Boer. He would reply, "Yes, yes; Roberts is a great man, a very great man indeed. So is Kitchener, so is General French, so is General Macdonald, so is General Methuen. Yet all those five men are attempting to get Cronje into a corner where they can capture him. They have ten times as many soldiers as Cronje has, ten times as many guns; therefore, what a really great man Cronje must be on your own showing."

That was before the fatal 27th of February on which Cronje surrendered.

I often asked them how they, representing a couple of small States, came to get hold of the idea that they could whip a colossal Power like Great Britain in a life or death struggle; and almost invariably they informed me that they had expected that one of the great European Powers would take an active part in the struggle on their behalf, and, furthermore, they had been taught to think that Britain's Empire was rotten to the core, so much so that as soon as war commenced in earnest all her colonies would fall away from her and hoist the flag of independence, and that India would leap once again into open and bloody mutiny. They expressed themselves as being dumbfounded when they heard that Australian troops were rallying under the Union Jack, and seemed to feel most bitterly that the men from the land of the Southern Cross were in arms against them. "We fell out with England, and we thought we had to fight England. Instead we find we have to fight people from all parts of the world, Colonials like ourselves. Surely Australia and Canada might have kept out of this fight, and allowed us to battle it out with the country we had a quarrel with."

"The Canadians and Australians are of British blood."

"Well, what if they are? Ain't plenty of the Cape Volunteers who are fighting under President Kruger's banner born of Dutch parents? Yet, because they fight against Englishmen, you call them all rebels, and talk of punishing them when the war is over, if you win, just because they lived on your side of the border and not on ours. Would you ask one Boer to fight against another Boer simply because he lived on one side of a river and his blood relation lived on the other? You Britishers brag of your pride of blood, and draw your fighting stock from all parts of the world in war time, but you have no generosity; you won't allow other people to be proud of their blood too."

I tried to persuade them that I did not for one moment think that Britain would be vindictive towards so-called rebels in the hour of victory, and pointed out that, in my small opinion, such a course would be foreign to the traditions of the Motherland; and was often met with the retort that if England did so the shame would be hers, not theirs. Many a time I was told to remember the Jameson raid and the manner in which the Boers treated not only the leaders of that band of adventurers, but the men also. "Look here," said one old fighting man to me, as he leant with negligent grace on his rifle, "I was one of those who helped to corner Jameson and his men, and I can tell you that we Boers knew very well that we would have been acting within our rights if we had shot Jameson and every man he had with him, because his was not an act of war--it was an act of piracy; and had we done so, and England had attempted to avenge the deed, half the civilised world would have ranged themselves on our side; but we did not seek those men's blood; we gave them quarter as soon as they asked for it, and after that, though we knew very well they had done all that men could do to involve us in a war of extermination with a great nation, we sent their leader home to his own country to be tried by his own countrymen, and the rank and file we forgave freely. We may be a nation of white savages, but our past does not prove it, and if Britain wins in the war now going on she will have to be very generous indeed before we will need to blush for our conduct."

"Why should not the white population of South Africa be ready to live under the protection of Britain? The yoke cannot be so heavy when men of all creeds, colours, and nationalities who have lived under that rule for years are now ready to volunteer to fight for her, even against you, who have admittedly done them no direct wrong?"

"Why should we live under any flag but our own?" replied the old fighting man passionately. "We came here and found the country a wilderness in the hands of savages; we fought our way into the land step by step, holding our own with our rifles; we had to live lives of fearful hardships, facing wild beasts and wilder men; we won with the strong hand the land we live in. Why should we bow our necks to Britain's yoke, even if it be a yoke of silk?" And as he spoke a murmur of deep and earnest sympathy ran through the ranks of the Boers who were standing around him.

"You, of course, blame all the Colonials, Australians and others, for coming to fight against you?" I asked. "I don't know that I do, or that my people do, in a sense," the veteran replied. "It all depends upon the spirit which animated them. If your Australians, who are of British blood, came here to fight for your Motherland, believing that her cause was a just and a holy one, and that she needed your aid, you did right, for a son will help his mother, if he be a son worth having; but if the Australians came here merely for the sake of adventure, merely for sport, as men come in time of peace to shoot buck on the veldt, then woe to that land, for though God may make no sign to-day nor to-morrow, yet, in His own time, He will surely wring from Australia a full recompense in sweat and blood and tears; for whether we be right or wrong, our God knows that we are giving our lives freely for what we in our hearts believe to be a holy cause."

"What do you fellows think of Australians as fighters?"

I asked the question carelessly, but the answer that I got brought me to my bearings quickly, for then I learnt that more than one gallant Australian officer dear to me had fallen, never to rise again, since I had been taken prisoner. The man who spoke was little more than a lad, a pale-faced, slenderly built son of the veldt. He had tangled curly hair, and big, pathetic blue eyes, soft as a girl's, and limbs that lacked the rugged strength of the old Boer stock; but there was that nameless "something," that indefinable expression in his face which warranted him a brave man. He carried one arm in a sling, and the bandage round his neck hid a bullet wound. "The Australians can fight," he said simply. "They wounded me, and--they killed my father." Perhaps it was the wind sighing through the hospital trees that made the Boer lad's voice grow strangely husky; possibly the same cause filled the blue eyes with unshed tears.

"It was in fair fight, lad," I said gently; "it was the fortune of war."

"Yes," he murmured, "it was in fair fight, an awful fight--I hope I'll never look upon another like it. Damn the fighting," he broke out fiercely. "Damn the fighting. I didn't hate your Australians. I didn't want to kill any of them. My father had no ill-will to them, nor they to him, yet he is out there--out there between two great kopjes--where the wind always blows cold and dreary at night-time." The laddie shuddered. "It makes a man doubt the love of the Christ," he said. "My father was a good man, a kind man, who never turned the stranger empty-handed from his door, even the Kaffirs on the farm loved him; and now he is lying where no one can weep over his grave. We piled great rocks on his grave. My cousin and I buried him. We had no shovels; we scooped a hole in the hard earth as well as we could, a long, shallow hole, and we laid him in it. I took his head and Cousin Gustave carried his feet. We folded his hands on his breast, laid his old rifle by his side, because he had always loved that gun, and never used any other when out hunting. Then we pushed the earth in on him gently with our hands, breaking the hard lumps up and crumbling them in our palms, so that they should not bruise his poor flesh. He had always been so kind, we could not hurt him, even though we knew he was dead, for he had been gentle to all of us in life; even the cows and the oxen at home loved him--and now who will go back and tell mother and little Yacoba that he is dead, that he will come to them no more? Oh, damn the war," the lad called again in his pain. "I don't know--only God knows--which side is right or wrong, but I do know that the curse of the Christ will rest on the heads of those who have made this war for ambition's sake or the greed of gold, and the good God will not let the widow and the orphan child go unavenged; blood will yet speak for blood, and it must rest either on the heads of Kruger and Steyn, or Chamberlain and Rhodes."

"Tell me, comrade, of the Australians who fell. They were my countrymen."

"It was a cruel fight," he said. "We had ambushed a lot of the British troops--the Worcesters, I think, they called them. They could neither advance nor retire; we had penned them in like sheep, and our field cornet, Van Leyden, was beseeching them to throw down their rifles to save being slaughtered, for they had no chance. Just then we saw about a hundred Australians come bounding over the rocks in the gully behind us. There were two great big men in front cheering them on. We turned and gave them a volley, but it did not stop them. They rushed over everything, firing as they came, not wildly, but as men who know the use of a rifle, with the quick, sharp, upward jerk to the shoulder, the rapid sight, and then the shot. They knocked over a lot of our men, but we had a splendid position. They had to expose themselves to get to us, and we shot them as they came at us. They were rushing to the rescue of the English. It was splendid, but it was madness. On they came, and we lay behind the boulders, and our rifles snapped and snapped again at pistol range, but we did not stop those wild men until they charged right into a little basin which was fringed around all its edges by rocks covered with bushes. Our men lay there as thick as locusts, and the Australians were fairly trapped. They were far worse off than the Worcesters, up high in the ravine.

"Our field cornet gave the order to cease firing, and called on them to throw down their rifles or die. Then one of the big officers--a, great, rough-looking man, with a voice like a bull--roared out, 'Forward Australia!--no surrender!' Those were the last words he ever uttered, for a man on my right put a bullet clean between his eyes, and he fell forward dead. We found later that his name was Major Eddy, of the Victorian Rifles. He was as brave as a lion, but a Mauser bullet will stop the bravest. His men dashed at the rocks like wolves; it was awful to see them. They smashed at our heads with clubbed rifles, or thrust their rifles up against us through the rocks and fired. One after another their leaders fell. The second big man went down early, but he was not killed. He was shot through the groin, but not dangerously. His name was Captain McInnerny. There was another one, a little man named Lieutenant Roberts; he was shot through the heart. Some of the others I forget. The men would not throw down their rifles; they fought like furies. One man I saw climb right on to the rocky ledge where Big Jan Albrecht was stationed. Just as he got there a bullet took him, and he staggered and dropped his rifle. Big Jan jumped forward to catch him before he toppled over the ledge, but the Australian struck Jan in the mouth with his clenched fist, and fell over into the ravine below and was killed.

"We killed and wounded an awful lot of them, but some got away; they fought their way out. I saw a long row of their dead and wounded laid out on the slope of a farmhouse that evening--they were all young men, fine big fellows. I could have cried to look at them lying so cold and still. They had been so brave in the morning, so strong; but in the evening, a few little hours, they were dead, and we had not hated them, nor they us. Yes, I could have cried as I thought of the women who would wait for them in Australia. Yes, I could have shed tears, though they had wounded me, but then I thought of my father, and of the mother, and little Yacoba on the farm, who would wait in vain for *him*, and then I could feel sorry for those, the wives and children of the dead men, no longer."

LIFE IN THE BOER CAMPS.

HEADQUARTERS, ORANGE RIVER COLONY.

It is an article of faith with many people that a Boer commando is a mere mob, that its leaders exercise no control over men in laager or on the field, and that punishment for crimes is a thing unknown. But this is far from being the case. It is quite true that a Boer soldier does not know how to click his heels together, turn his toes to an acute angle, stiffen his back, and salute every time an officer runs against him. He could not properly perform any of the very simplest military evolutions common to all European soldiers if his immortal welfare depended upon it. That is why he is such a failure as an attacking agent. Still, in spite of these things, the Boer on commando has to submit to very rigid laws. The penalty for outrage, or attempted outrage, on a woman is instant death on conviction, no matter what the woman's nationality may be. For sleeping on sentry duty the punishment is unique; it is a punishment born of long dwelling in the wilderness. It is of such a nature that no man who has once undergone it is calculated ever to forget. When a clear case is made out against a burgher by trial before his commandant the whole commando in laager is summoned to witness the criminal's reward. He is taken out beyond the lines to a spot where the sun shines in all its unprotected fierceness. He is led to an ant-hill full of busy, wicked, little crawlers; the top of the ant-hill is cut off with a spade, leaving a honeycombed surface for the sleepy one to stand upon (not much fear of him sleeping whilst he is there). He is ordered to mount the hill and stand with feet close together. His rifle is placed in his hands, the butt resting between his toes, the muzzle clasped in both hands. Two men are then told off to watch him. They are picked men, noted for their stern, unyielding sense of duty and love for the cause they fight for.

These guards lie down in the veldt twenty-five yards away from the victim. They have their loaded Mausers with them, and their orders are, if the prisoner lifts a leg, to put a bullet into it; if he lifts an arm, a bullet goes into that defaulting member; if he jumps down from his perch altogether, the leaden messengers sent from both rifles will cancel all his earthly obligations. The sun shines down in savage mockery; it strikes upon the bare neck of the quivering wretch, who dare not lift a hand to shift his hat to cover the blistering skin. It strikes in his eyes and burns his lips until they swell and feel like bursting. The barrel of his rifle grows hotter and hotter, until his fingers feel as if glued to a gridiron. The very clothes upon his body burn the skin beneath. He feels desperate; he must shift one arm, for the anguish is intolerable. He makes an almost imperceptible movement of his shoulder, and glances towards his guards. The man on his right front lays his pipe quickly in the grass, and swiftly lifts his Mauser to his shoulder. The wretch on the ant-heap closes his eyes with a groan, and stands as still as a Japanese god carved out of jute-wood. The guard lays down his rifle and picks up his pipe.

The sun climbs higher and higher, until it gleams down straight into the ant-heap; the scorching heat penetrates into the unprotected cells, and enrages the dwellers inside. They swarm out full of fight, like an army lusting for battle. Their home has been ravished of the protection they had raised with half a lifetime of labour, and in their puny way they want vengeance. They find a foe on top, a man ready to their wrath. They crawl into his scorched boots, over his baked feet, guiltless of stockings; they charge up the legs, on which the trousers hang loosely, and as they charge they bite, because they are out for business, not for a picnic. The very stillness of their victim seems to enrage them. The first legion retires at full speed down into the ant-heap again. They have gone for recruits. In a few seconds up they come again, until the very top of the heap is alive with them. They climb one over another in their eagerness to get in their individual moiety of revenge. Down into the veldtschoon, up the bare, hairy legs, over the hips, round the waist, over the lean ribs, along the spine, under the arms, round the neck, over the whole man they go, as the Mongolian hordes will some day go over the Western world. And each one digs his tiny prongs into the smarting, burning, itching poor devil on top of their homestead. He shifts a leg the hundredth part of an inch. The guard on the left gives his bandolier a warning twist, and glances along the long brown barrel that nestles in the hollow of his left hand.

The commandant comes out of the circle of burghers, looks at the victim, sees that the eyes are bloodshot and protruding far beyond the normal position. He is not a hard man, but he knows that the culprit has endangered the lives and liberties of all. "You will remember this," he says sternly; "you will not again sleep when it is your turn to watch." "Never, so help me God!" gasps the prisoner. "Stand down, then; you are free." Quicker than a swallow's flight is the movement of the liberated man. He drops his rifle with a gasp of relief, tears every stitch of clothing from his body, throws the garments from him, and pelts his veldtschoon after them. Some sympathetic veteran, who has possibly, in earlier wars, been through the ordeal himself, runs up with a drink of blessed water. He does not drink it; he pours it down his burning throat, then sits on the grass, drawing his breath in long, sobbing sighs, all the more terrible because they are tearless. From head to heel he is covered with tiny red marks, just like a schoolboy who has had the measles; in three days there will not be a mark on him, but he won't forget them, all the same, not in thirty-three years, or three hundred and thirty-three, if he happens to have a memory of any kind at that period.

This mode of punishing recalcitrant persons was picked up, I am told, from one of the savage tribes. I do not know if this is so or not, but there is no doubt that the niggers know all about it, because one day, when I found that one of my niggers had been helping himself lavishly to my tobacco, I promised to stand him on an ant-heap as soon as I had finished shaving. Five minutes later my other nigger, Lazarus, came into my tent and informed me that Johnnie had bolted. I went out, and by the aid of my glasses I could just espy a black dot away out on the veldt, making a rapid and direct line for the land of the Basutos; and that was the last I ever saw or heard of tobacco-loving, work-dodging, truth-twisting Johnnie.

There is a distinctly humorous side to the Boer character, which crops out sometimes in his methods of dealing out justice to those who have done the thing that seems evil in his sight. If there is a fellow in laager who is not amenable to orders, one of those malcontents who desires to have everything his own way--and there generally is one of these cherubs in every large gathering of men all the world over--the commandant first calls him up and warns him that he is making himself a pest to the whole commando, and exhorts him to mend his manners. As a general thing the commandant throws a few slabs of Scripture appropriate to the occasion at the disturber's ears, and mixes it judiciously with a good deal of worldly wisdom, all of which tending to teach the fellow that he is about as desirable as a comrade as a sore eye in a sand-storm. Should the exhortation not have the desired effect, and the offender continue to stir up strife in laager, as a lame mule stirs up mud in midstream, then the commandant sends a guard of young men to gather in the unruly one. He is captured with as little ceremony as a nigger captures a hog in the midst of his mealy patch. They strip him bare to the waist, and put a bridle on his head; the bit is jammed into his mouth, and firmly buckled there, and then the circus begins. One of the guards takes the reins, usually a couple of long lengths of raw hide; another flicks the human steed on the bare ribs with a sjambok, and he is ordered to show his paces. He has to walk, trot, canter, gallop, and "tripple" all around the laager several times, amidst the badinage and laughter of the burghers, and he gets enough "chaff" during the journey to last the biggest horse in England a lifetime.

It is bad enough when there are only men there, but when there are, as is often the case, a dozen or two of women and girls present his woe is served up to him full measure and brimming over. The men roar with laughter, and pelt him with crusts of rusks, but the women and girls make his life an agony for the time being. They smile at him sweetly, and ask him if he feels lonely without a cart, or they pull up a handful of grass and offer it to him on the end of a stick, making a lot of "stage aside" remarks concerning the length of his ears the while, until the fellow's face crimsons with shame.

They are wonderfully patriotic, these Boer girls and women, and are merciless in their contempt for a man who will not do his share of fighting, marching, and watching cheerfully and uncomplainingly. The hardships and privations they themselves undergo without murmuring, in order to assist their husbands, brothers, and lovers, is worthy of being chronicled in the pages of history, for they are the Spartans of the nineteenth century. They are swift to help those who need help, but unsparing with their scorn for those who are unworthy. The treatment meted out to the grumbler and mischief-maker usually presents more of the elements of comedy than anything else, and it is his own fault if he does not get off lightly. But if he cuts up rough, tries to strike or kick his drivers or tormentors, or if he goes in for a course of sulks, and flops himself down, refusing to be driven, then the comic element disappears from the scene. Out come the sjamboks, and he is treated precisely as a vicious or sulky horse would be treated under similar circumstances. As a rule, it does not take long to bring a man of that kind to his proper senses. Should he talk of deserting or of avenging himself later on, he is watched, and a deserter soon learns that a rifle bullet can travel faster than he can. As for revenge, the sooner he forgets desires or designs of that kind the better for his own health.

For minor offences, such as laziness, neglecting to keep the rifle clean and in good shooting order, attempting to strike up a flirtation with a married woman, to the annoyance of the lady, or any other little matter of the kind, the wayward one is "tossed." Tossing is not the sort of pastime any fellow would choose for fun, not if he were the party to be tossed, though it is a beanfeast for the onlookers. They manage it this way. A hide, freshly stripped from a bullock, smoking, bloody, and limber as a bowstring, is requisitioned; the hairy side is turned downwards, two strong men get hold of each corner, cutting holes in the green hide for their hands to have a good grip; they allow the hide to sag until it forms a sort of cradle, into which the unlucky one is dumped neck and crop. Then the signal is given, the hide sways to and fro for a few seconds, and then, with a skilful jerk, it is drawn as taut as eight pairs of strong arms can draw it. If the executioners are skilful at the business the victim shoots upwards from the blood-smeared surface like a dude's hat in a gale of wind. Sometimes he comes down on his feet, sometimes on his head, or he may sprawl face downwards, clutching at the slimy surface as eagerly as a politician clutches at a place in power. But his efforts are vain; a couple more swings and another jerk, and up he goes, turning and twisting like a soiled shirt on a wire fence. This time he comes down on his hands and knees, and promptly commences to plead for pity, but before he can open his heart a neat little jerk sends him out on his back, where he claws and kicks like a jackal in a gin case, whilst the more ribald amongst the onlookers sing songs appropriate to the occasion, but the more devout chant some such hymn as this:

Lord, let me linger here,
For this is bliss.

A man is very seldom hurt at this game, though how he escapes without a broken neck is one of the wonders of gravitation to me. One second you see the poor beggar in mid air, going like a circular saw through soft pine. Just when you are beginning to wonder if he has converted himself into a catherine-wheel or a cork-screw, he straightens himself out horizontally, remains poised for the millionth part of a second like a he-angel that has moulted his wings; then down he dives perpendicularly like a tornado in trousers, skinning forehead, nose, and chin as he kisses the drum-like surface of the hide. No, on the whole, I do not consider it healthy to try to fool with a married woman in a Boer fighting laager, apart altogether from the moral aspect of the affair. If some of the amorous dandies I wot of, who claim kindred with us, got the same sort of treatment in Old England, many a merry matron would be saved much annoyance.

For rank disobedience of orders, brutality of conduct, cowardice in the face of the enemy, flagrant neglect of the wounded, or any other very serious military crime, the punishment is sjamboking, which is simply flogging, as it existed in our Army and Navy not so many years ago. On board ship they used to use the "cat," a genteel instrument with a handle attached. The Boer sjambok is a different article altogether; it has not nine tails, but it gets there just the same. The sjambok dear to the Boer soul is that made out of rhinoceros hide. It is a plain piece of hide, not twisted in any way; just clean cut out and trimmed round all the way down. It is about three feet long, and at the end which the flogger holds it is about two and a half inches in circumference, tapering down gradually to a rat-tail point. It is a terrible weapon when the person who wields it is bent on business, and is not manufacturing poetry or mingling thoughts of home and mother with the flogging. Truth to tell, I don't think they do much flogging--not half as much as they are credited with--but when they do flog, the party who gets it wants a soft shirt for a month after, and it's quite a while before he will lie on his back for the mere pleasure of seeing the moon rise.

BATTLE OF CONSTANTIA FARM.

THABA NCHU.

The Battle of Constantia Farm will not rank as one of the big events of this war, but it is worthy of a full description, because in this battle the Briton for the first time laid himself out from start to finish to fight the Boer pretty much on his own lines, instead of following time-honoured British rules of war. Before attempting to portray the actual fighting, I think a brief sketch of our movements from the time we left the railway line to cross the country will be of interest to those readers of **The Daily News** who desire to follow the progress of the war with due care.

The Third Division, which had been at Stormberg, and had done such excellent, though almost bloodless, work by sweeping the country between the last-named place and Bethany, rested at the latter place, and built up its full strength by incorporating a large number of men and guns. General Gatacre, who had retrieved his reverse at Stormberg by forcing Commandant Olivier to vacate his almost impregnable position without striking a blow, and later by his masterly move in swooping down on Bethulie Bridge and preventing the Boers from wrecking the line of communication between Lord Roberts and his supplies from Capetown, only remained long enough with his old command to see them equipped in a manner fit to take the field, and then retired in favour of General Chermside. It was under this officer that we marched away from the railway line across country known to be hostile to us. Almost due east we moved to Reddersburg, about twelve and a half miles. We had to move slowly and cautiously, because no living man can tell when, where, or how a Boer force will attack. They follow rules of their own, and laugh at all accepted theories of war, ancient or modern, and no general can afford to hold them cheap.

A day and a half was spent at Reddersburg, and then the Third Division continued its eastward course in wretched weather, until Rosendal was arrived at. This is the spot where the Royal Irish Rifles and Northumberland Fusiliers had to surrender to the Boers. We had to camp there for the best part of three days on account of the continuous downpour of rain, which rendered the veldt tracks impassable for our transport. To push onward meant the absolute destruction of mules and oxen, and the consequent loss of food supplies, without which we were helpless, for in that country every man's hand was against us, not only in regard to actual warfare, but in regard to forage for man and beast.

Here we were joined by General Rundle with the Eighth Division, which brought our force up to about thirteen thousand men, thirty big guns, and a number of Maxims. When the weather cleared slightly we moved onward slowly, the ground simply clinging to the wheels of the heavily laden waggons, until it seemed as if the very earth, as well as all that was on top of it, was opposed to our march. Our scouts constantly saw the enemy hovering on our front and flanks, and more than once exchanged shots with them. General Rundle, who was in supreme command, thus knew that he could not hope to surprise the wily foe, for it was evident to the merest tyro that the Boer leader was keeping a sharp eye upon our movements, and would not be taken at a disadvantage. We expected to measure the enemy's fighting force at any hour, but it was not until about half-past ten on the morning of Friday, the 20th of April, that we were certain that he meant to measure his arms with ours, though early on that morning our scouts had brought in news that a commando, believed to be about two thousand five hundred strong, with half a dozen guns, commanded by General De Wet, was strongly posted right on our line of march. Slowly we crept across the open veldt, our men stretching from east to west for fully six miles. There was no moving of solid masses of men, no solid grouping of troops; no two men marched shoulder to shoulder, a gap showed plainly between each of the khaki-clad figures as we moved on to the rugged, broken line of kopjes. There was no hurry, no bustle, the men behaved admirably, each individual soldier seeming to have his wits about him, and proving it by taking advantage of every bit of cover that came in his way. If they halted near an ant-hill, they at once put it between themselves and the enemy.

Slowly but steadily they rolled onward, like a great sluggish, but irresistible, yellow wave, until we saw the scouts slipping from rock to rock up the stony heights of the first line of hills. Breathlessly we watched the intrepid "eyes of the army" advance until they stood silhouetted against the sky-line on the top of the black bulwarks of the veldt. Then we strained our ears to catch the rattle of the enemy's rifles, but we listened in vain; and we were completely staggered. What did it mean? Was it a trap? Was there some devilish craft behind that apparent peacefulness? Trap or no trap, we had not long to wait. The long, yellow wave curled inwards from both flanks, the men going forward with quick, lithesome steps. The mounted infantry shot forward as if moved by magic, and, before the eye could scarcely grasp the details, our fellows held the heights, and men marvelled and wondered whether the Boers had bolted for good. But they soon undeceived us, for the hills shook with the far-reaching roar of their guns, and shells began to make melody which devils love; but they did no harm. Not a man was touched. Then came the short, sharp word of command from our lines. Officers bit their words across the centre, and threw them at the men. The Horse Artillery moved into position, some going at a steady trot, others sweeping along the valleys as if they were the children of the storm. The left flank swung forward and encircled the base of an imposing kopje. The men swarmed up with tiger-like activity, quickly, and in broken and irregular lines; but there was no confusion, no wretched tangle, no helpless muddle. They did not rush madly to the top and stand on the sky-line to be a mark for their foes. When they almost touched the summit they paused, formed their broken lines, and carefully and wisely topped the black brow; and as they did so the Boer rifles spoke from a line of kopjes that lay behind the first. Then our fellows dropped to cover, and sent an answer back that a duller foe than the Boers would not have failed to understand. The Mauser bullets splashed on the rocks, and spat little fragments of lead in all directions; but few of them found a resting-place under those thin yellow jackets. By-and-by the shells began to follow the Mauser's spiteful pellets, but the shells were less harmful even than the little hostile messengers; for, though well directed, the shells never burst--they simply shrieked, yelled, and buried themselves. Our gunners got the ground they wanted, and soon gun spoke to gun in their deep-throated tones of defiance. The Boers were not hurting us; whether we were injuring them we could not tell.

In the meantime our whole transport came safely inside a little semi-circular valley, and arranged itself with almost ludicrous precision. The nigger drivers chaffed one another as the shells made melody above their heads, and made the air fairly dance with the picturesque terms of endearment they bestowed upon their mules, between the welts they bestowed with their long two-handed whips. When two of their leaders jibbed and refused to budge, they howled and called them Mr. Steyn and Ole Oom Paul; but when they got down solid to their work they laughed until even their back teeth were showing beyond the dusky horizon of their lips, and endowed them with the names of Cecil Rhodes and Mistah Chamberlain, which may or may not appear complimentary to the owners of those titles--anyway, the mules did not seem to be offended. One thing was made manifest to me then, and confirmed later on, viz., the nigger is a game fellow; give him a little excitement, and he is full of "devil"--it's the doing of deeds in cold blood that finds him out. After seeing the way the transport was handled, I moved along to look at the ambulance arrangements, and found them practically perfect. The medical staff was cool and collected, the helpers were alert and attentive to business; the waggons, with their conspicuous red crosses, were all well and carefully placed--though in such a fight it was a sheer impossibility to dispose them so as to render them absolutely immune from danger, for shells have a knack of falling where least expected, and when they burst he is a wise man who falls flat on his face and leaves the rest to his Creator and the fortune of war. My next move was to secure a position on the top of a kopje, to try to gather some idea concerning the actual strength of the Boer position. It needed no soldier's training to tell a man who knew the rugged Australian ranges thoroughly that the enemy had chosen his ground with consummate skill. To get at the Boers our men had either to go down the sides of the kopjes in full view of the clever enemy, or else make their way between narrow gullies, where shells would work havoc in their packed ranks. After they had reached the open, level ground, they had to cross open spaces of veldt commanded by the Boer guns and rifles, whilst the Boers themselves sat tight in a row of ranges that ran from east to west, mile after mile, in almost unbroken ruggedness. If we turned either flank, they could promptly fall back upon another line of kopjes as strong as those they held. Away behind their position the grim heights of Thaba Nchu rose towards the blue sky, solemn and stately. Far away to the eastward, a little south of east perhaps, I could see the hills that hid Wepener, distant about eighteen miles from the Boer centre. There we knew, and the enemy knew, that the Boers held a British force pinned in. They knew, and we knew, that Commandant Olivier, with eight or nine thousand men and a lot of guns, held the reins in his hands; and the men our force were engaging knew that unless they could keep us in check Olivier would soon be the hunted instead of the hunter.

By-and-by the rifle fire on our left flank grew weaker and weaker--our guns were searching the kopjes with merciless accuracy--and before sundown it died away altogether, and we had time to collect our wounded and ascertain our losses, though we could not even guess how the Boers had fared Our wounded amounted to eight men all told, none of them dangerously hurt; of dead we had none, not one. When their fire slackened the enemy doubtless expected to see an onward dash of troops from our position, but it was not to be. General Rundle had decided to play "patience" and save his men; there was no necessity for him to rush on and force the Boer position, and he chose the better part. Steadily our fellows were worked into position, until every bit of ground that could bear upon the foe was lined with British troops. Every available point, front or flank, where a gun could be placed to harass the foe was taken advantage of; nothing was left to chance, nothing was rashly hurried. Carefully, methodically the work was done. There was to be no carnival of death on our side, no trusting to the "luck of the British Army," no headlong rush into the arms of destruction, no waving line of bayonets. The Boer was to play a hand with the cards he loves to deal. He was to be shelled and sniped. If he wanted straight-out fighting, he had to come out into the open and get it. He was to have no chance to sit in safety and slaughter the British soldiers like shambled deer, as he had so often done before. As the sun went down our men bivouacked where they stood, and nothing was heard through the long, cold night except at intervals the grim growling of a gun, the sentinels' swift, curt challenge, or the neighing of horses as steed spoke to steed across the grass-grown veldt.

At the breaking of the dawn I was aroused from sleep by the simultaneous crashing of several of our batteries. It was Britain's morning salutation to the Boer. I hurried up to a spot on the kopje where a regiment of Worcesters lay amongst the broken ground, and saw that the battle was just about to commence in deadly earnest. It was a huge, flat-topped kopje where I located myself. The outer edges of the hill rose higher than the centre, a little rivulet ran across tiny indentations on the crown of that rampart, and there was ample space for an army to lie concealed from the eyes of enemies. If the Boers were strongly posted, so were the British. Away past our right flank Wepener range was plainly visible in the clear morning light, and just behind Wepener lay the Basuto border, with its fringe of mountains. About two thousand yards away, directly facing our centre, a white farmhouse stood in a cluster of trees. This farmhouse gave the battlefield its name, Constantia Farm. The enemy could be seen by the aid of glasses slipping from the kopjes down towards this farm and back again at intervals. Cattle, horses, goats, and sheep went on grazing calmly, the roaring of the guns doubtless seeming to them but as the tumult of a storm.

Turning my eyes towards the valley behind our position, I saw that we intended to try to turn the enemy's left flank. Little squads of mounted men, 95 in each group, swept along the valley at a gallop. They were the Yeomanry and mounted infantry, and numbered about 600. A more workmanlike body of fellows it would be hard to find anywhere. They sat their horses with easy confidence, and looked full of fight. Some of them carried their rifles in their hands, muzzle upwards, the butt resting on the right thigh; others had their guns slung across their shoulders. Group after group went eastward, and the Boers knew nothing of the movement, because we were for once employing their own tactics. I watched them out of sight, and then turned my attention to the guns. There was very little time wasted by our people. The gunners on our left flank poured in a heavy fire, the centre took up the chorus, and the guns on the right repeated it. For miles along their front the Boers must have been in deadly peril. We seldom saw them. Now and again a group of roughly clad horsemen would flash into view and disappear again as if by magic, with shells hurtling in their wake. Our artillery could not locate their main force with any degree of certainty, nor could they place us properly. They were not idle; their guns, of which they had a decent number, sought for our position with dauntless perseverance. Their shells soon began to drop amongst us, but they did no harm at all. They fell close enough to our troops in many instances, but they were so badly made that they would not explode, or if they did they simply fizzed, and were almost as harmless as seidlitz powders.

The spiteful little pom-poms cracked away and kept us on the alert, until one grew weary of the everlasting noise of cannon. At mid-day, tired of the monotony of the game, I turned my horse's head towards camp, and, in company with three other correspondents, soon sat down to a lunch of mealies and boiled fowl; but we were destined not to enjoy that meal, for before the first mouthful had left my plate there came a wailing howl through the air, then a strange jarring noise, and a shell plunged into the earth forty yards away from the tent. A few minutes later another visitor from the same direction crashed on top of one of the transport waggons within a stone's throw of our tent. That decided me; in a few seconds I had scrambled up the side of a kopje, with the leg of a fowl in one hand and a soldier's biscuit in the other. The shells had not burst, but no man could say when one would, and I had no particular interest in regard to the inside of any shell myself. I was not the only one who made a hasty exit from the camp; in ten seconds the side of the kopje was alive with men. The shells continued to fall right amongst the waggons every few minutes for over two hours; yet only one man was killed, a negro driver being the victim, a shell dropping right against his thigh. The range of the Boer gun was absolutely perfect, but the shells were mere rubbish. Had they been as good as ours, half our transport would have been in ruins. The British gunners manoeuvred in all directions in order to locate that particularly dangerous piece of ordnance. They blazed at it in batteries; they tried to find it by means of cross-firing; they lined men up on the sky-line of kopjes to draw the fire; they limbered up and galloped far out on the veldt, until the enemy's rifle fire drove them in again; but all in vain. The Boer leader had placed his gun with such skill that the British could not locate it, and it kept up its devilish jubilee until the night set in.

That day our scouts captured one Free State flag from the enemy; the Yeomanry and mounted infantry did not succeed in their efforts to turn the Boers' left flank, but they checked the enemy from advancing in that direction, which was an important item in the day's work. We did not want the Boer left to overlap our right; had they done so they could then get behind us and harass our convoys coming from the direction of Bethany railway station. We had very little dread of them turning our left flank, because we knew that General French was moving towards us on that side from Bloemfontein, with the object of getting the Boers on the inside of two forces, and so giving them no chance of escape. We had only a few men wounded, one petty officer of the Scouts killed, and a negro driver killed, which was simply marvellous when one considers the terrible amount of ammunition used during the day. That night all the correspondents had to sleep, or try to sleep, with the transport. It was a wretched night; we knew the Boers had the range, and we fully expected to get a hot shelling between darkness and dawn, but, curiously enough, the foe kept their guns still all the night But the suspense made the night a weary one.

The following day was Sunday, and at a very early hour our scouts informed us that the Boers had made a wide detour towards Wepener, and had overlapped our right flank. They slipped up into a kopje, which would have enabled them to enfilade our position in a most masterly manner; but before they could get their guns there our artillery was at them, and the kopje was literally ploughed up with shells. It was too warm a corner for any man on earth to attempt to hold, and they soon took their departure, falling back in good order, and leaving no dead or wounded behind them. The Yeomanry had advanced on the kopje, under the protection of the shell firing, and when close to the position they fixed bayonets and dashed up the hill; but when they topped it they found that the Boers had retired. It was a quick bit of work, neatly and expeditiously done. Had the Boers held the hill long enough to get their guns in position they would have played havoc with us, for they could then have swept our whole line. From morning until night-fall we kept at them with our big guns; whenever a cloud of dust arose from behind a range of kopjes we dropped shells in the middle of it; wherever a cluster of Boers showed themselves for a second a shell sought them out. No matter how well they were placed, they must have had a lively time of it. During the Sabbath they scarcely used their guns at all, but they opened on our troops with rifle fire as soon as they made a forward move at any part of the line, showing clearly that they were watching as well as praying. The day closed without incident of any particular character; we had a few wounded, but no deaths, and could form no idea how the Boers were faring. Now and again during the night one or another of our guns would bark like sullen watchdogs on the chain, but the Boer guns were still.

Monday morning broke crisp and clear, and once more the big-gun duel began, only on this occasion the Boers made great use of a pom-pom gun This spiteful little demon tossed its diminutive shells into camp with painful freeness. They knocked three of the Worcesters over early in the day, killing two and badly damaging the other. As on all other occasions in this peculiar engagement, the Boer gunnery was simply superb; but their shells were worthless. Shells grew so common that the "Tommies" scarcely ducked when they heard the report of a gun they knew was trying to reach them, but smoked their pipes and made irreverent remarks concerning things made in Germany. About midday a party of Boers, who had somehow dodged round to our rear, made a dashing attempt to raid some cattle that were grazing close under our eyes; but they had to vanish in a hurry, and were particularly lucky in being able to escape with their lives, for a party of scouts darted out after them at full gallop on one side, whilst another party of mounted infantry rode as hard as hoofs could carry them on the other side of the bold raiders. They unslung their rifles as they dashed across the veldt, and the Boers soon knew that the fellows behind them were as much at home as they were themselves at that kind of business.

Late on Monday evening the Boers located a little to the left of our centre moved forward a bit. Though with infinite caution, and commenced sniping with the rifle. It was an evidence that they were growing weary of our tactics, and would greatly have liked us to attempt to rush their position with the bayonet, so that they could have mowed our fellows down in hundreds. But this General Rundle wisely declined to do; it was victory, not glory, he was seeking, and he was wise enough to know that a victory can be bought at far too high a price in country of this kind against a foe like the wily Boer. On Sunday night our strength was augmented by the arrival of three regiments of the Guards, and on Monday night we, knew for a certainty that General French was close at hand. The Boer was between two fires, and he would need all his "slimness" to pull him out of trouble. During a greater part of the night our guns continued to rob sleep of its sweetness, and the enemy's pom-pom mingled with our dreams. On Tuesday morning news came to us that Wepener had been relieved by Brabant and Hart, and that the Boers who had invested that place were drawing off in our direction, so that our right flank needed strengthening. The Boers displayed no sign of quitting their position, though they must have known that Brabant and Hart would be on their track from the south-east, and General French from the north-west. They held their ground with a grim stubbornness against overwhelming odds of men and guns, and dropped shells amongst us in a way that made one feel that no spot could be labelled "absolutely safe."

At about 7 p.m. we sent a force out south, consisting of about 4,000 men, under

General Boyes. Amongst that force were the West Kents, Staffords, Worcesters, Manchesters, all infantry. The Imperial Yeomanry and mounted infantry also accompanied the expedition. But there was little for them to do except hold the enemy in check, which they did. There were some phenomenally close shaves during the day. On one occasion the enemy got the range of one of our guns with their pom-pom, and the way they dropped the devilish little one-pound shells amongst those gunners was a sight to make a man's blood run chill. The little iron imps fell between the men, grazed the wheels, the carriage, and the truck of the gun; but

He, watching over Israel, slumbers not nor sleeps.

Nothing short of angel-wings could have kept our fellows safe. The men knew their deadly peril, knew that the tip of the wand in the Death Angel's hand was brushing their cheeks. One could see that they knew their peril. The hard, firm grip of the jaw, the steady light in the hard-set eyes, the manly pallor on the cheeks, all told of knowledge; yet not once did they lose their heads. Each fellow stood there as bravely as human flesh and blood could stand, and faced the iron hail with unblenching courage and intrepid coolness. Had those khaki-clothed warriors been carved out of bronze and moved by machinery, they could not have shown less fear or more perfect discipline. The pom-pom is a gun which I have been told the British War Office refused as a toy some two years back. I have had the doubtful pleasure of being under its fire to-day, and all I can say is that I would gladly have given my place to any gentleman in the War Office who happens to hold the notion that the pom-pom is a toy.

Somehow the enemy got hold of the position where General Rundle and staff were located, and all the afternoon they swept the plain in front of the tents, the hills above, and the hill opposite with shells; but they could not quite drop one in the little ravine itself. Half an hour before sundown I had to ride with two other correspondents to headquarters to get a dispatch away. We got across safely, but had not been there five minutes before a grandly directed shell sent the General and his staff off the brow of the hill in double quick time. We delivered our dispatches, and were getting ready for a gallop over the quarter mile of veldt, when, ***pom, pom, pom, pom***, came a dozen one-pounders a few yards away right across our track. It made our hearts sit very close to our ribs, but there was nothing for it but to take our horses by the head, drive the spurs home, and ride as if we were rounding up wild cattle. I want it to stand on record that I was not the last man across that strip of veldt. There was not much incident in the day's fighting; there seldom is in an artillery duel, carried on by men who know the game, in hilly country. Once during the afternoon the big gun belonging to the Boers became so troublesome that half a dozen of ours were trained upon it, and for best part of an hour it sounded as if a section of Sheol had visited the earth, so deadly was the fire, so fierce the bursting missiles, that not a rock wallaby, crouching in its hole, could have lived twenty minutes in the location. We heard no more from that gun.

As I rode from position to position our fellows greeted me with the cry: "Any news, sir? Heard if we are going to have a go at 'em with the spoons (bayonets)?" One midget, a bugler kiddie, so small that an ordinary maid-of-all-work could comfortably lay him across her knee and spank him, yawned as he knelt in the grass, and desired to know when "we was goin' ter 'ave some real bloomin' fightin'. 'E was tired of them bloomin' guns, 'e was; they made his carmine 'ead ache with their blanky noise. 'E didn't call that fightin'; 'e called it an adjective waste of good hammunition. 'E liked gettin' up to 'is man, fair 'nd square, 'nd knockin' 'ell out of 'im." He meant it, too, the little beggar, and I could not help laughing at him when I considered that lots of the old fighting Boers I had seen could have dropped the midget into their lunch bags, and not have noticed his weight.

The Yeomanry did a lot of useful work, and are as eager for fight as a bull ant on a hot plate. They are as good as any men I have seen in Africa, full of ginger, good horsemen, wear-and-tear, cut-and-come-again sort of men. They adapt themselves to circumstances readily, are jolly and good-humoured under trying circumstances. Their officers are, as a rule, first-class soldiers, equal to any emergency. On Tuesday the Boers kept their guns going at a great rate, and we really thought that they had made up their minds to see the thing right out at all costs. Personally I did not for a moment think that they were ignorant of General French's rapid advance. I do not believe it possible for any large body of hostile troops to move in South Africa without the Boers being thoroughly cognisant of every detail connected with the move, partly because they are the most perfect scouts in the world, and partly because the scattered population on every hand is positively favourable to them. Our artillery dropped a storm of shells during the day, and that night it was whispered in camp that there was to be a general attack next morning. On Tuesday evening General French advanced right on to the Boer rear, and some smart fighting took place, the enemy suffering considerably, though our losses were small.

At dawn on Wednesday we moved forward rapidly, and in a few hours' time our infantry were standing in the trenches and upon the hills that the Boers had occupied the day before. Our mounted men rode at a gallop through the gullies, but nothing was to be seen of the foe except a few newly dug graves. The Boers had vanished like a dream, taking all their guns with them. Louis Botha, the commander-in-chief, had come in person to them, and the retreat was carried out under his eyes. We followed to Dewetsdorp, and from there on to Thaba Nchu (pronounced Tabancha).

On Friday night the enemy exchanged a few shots with us from the heights beyond, but no harm was done on either side. The Third Division, to which I had attached myself, under General Chermside, has been ordered towards Bloemfontein. French is in command, and, judging by his past performances, I fully expect we shall have some busy times, though French may go away and leave the Eighth Division under General Rundle.

WITH RUNDLE IN THE FREE STATE.

ORANGE FREE STATE.

Since the Boers bolted from Constantia Farm we have done but little beyond following them from spot to spot through the Free State, in the conquered territory along the Basuto border. At Constantia Farm they gave us a gunnery duel, which, though incessant and continuous, did little real damage to either side. After that, when General French joined issue with us, the Boers shifted their ground with consummate skill. We moved on to Dewetsdorp, and there the Third Division, under Chermside, parted company with us. We moved onward to Thaba Nchu, Brabant keeping well away towards the Basuto border with his flying column. At Thaba Nchu it looked day by day as if we were in for something hot and hard, the Boers having, as usual, taken up a position of vast natural strength. But Hamilton was the only one to get to close quarters with the veldt warriors, when executing a flanking movement. I have since learned that the enemy suffered very severely on that occasion.

They can give some of the British journalists a wholesome lesson in regard to manliness of spirit, these same rough fellows, bred in the African wilds. Speaking to me of the charge the Gordons made, when led by Captain Towse, they were unstinted in their praises. "It was grand, it was terrible," they said, "to see that little handful of men rush on fearless of death, fearless of everything." It was bravery of the highest kind, and they admired it, as only brave men do admire courage in a foeman. The people of Britain who read extracts taken from Boer newspapers, extracts which ridicule British pluck and all things British, must not blame the Boers for those statements. In nearly every case the papers published inside Burgher territory are edited by renegade Britons, and it is these renegades, not the fighting Boers, who defame our nation, and take every possible opportunity of hitting below the belt.

When we left Thaba Nchu, General French left us, as did also Hamilton and Smith-Dorien. Brabant hugged the Basuto border, and swept the land clean of everything hostile. General Rundle (the flower of courtesy and chivalry) kept the centre; General Boyes looked after our left wing; General Campbell picked up the intermediate spaces as occasion demanded; and so we moved on, trying, but trying in vain, to draw a cordon round the ever-shifting foe. There was no chance for a dashing forward move; the country through which we passed was lined by kopjes, which were simply appalling in their native strength. What prompted the Boer leaders to fall back from them, step by step, will for ever remain a mystery to me. It was not want of provisions, for we knew that they had huge supplies of beef and mutton, whilst there were in their possession almost inexhaustible stores of grain. It was not want of fodder for their horses, for the valleys and veldt were covered with beautiful grass, almost knee-deep. Water was plentiful in all directions, and they apparently possessed plenty of ammunition. Prisoners assert that Commandant Olivier was absolutely furious when compelled to fall back, by order of his superiors. It is also asserted that he is now in dire disgrace on account of his refusal to obey promptly some of his superior's commands. It is further stated that he is to be deposed from his command, and will cease to be a factor of any importance in the war. It is hard to fathom Boer tactics. It does not follow because a line of kopjes are abandoned to-day that the burghers have retreated; they fall back before scouting parties; their pickets watch our scouts return to camp, knowing that they will convey the news to headquarters that the kopjes are empty of armed men. Then, with almost incredible swiftness, the light-armed Boers swarm back by passes known only to themselves, and secretly and silently take up positions where they can butcher an advancing army. If General Rundle had been a rash, impetuous, or a headstrong man, he could comfortably have lost his whole force on half a dozen occasions; but he is not. He is essentially a cautious leader, and pits his brain against that of the Boer leaders as a good chess player pits his against an opponent. He may believe in the luck of the British Army, but he trusts mighty little to it. Better lose a couple of days than a couple of regiments is his motto, and a wise motto it is. Had he flung his men haphazard at any of the positions where the Boers have made a stand, he would have been cut to pieces.

Rundle plays a wise game. When the enemy looks like sitting tight, Rundle at once commences a series of manoeuvres directed from his centre. This keeps the enemy busy, and gives them a lot of solid thinking to do, and whilst they are thinking he moves his flanks forward, overlapping them in the hope of surrounding them. The Boer hates to have his rear threatened, and invariably falls away. His method of falling back is unique. As soon as he smells danger, all the live stock is sent off and all the waggons. Cape carts are kept handy for baggage that cannot be sent with the heavy convoy. Most of the big guns go with the first flight; one or two, which can easily be shifted, are kept to hold back our advance, and the deadly little pom-poms are dodged about from kopje to kopje. The pom-pom is not much to look at, but it is a weapon to be reckoned with in mountain warfare. It throws only a one-pound shell, and throws it from the most impossible places imaginable. The beauty of the pom-pom is that it drops its work in from spots from which no sane man ever expects a shell to come.

When the Boer finds that his position is untenable on account of a flanking move, the horses are hitched up to the light Cape carts, the loading is packed, and off they fly at a gallop, and the guns follow suit; whilst the rifles hold the heights. That is why we so seldom get hold of anything worth having when we do take a position. Our losses have been paltry, because the Boer is a defensive, not an offensive, fighter. He waits to be attacked, he does not often attack; and our general is a man who does not throw men's lives away. He believes in brains before bayonets, and England may be thankful for the possession of General Rundle. Had he been a madcap general, there would have been a few thousand more widows in the old country to-day than there are. At the same time, he is a man of immense personality. Should he ever get a chance to engage the enemy in a pitched battle, he will prove to the world that he is capable of great things. There will be no half-hearted work in such an hour. If he has to sacrifice men on the altar of war, he will surely sacrifice them, but not until he is compelled to do so. Brabant is a wild daredevil, who rushes on like a mountain torrent Boyes is brainy; careful, and yet dashing.

I want to state here that I have never lost a single opportunity, whilst travelling through the enemy's country, of looking at the "home" life of the people--and I may say that I have been in a few back-country homes in America, in Australia, and in other parts of the world--and I want to place it on record that in my opinion the Boer farmer is as clean in his home life, as loving in his domestic arrangements, as pure in his morals, as any class of people I have ever met. Filth may abound, but I have seen nothing of it. Immorality may be the common everyday occurrence I have seen it depicted in some British journals, but I have failed to find trace of it. Ignorance as black as the inside of a dog may be the prevailing state of affairs; if so, I have been one of the lucky few who have found just the reverse in whichsoever direction I have turned. After six months', or nearly six months', close and careful observation of their habits, I have arrived at the conclusion that the Boer farmer, and his son and daughter, will compare very favourably with the farming folk of Australia, America, and Great Britain. What he may be in the Transvaal I know not, because I have not yet been there; but in Cape Colony and in the Free State he is much as I have depicted him, no better, no worse, than Americans and Australians, and as good a fighting man as either--which is tantamount to saying that he is as good as anything on God's green earth, if he only had military training.

Ask "Tommy" privately, when he comes home, if this is not so--not "Thomas," who has been on lines of communication all the time--but "Tommy," who has fought him, and measured heart and hand with him. I think he will tell you much as I have told you. For "Tommy" is no fool; he is not half such a braggart, either, as some of the Jingoes, who shout and yell, but never take a hand in the real fighting; those wastrels of England, who are at home with a pewter of beer in their hands--hands that never did, and never will, grip a rifle.

Whilst at Trummel I took advantage of a couple of days' camping to go out three miles from camp to have a look at a diamond mine. I found a red-whiskered Dutchman in charge, who knew less English than I knew Dutch, and as my Dutch consists of about twelve words we did not do much in the conversational line; but I made him understand by pantomimic telegraphy that I wanted to have a look round, to size up things. He took me to a "dump," where the ore at grass was stored, and converted himself into a human stone-cracking machine for my benefit, until I had seen all that I wanted to see in regard to the "ore at grass." He was very much like mine managers the world over--very ready to play tricks on anyone he considered "green" at the business. It was not his fault that he did not know that I had been a reporter on gold, silver, copper, lead, tin, and coal mines for about twenty years.

Thinking, doubtless, that I was like unto the ordinary city fellow who comes at rare intervals to look at a mine, he made me a present of a piece of rock with some worthless garnets in it, also a sample of country rock pregnant with mundic; the garnets and the mundic glittered in the sunshine. I rose to the bait, as I was expected to do, and intimated that I would like a lot of it. This delighted the Dutchman, and he beamed all over his expansive face, all the time cursing me for the second son of an idiot, as is the way with mine managers. But he stopped grinning before the afternoon wore out, for I set him climbing and clambering for little pieces of mundic and tiny patches of garnets in all the toughest places I could find in that mine, and went into ecstasies over each individual piece, until I had quite a load of the rubbish. Then I intimated gently that I would be back that way when the war was over, and would surely send my Cape cart for them if he would be good enough to mind them for me. I fancy an inkling of the truth dawned in that Dutchman's soul at last, for he made no further reference to either garnets or mundic. I satisfied myself with a sample of the matrix in which diamonds are found, and also with a specimen of the country rock for geological reference, but the garnets are on the heap still.

The mine, which is named the "Monastery," is very crudely worked; everything connected with it is primitive. A huge quarry, about 600 feet in circumference, and about 40 feet deep, had been opened up. There was nothing in it in the shape of lode or reef, but a large number of disconnected "stringers," or leaders of rocky matter, in which diamonds are often found. At the bottom of the quarry the water lay fully eight feet deep, owing to the fact that the mine had lain unworked during the war. A vertical shaft had been sunk a little distance from the quarry to a depth of 150 feet, but there was a hundred feet of water in it, so that I am unable to say anything concerning the Monastery diamond mine at its lower levels. One or two tunnels had been drawn from the quarry into the adjoining country on small leaders, and from what I could gather from my guide diamonds had been discovered. Whilst I went below, I left my Kaffir boy on top to pick up what he could in the shape of rumour or gossip from the natives, and he informed me that the niggers had been the cause of the opening of the mine, they having found diamonds near the surface in some of the leaders, which consisted of a rock known in Australian mining circles as illegitimate granite. The white folk, fearing that the poor heathen might become debauched if they possessed too much wealth, had gathered those diamonds in-- when they could--and later had started mining for the precious gems, with what success the heathen did not know. I tried the Dutchman on the same point, but I might as well have interviewed an oyster in regard to the science of gastronomy. He dodged around my question like a fox terrier round a fence, until I gave him up in despair. But, for all that, I rather fancy they have found diamonds round that way, only they don't want the British to know anything about it.

RED WAR WITH RUNDLE.

In our rear lies the little village of Senekal, a shy little place, seemingly too modest to lift itself out of the miniature basin caused by the circumambient hills. Khaki-clad figures, gaunt, hungry, and dirty, patrol the streets; the few stores are almost denuded of things saleable, for friend and foe have swept through the place again and again, and both Boer and Briton have paid the shops a visit. At the hotel I managed to get a dinner of bread and dripping, washed down with a cup of coffee, guiltless of both milk and sugar. But, if the bill of fare was meagre, the bill of costs made up for it in its wealth of luxuriousness. If I rose from the table almost as hollow as when I sat down, I only had to look at the landlord's charges to fancy I had dined like one of the blood royal. Opposite the hotel stands the church, a dainty piece of architecture, fit for a more pretentious town than Senekal. It is fashioned out of white stone, and stands in its own grounds, looking calm and peaceful amidst all the bustle and blaze of war. Someone has turned all the seats out of the sacred edifice, preparatory to converting it into a hospital. The seats are not destroyed; they are not damaged; they are stacked away under a neighbouring verandah.

I do not think it wrong so to utilise a church. It is the only place fit to put the wounded men in in all the town. The great Nazarene in whose name the church was erected would not have allowed the sick to wither by the wayside in the days when the Judean hills rang to the echo of His magnetic voice, nor do I think it wrongful to His memory to convert His shrine into an abiding place for the sick and suffering.

Far away on our left flank the enemy hold the heights, and watch us moving outward, whilst between them and us, stretching mile after mile in a line with our column, ripples a line of scarlet flame, for the foe has fired the veldt to starve the transit mules, horses, and oxen. Like a sword unsheathed in the sunlight, the flames sparkle amidst the grass, which grows knee-deep right to the kopje's very lips. Birds rise on the wing with harsh, resonant cries, flutter awhile above their ravished homes, then wheel in mid-air and seek more peaceful pastures. Hares spring up before the crackling flames quite reach their forms, and, like grey streaks in a sailor's beard on a stormy day, flash suddenly into view, and as suddenly disappear again. Here and there a graceful springbok dashes through the smoke, with head thrown back and graceful limbs extended, his glossy, mottled hide looking doubly beautiful backed by that red streak of fire. The wind catches the quivering crimson streak, and for awhile the flames race, as I have seen wild horses, neck to neck, rush through the saltbush plains at the sound of the stockman's whip. Then, as the wind drops, the flames curl caressingly around the wealth of growing fodder, biting the grass low down, and wrapping it in a mantle of black and red, as flame and smoke commingle.

Here and there a pool of water, hidden from view until the fire fiend stripped the veldt land bare, leaps to life like a silver shield in the grim setting of the bare and blackened plain. Small mobs of cattle stand stupidly snuffing the smoke-laden air, until the breath of the blaze awakens them to a sense of peril; then, with horns lowered like bayonets at the charge, with tails stiff and straight behind them as levelled lances, they leap onward, over or through everything in front of them, bellowing frantically their brute beast protest against the red ruin of war. The flames roll on; they reach the stone walls of a cattle pen, and leap it as a hunter takes a brush fence in his stride; onward still, until a Kaffir kraal is reached. The soft-lipped billows kiss the uncouth mud wall, and for a moment transfigure them with a nameless beauty, the beauty that precedes ruin. Only a moment or two, and then the resistless destroyer flaunts its pennons amidst the reed-thatched roofs; the sparks leap up, the black smoke curls towards the sky, whilst on the neighbouring hills the negro women, with their babes in their arms, wail woefully, for those rude huts, with all their barbarous trappings, meant home--aye, home and happiness--to them. The flames roll onward now in two long lines, for the Kaffir encampment had sundered them, and now they look, with their beautifully rounded curves sweeping so gracefully out into the unknown, like the rich, ripe lips of a wanton woman in the pride of her shameless beauty. All that they leave behind is desolation, darkness, despair, ruin unutterable, only blackened walls, simmering carcases, weeping women, and wailing children.

Away on our right flank we can just make out the skeletons of what a few hours before had been a cluster of smiling farmhouses. They do not smile now; they grin horribly in the sunlight, grin as the fleshless skulls of dead men grin on a battlefield after those sextons of the veldt the grey-hooded, curved-beaked vultures have screamed their final farewell to the charnel-houses of war--noble war, splendid war, pastime of potentates and princes, invented in hell and patented in all the temples of sorrow.

As we look on those grim relics of this dreary time we catch the maddening sound of distant guns. The chargers prick their ears, and quiver from muzzle to coronet. The khaki-clad figures on the plain throw up their heads and turn their eyes towards the sound; the tired shoulders square themselves, each foot seems to tread the blackened plain with firmer, prouder tread. The sound of guns is like the rush of wine through sluggish veins, and men forget that they are faint with hunger, weary to the verge of wretchedness with ceaseless marching. The sound of guns bespeaks the presence of the foe, and those gaunt soldiers of the Queen are galvanised to life and lust of battle by the very breath of war. A ripple runs along the line, the farthest flanks catch the gleam of the sun on distant rifle barrels. An order rings out sharp and crisp; the column stands as if each man and horse were carved in rock.

The infantry lean lightly on their guns, the cavalry crane forward in their saddles. We pause and wait until we see the green badge of O'Driscoll's scouts on the hats of the advancing riders. O'Driscoll rides towards the staff with loosened rein, and every spur in all his gallant little troop shows how the scouts had ridden. We strain our ears to catch the news the Irish scout has brought. It comes at last Clements has met the foe, and death is busy in those distant hills.

Rundle sits silently, hard pressed in his saddle--a gallant figure, with soldier and leader written all over him. We wait his verdict anxiously, for on his word our fate may hinge. We have not long to wait--Clements can hold his own; Brabant will outflank the Boers. Forward, march! The men droop as wheat fields droop in the sultry air of a seething day. They are tired, deadly tired; not too tired to fight, but weary of the endless marching from point to point to keep the enemy from breaking through their lines and striking southward.

Away in front of us we note the snow-crowned hills which girdle Basutoland, snow crowned and sun kissed; every hilltop sparkling like a giant gem, and over all a pale blue sky, curtained by flimsy clouds of gauzy whiteness, through which the sun laughs rosily, the handiwork of the Eternal. And underfoot only the deep dead blackness of the blistered veldt, ravished of its wondrous wealth of living green, the rude, rough footprint of the god of war--sweet war; kind, Christian war!

Now, overhead, betwixt the smoking earth and smiling sky, flocks of vultures come and go, fluttering their great pinions noiselessly. To them the sound of guns is merriest music; it is their summons to the banquet board. Foul things they look as the float over us, silent as souls that have slipped from some ash heap in Hades, grey with the greyness that grows on the wolf's hide; their feathers hang upon them in ridges, unkempt, unlovely, soiled with blood and offal. They float above our heads, they wheel upon our flanks.

A horse drops wearily upon its knees, looks round dumbly on the wilderness of blackness, then turns its piteous eyes upward towards the skies that seem so full of laughing loveliness; then, with a sob which is almost human in the intensity of its pathos, the tired head falls downwards, the limbs contract with spasmodic pain, then stiffen into rigidity; and one wonders, if the Eternal mocked that silent appeal from those great sad eyes, eyes that had neither part nor lot in the sin and sorrow of war, how shall a man dare look upwards for help when the bitterness of death draws nigh unto him? The grey lines above, on flank, and front, and rear, were with greedy speed converging to one point, until they flock in a horrid, struggling, fighting, revolting mass of beaks and feathers above the fallen steed, as devils flock around the deathbed of a defaulting deacon. A soldier on the outer edge of the extended line swings his rifle with swift, backhanded motion over his shoulder, and brings the butt amidst the crowd of carrion. The vultures hop with grotesque, ungainly motions from their prey, and stand with wings extended and clawed feet apart, their necks outstretched and curved heads dripping slime and blood, a fitting setting amidst the black ruin of war. The charger now looks upward from eyeless sockets; his gutted carcass, flattened into a shapeless streak, shrinks towards the earth, as if asking to be veiled from the laughter of the skies. But there is neither pity from above nor shelter from below as the red wave of war, like the curse of the white Christ, sweeps over the land. God grant that merry England may never witness, on her own green meadow lands, these sights and sounds which meet the eye and ear on African soil.

Oh, England, England, if I had a voice whose clarion tones could reach your ears and stir your hearts in every city and town, village and hamlet, wayside cot and stately castle, in all your sea-encircled isle, I would cry to you to guard your coasts! Better, it seems to me, writing here, with all the evidences of war beneath my eyes, that every man born of woman's love on British soil should die between the decks, or find a grave in foundering ships of war, than that the foot of a foreign foe should touch the Motherland. Better that your ships be shambles, where men could die like men, sending Nelson's royal message all along the armoured line; better that our best and bravest found a grave where grey waves curl towards our coastline, than that our womanhood should look with woe-encircled eyes into the wolfish mouth of war. Better that our strong men perished, with the brine and ocean breezes playing freshly on the gaping wounds through which their souls passed outward, than that our little maids and tiny, tender babes should face the unutterable shame, the anguish, and the suffering of a war within our borders.

Do not laugh the very thought to scorn and brand the thing impossible, for fools have laughed before to-day whilst kingdoms tottered to their fall You who stay at home miss much that others know--and, knowing, dread. If England at this hour could only realise what manner of men control her destinies, then all the lion in the breed would spring to life again. I do not know if lack-brains of a similar strain control the supplies for England's Navy; but if, in time of war, it proves to be the case, then God help us, God help the old flag and the stout hearts who fight for it.

Lend me your ears, and let me tell you how our army in Africa is treated by the incompetent people in the good city of London. I pledge my word, as a man and a journalist, that every written word is true. I will add nothing, nor detract from, nor set down aught in malice. If my statements are proven false, then let me be scourged with the tongue and pen of scorn from every decent Briton's home and hearth for ever after, for he who lies about his country at such an hour as this is of all traitors the vilest. I will deal now particularly with the men who are acting under the command of Lieutenant-General Sir Leslie Rundle. This good soldier and courteous gentleman has to hold a frontage line from Winburg, *via* Senekal, almost to the borders of Basutoland. His whole front, extending nearly a hundred miles, is constantly threatened by an active, dashing, determined enemy, an enemy who knows the country far better than an English fox-hunting squire knows the ground he hunts over season after season. To hold this vast line intact General Rundle has to march from point to point as his scouts warn him of the movements of the tireless foe. He has stationed portions of his forces at given points along this line, and his personal work is to march rapidly with small bodies of infantry, yeomanry, scouts, and artillery towards places immediately threatened. He has to keep the Boers from penetrating that long and flexible line, for if once they forced a passage in large numbers they would sweep like a torrent southwards, envelop his rear, cut the railway and telegraph to pieces, stop all convoys, paralyse the movements of all troops up beyond Kroonstad, and once more raise the whole of the Free State, and very possibly a great portion of the Cape Colony as well.

General Rundle's task is a colossal one, and any sane man would think that gigantic efforts would be made to keep him amply supplied with food for his soldiers. But such is not the case. The men are absolutely starving. Many of the infantrymen are so weak that they can barely stagger along under the weight of their soldierly equipment. They are worn to shadows, and move with weary, listless footsteps on the march. People high up in authority may deny this, but he who denies it sullies the truth. This is what the soldiers get to eat, what they have been getting to eat for a long time past, and what they are likely to get for a long time to come, unless England rouses herself, and bites to the bone in regard to the people who are responsible for it.

One pound of raw flour, which the soldiers have to cook after a hard day's march, is served out to each man every alternate day. The following day he gets one pound of biscuits. In this country there is no fuel excepting a little ox-dung, dried by the sun. If a soldier is lucky enough to pick up a little, he can go to the nearest water, of which there is plenty, mix his cake without yeast or baking-powder, and make some sort of a wretched mouthful. He gets one pound of raw fresh meat daily, which nine times out of ten he cannot cook, and there his supplies end.

What has become of the rations of rum, of sugar, of tea, of cocoa, of groceries generally? Ask at the snug little railway sidings where the goods are stacked--and forgotten. Ask in the big stores in Capetown and other seaport towns. Ask in your own country, where countless thousands of pounds' worth of foodstuffs lie rotting in the warehouses, bound up and tied down with red tape bandages. Ask--yes, ask; but don't stop at asking--damn somebody high up in power. Don't let some wretched underling be made the scapegoat of this criminal state of affairs, for the taint of this shameful thing rests upon you, upon every Briton whose homes, privileges, and prosperity are being safeguarded by these famishing men. The folk in authority will probably tell you that General Rundle and his splendid fellows are so isolated that food cannot be obtained for them. I say that is false, for recently I, in company with another correspondent, left General Rundle's camp without an escort. We made our way in the saddle, taking our two Cape carts with us, to Winburg railway station; leaving our horseflesh there, we took train for East London. Then back to the junction, and trained it down to Capetown, where we remained for forty-eight hours, and then made our way back to Winburg, and from Winburg we came without escort to rejoin General Rundle at Hammonia. If two innocent, incompetent (?) war correspondents could traverse that country and get through with winter supplies for themselves, why cannot the transport people manage to do the same? These transport people affect to look with contempt upon a war correspondent and his opinions on things military; but if we could not manage transport business better than they do, most of us would willingly stand up and allow ourselves to be shot. We are no burden upon the Army; we carry for ourselves, we buy for ourselves, and we look for news for ourselves; and we take our fair share of risks in the doing of our duty, as the long list of dead and disabled journalists will amply prove.

It is not, in my estimation, the whole duty of a war correspondent to go around the earth making friends for himself, or looking after his personal comfort, or booming himself for a seat in Parliament on a cheap patriotic ticket. It is rather his duty to give praise where praise is due, censure where censure has been earned, regardless of consequences to himself. Such was the motto of England's two greatest correspondents--Forbes and Steevens--both of whom have passed into the shadow-land, and I would to God that either of them were here to-day, for England knew them well, and they would have roused your indignation as I, an unknown man, dare not hope to do. But though what I have written does not bear the magical name of Steevens or of Forbes, it bears the hallmark of the eternal truth. Our men on the fields of war are famishing whilst millions worth of food lies rotting on our wharves and in our cities, food that ought with ordinary management to be within easy reach of our fighting generals. Britain asks of Rundle the fulfilment of a task that would tax the energies and abilities of the first general in Europe; and with a stout heart he faces the work in front of him, faces it with men whose knees knock under them when they march, with hands that shake when they shoulder their rifles--shake, but not with fear; tremble, but not from wounds, but from weakness, from poverty of blood and muscle, brought about by continual hunger. Are those men fit to storm a kopje? Are they fit to tramp the whole night through to make a forced march to turn a position, and then fight as their fathers fought next day?

I tell you no. And yours be the shame if the Empire's flag be lowered--not theirs, but yours; for you--what do you do? You stand in your music-halls and shout the chorus of songs full of pride for your soldier, full of praise for his patience, his pluck, and his devotion to duty; and you let him go hungry, so hungry that I have often seen him quarrel with a nigger for a handful of raw mealies on the march. It is so cheap to sing, especially when your bellies are full of good eating; it costs nothing to open your mouths and bawl praises. It is pleasant to swagger and brag of "your fellows at the front;" but why don't you see that they are fed, if you want them to fight? Give "Tommy" a lot less music and flapdoodle, and a lot more food of good quality, and he'll think a heap more of you. It is nice of you to stay in Britain and drink "Tommy's" health, but there would be far more sense in the whole outfit if you would allow him to "eat his own" out here.

THE FREE STATERS' LAST STAND.

SLAP KRANZ.

At last the blow has fallen which has shattered the Boer cause in the Free State. There will be skirmishes with scattered bands in the mountain gorges beyond Harrismith, but the backbone of the Republic has been broken beyond redemption. Sunday, the 30th of July, was big with fate, though we who sat almost within the shadow of the snow enshrouded hills of savage Basutoland at the dawning of that day knew it not. It was a joyful day for us, though pregnant with sorrow for the veldtsmen who had fought so long and well for their doomed cause, for on that day our generals reaped the harvest which they had sown with infinite patience and undaunted courage. General Hunter, to whom the chief command had just been given, was there, surrounded by his staff, a soldierly figure worthy of a nation's trust; Clements, keen faced, sharp voiced, with alertness written in each lineament; Paget, whose fiery spirit spoke from his mobile face, his blood, hot as an Afghan sun, flashing the workings of his mind into his face as sunlight flashes from steel; and Rundle, hawk-eyed and stern, no friend to Pressmen, but a soldier every inch, one of those men whose hands build empires. Had he been stripped of modern gear that day, and placed in Roman trappings, one would have looked behind him to see if Caesar meant to grace the show; but Caesar was not there.

One of the greatest soldiers since the world began was missing from our ranks, the hero Roberts, whose great intellect had planned the *coup* which his generals had carried to maturity. Yet, though Lord Roberts planned each general move, an immense amount of actual work was left to the generals. The country they had to pass through was rugged and inhospitable. The foe they had to fight was brave, resourceful, and well supplied with all munitions of war; a single mistake on the part of any one of them would have wrecked the magnificent plan of the Commander-in-Chief. But no mistakes were made; each general worked as if his soul's salvation depended upon his individual efforts. Where all are good, as a rule it is hard to make a distinction; but in this instance one man stands out above his fellows, and that man is General Sir Leslie Rundle, the commander of the Eighth Division. His task from the first was herculean. He had to hold a line fully one hundred miles in length; day after day, week after week, the enemy tried to break that line and pour their forces into the territory we had conquered. Had they succeeded, they would have shaken the whole of South Africa to its very centre. This task kept Sir Leslie Rundle busy night and day. Wherever he camped, spies dogged his footsteps; black men and white men constantly upon his track. His every move was rapidly reported to our ever-watchful enemies. But, quick as the enemy undoubtedly were in all their movements, General Rundle nullified their efforts by his rapidity. So terribly hard did he work his men that they nicknamed him "Rundle, the Tramp." How the men stood it I cannot understand. I know of no other men in all the world who would have gone on as they did, obeying orders without a murmur or a whimper. They were savage at times over the food they got, and small blame to them, but they never blamed their general. They knew that he gave them plenty of the class of food that he could lay hands upon. Had the general's supplies been in this part of the country, instead of being tied up in red-tape packages on the railway line, General Rundle would have kept his Division fully supplied. The only food which he could command, beef and mutton, he gave without stint. Had the War Office authorities attended to their end of the work with the same commendable zeal, half the hardships of the campaign would have been averted.

If ever war was reduced to an absolute science, it was upon this occasion. On the one hand, some six thousand Boers on the defensive, armed with the handiest quick-firing rifle known to modern times, with from eight to ten guns, well supplied with food and ammunition, and backed by some of the most awful country the eye of man ever rested upon--a country which they knew as a child knows its mother's face. On the other hand, an attacking force of 30,000 men and guns. To read the number of the opposing forces one would think the Boer task the effort of madmen, bent upon national extinction; but one glance at the country would upset those calculations entirely. Every kopje was a natural fortress, every sluit a perfect line of trenches, and every donga a nursery for death.

To attempt to go into every move made by our troops during the months of May, June, and the early parts of July would only prove wearisome to the average reader; suffice it to say that finally we got the burgher forces into the Caledon Valley. This valley is about twenty-eight miles in length, and from fourteen to fifteen miles across its widest part. Properly speaking, it was not a valley at all, but a series of valleys interspersed by great kopjes, nearly all of which presented an almost impregnable appearance. The valley had a number of outlets, which the Boers fondly believed our people to be unacquainted with. These outlets were known as "neks," and were, without exception, terribly rough places for a hostile force to attack. Commando Nek was upon the south-east, facing towards Basutoland. This was merely a narrow pass, running up over a jagged kopje, with two greater kopjes on each side of it. The hills all round it were so placed that a number of good marksmen, hidden in the rocks, could easily sweep off thousands of an enemy who attempted to take it by storm. But that pass had to be taken before we could claim to hold the Free State in the hollow of our hand. Slabbert's Nek was merely a huge gash in the face of a cliff. It was the Boers' causeway towards the north, their highway to safety. Retief's Nek lay to the westward, and formed a grinning death trap for any general who might try the foolish hazard of a single-handed attack Naauwpoort Nek, ugly and uninviting, faced south-east towards Harrismith. Golden Gate, named by a satirist--or a satyr--was merely a narrow chasm worn by wind and weather through the girdle of mountains. It looked towards the east, and was a mere pathway, which none but desperate soldiers, driven to their last extremity, would think of using.

The Boers never dreamed that it was possible for our troops to move with such machine-like precision as to hold every nek at our mercy. But whilst Rundle held the ground to the south, and kept the Boers for ever on the move by his restless activity, Clements and Paget moved on Slabbert's Nek, Hunter swept down on Retief's Nek, Naauwpoort Nek was invested by Hector Macdonald, Bruce Hamilton closed in upon Golden Gate, and the great net was almost perfect in its meshes. The enemy did not realise their danger until it was too late for the great bulk of their force to escape. Commandant De Wet saw the impending peril at the eleventh hour, and tried hard to get his countrymen to follow him in a dash through Slabbert's Nek; but very few of the burghers would believe that the sword of fate was hanging by so slim a thread over their heads. In vain this able soldier of the Republic harangued them. Vain all his threats and protestations. They could not and would not believe him. Sullenly they sat in their strongholds and watched Rundle--they could see him, and that danger which was present to their eyes was the only danger they would believe in; and day by day, hour by hour, the cordon of Britain's might drew closer and closer, until every link in the vast chain was practically flawless. Then Commandant De Wet gathered around him about 1,800 of his most devoted followers, and with Ex-President Steyn in their ranks they passed like ghosts of a fallen people through Slabbert's Nek on towards the Transvaal. How they managed to elude the incoming khaki wave some other pen must tell. It was a splendid piece of work on the Republican Commandant's part, and history will not begrudge him the full measure of praise due to him. Had General Prinsloo and his burghers been guided by him, these pages had never been written, for where De Wet took his 1,800 burghers he could as easily have taken 6,000.

Scarcely had De Wet made his escape ere the truth was borne in upon the burghers with an iron hand that their doom was sealed. General Rundle's force, which all along had been essentially a blocking force, and not a striking force, made a move on the 23rd of July. All day the cannons spoke to the burghers from Willow Grange, all day long the rifles rippled their leaden waves of death. We could see but little of the enemy; they lay concealed behind the loose rocks, and our men had little else to do but lift their rifles and pull the trigger, trusting to the powers that rule the destinies of war to speed the bullets to some foeman's resting place. But we knew they were there if we could not see them, for the snap and snarl of the Mauser rifles came readily to our ears, and the booming of their guns answered ours, as hound answers hound when the scent grows hottest. We pounded them with shrapnel and pelted them with common shell until the air around them rained iron. Our guns were six to one, yet those brave veldtsmen held their own with a stubborn courage worthy of the noblest traditions in all the red pages of war. They gave us a parting shot at sundown, and at night, when the thick mists from the snow-draped mountains behind us came down upon the land and added to the darkness of the winter's night, they moved their gun and fell back with it to a place where they could renew the battle on the morrow. And at the dawning they testified their vitality by dropping a couple of shells right into the midst of the Imperial Yeomanry camp.

Whilst we were busy at Julies Kraal, drawing the Boers' attention from other points, feinting as if we intended to push right on into Commando Nek, General Sir Archibald Hunter made a dash at Relief's Nek with his force, and our cannon were busy at almost every point around the valley where the Boers were stationed. General Prinsloo, who was in supreme command of the enemy's forces, had no means of knowing where the British really meant to strike. In vain he pushed men to anticipate Rundle's threatened move, vainly he turned like a trapped tiger towards Hunter's marching men. Turn where he would, the khaki wave met him, rolling resistlessly inward and onward. Hunter broke through with small loss, for the force which should have checked him at Retief's Nek was waiting at Commando Nek for Rundle and the Eighth Division. It was a master stroke, for when once Hunter was upon the inside of the valley he was in a position to threaten the rear of the Boer forces at Commando Nek, and that was a state of affairs which the enemy could not stand upon any terms. A number of them, under clever Commandant Olivier, slipped away through Golden Gate. They did not face the more open country even inside the big valley, but made their way through a piece of ground known as Witzies Hoek, and thence through a ravine which almost beggars description. Later on I went with Driscoll's Scouts in search of the tracks of these men, and followed along the same road they had taken. The ravine was a long, narrow gap between mountain ranges of immense height. The sides of the mountains were covered with loose boulders, sufficient to protect the whole Boer army from our artillery fire. The only track which a horseman could possibly follow wound in and out alongside the face of the cliffs, so narrow that even the horses bred in the country found it difficult to keep their feet upon it, and could only proceed, at funeral pace, in single file. A handful of men could have held that place against an army. With De Wet and Olivier gone, half our task was over. The Boers made a blind rush, first to one nek, then to the next, only to find that Britain's sons guarded them all. Small bodies of men might escape, but the vast supplies of mealies, waggons, guns, and all the cumbrous appliances of war, without which an army is useless, were penned in. The hand of the Field-Marshal was on them. The blocking forces held the neks, and now those forces which had to strike were ordered to move. No sooner did General Rundle receive his orders to advance than he rolled forward with the impetuosity of a storm breaking upon a southern coast. They on the spot knew that all the enemy's hopes lay centred round a town in the middle of the valley. This town was Fouriesburg. The general who could strike that town first would deal the death blow to the Boer forces in the Free State. Rundle was furthest from the town; the pathway his troops would have to pursue was rougher and more rugged than that which lay open to the rest of the forces.

But Rundle knew his men; he knew their mettle; he had tried them with long, weary marching, and he knew that they were worthy of his trust. He gave his orders. The Leinsters and the Scots Guards, tall, gaunt, hunger-stricken warriors, whose ribs could be counted through their ragged khaki coats, swung out as cheerily as if they had never known the absence of a meal or the fatigue of a dreary march. The Irishmen chaffed the Scots, and the Scots yelled badinage back to the sons of Erin, and onward they went, onward and upward, over the rock-strewn ground, through the narrow passes, fixing their bayonets where the ground looked likely to hold a hidden foe, ready at a moment's notice to charge into the blackness that lay engulfed in those dreary passes. But the enemy did not wait for them. As the Eighth Division advanced, making the rocky headlands ring with the rhythm of their martial tread, the Boers fell back like driven deer, and the bugle spoke to the Scottish bagpipe until the silent hills gave tongue, and echo answered echo until the wearied ear sickened for silence. Onward we swept, until Commando Nek lay like a grinning gash in the face of nature far in our rear. When we did halt the men threw themselves down on the freezing earth, and wolfed a biscuit; then, stretching themselves face downwards on the grass, they slept with their rifles ready to their hands, their greatcoats around them, and above only the stars, that seemed to freeze in the boundless billows of eternal blue. Onward again, before the silver sentinels above us had faded before the blushing face of the dawning. With faces begrimed with dirt, with feet blistered by contact with flinty boulders, with tattered garments flapping around them like feathers on wounded waterfowl, officers and men faced the unknown, as their fathers faced it before them. Meanwhile Hunter was pressing towards Fouriesburg from Relief's Nek, his scouts--the well-known "Tigers," under Major Remington--well in advance of his main column.

Rundle gave an order to Driscoll, Captain of the Scouts, who had done such good service to the Eighth Division. What passed between the general and the Irish captain no man knows, probably no man will ever know. But when Driscoll rode up at the mad gallop so characteristic of the man there was that in his hard, ugly, wind-tanned face which spoke of stern deeds to be done. He did not ride alone, this Irish-Indian Volunteer captain--Rundle's own *aide*, Lord Kensington, of the 15th Hussars, was on his right hand, and on his left Lieutenant Roger Tempest, of the Scots Guards, for a squad of the Scots Guards who had been learning scouting under Driscoll were to accompany Driscoll's Scouts. That little group was characteristic of the future of the British Empire. Two aristocrats riding shoulder to shoulder with a wild dare-devil, whose rifle had cracked over half the earth. England, Ireland, and Scotland rode alone in front of the adventurous band that day. It was a reckless ride; the captain, on his grey stallion, half a length in front. They darted through gullies, drew rein and unslung rifles up hill, now standing in the stirrups to ease their cattle, now sitting tight in the saddle to drive them over the open veldt, taking every chance that a dare-devil crew could take, pausing for nothing, staying for nothing. Right into the town of Fouriesburg they galloped, down from their saddles they leaped, up went the rifles; the foe poured in a few shots, and, appalled by the devil-ish audacity of the deed, fled before a handful. It was a proud moment then, when, in the last stronghold of the foe in all the Free State, Kensington, the *aide* of the General of the Eighth Division, with a little band of officers grouped around him, with the Scouts and Scots Guards lying behind cover, rifle in hand, pulled down the Orange Free State flag in the very teeth of the foe. Only a little band of officers--Kensington, Driscoll, Davies, and Tempest. May their names be remembered when the wine cups flow!

On the night of the 28th of July Colonel Harley, Chief Staff Officer Eighth Division, led two companies of the Leinsters and the full strength of the Scots Guards in a night attack on De Villier's Drift, which was to clear the way for the whole of the Eighth Division towards Fouriesburg. The movement had been well and carefully planned, and was neatly and expeditiously carried out. The following day we advanced in open order over the rolling veldt; now and again a man paused, lurched a little to one side, staggered and fell, as shot and shell dropped amongst us, but the march forward never ceased, never paused Paget and Hunter were with us now, and the lyddite guns seemed to drive all the fight out of the foe. They would not stand. Paget's artillerymen dashed forward, unlimbered, and loosed on the enemy with a recklessness of personal safety that was almost wanton.

Every branch of the Service was vying with its neighbour to see who could take the most chances in the game of war, and the very recklessness of the men was their safeguard, for their dash whipped the foe, who now seemed to realise that their evil hour had at last dawned. They sent in a flag of truce, asking for the terms on which they might surrender.

On the evening of the 29th July we knew that the enemy were negotiating for terms of peace, though things were kept as secret as possible until the following day. Then we saw General Prinsloo ride in with his *aide* and surrender. He met General Rundle first, and a few minutes later General Hunter, and the three leaders rode through the lines together. They were closeted closely for some hours before the final agreement could be arrived at. Prinsloo wanted terms for his men which the British generals would not concede, the final agreement being that the burghers were to ride in and throw down their arms under our flag. They were to be allowed a riding hack to convey them to the railway station, and each man was to remain in possession of his private effects. More than this General Hunter would not concede upon any terms. At one period of the negotiations things became so strained that hostilities were almost renewed, but the Hoof Commandant was wise enough to realise that destiny had decided against him and his burgher band. He came from the conclave at last, and gave an order in Dutch to his *aide*, and in a moment the horseman was flying towards the Boer laager with the news that, so far as they were concerned, the great war of 1899 and 1900 was at an end.

Our troops had been drawn up in long parallel lines, up over the slopes, over the crest, and along the edge of "Victory Hill." They formed a lane of blood and steel, down which the conquered veldtsmen had to march. Their guns were on their flanks, the generals grouped in the centre. Everything was hushed and still; there was no sign of braggart triumph, no unseemly mirth, no swagger in the demeanour of the troops. They had worked like men; they carried their laurels with conscious power and pride, but with no offensive show. It was a sight which few men ever behold, and none ever forget. The glory of the skies, where everything that met the eye was brightest blue, edged with stainless whiteness, was above us; and beneath our feet, and to right and left, were great valleys--not smiling like our English vales, where sunlight runs through shadows like laughter through tears,

but vast uncultivated gaps that grinned in sardonic silence at conqueror and conquered, as though to remind us that we were but puppets in a passing show. Kopjes
and valleys may have looked upon many a grim page in war's history. Savage chiefs,
backed by savage hordes, have swept across them many a time and oft. Possibly, if
the rocks had tongues, they could tell us much of ancient armies, for this land of
Africa is old in blood and warlike doings. But few more remarkable sights than this
upon which my eyes rested upon the 30th July, 1900, have ever graced even this
land of many wonders.

I looked along our lines, and saw our soldiers standing patiently waiting for the
curtain to fall. I was proud of them, and of the men who led them, for they had won
without one cruel stroke. No single human life had wantonly been wasted, no dis-
honourable deed had smirched their arms, no smoking ruins cried aloud to God for
retribution, no outraged women sobbed dry-eyed behind us, no starving children
fled before the khaki wave; and in this last hour, an hour pregnant with humiliation
and pain to our enemies, there was the steady manliness which spoke of the great
dignity of a great nation. Out from the stillness a bugle spoke from the lines of the
Leinsters; the Scottish bagpipes, far away down the hillside, took up the note with
a shrill scream of triumph, like the challenge of an eagle in its eyrie. A rustle ran
along the lines. We caught the hum of many voices, then the tramp of horses' hoofs.
A soldier slipped towards the spot where our country's flag was furled and ready; a
moment later the Union Jack spread out and hugged the breezes. Our foemen rode
towards the flag between the lines of those whose hands had placed it there, and
when they came abreast of it they dropped their rifles and their bandoliers, and
with bent heads passed onwards.

Some were boys, so young that rifles looked unholy things in hands so childlike; others were old men, grey and grizzled, grim old tillers of the soil, who looked
as hard as the rocky boulders against which they leant, many were in the pride of
manhood; but old or young, grey beard or no beard, all of them seemed to realise
that they were a beaten people. All day, and for many days, they came to us and
laid their arms aside, until fully 4,000 men had owned themselves our prisoners.
We gathered in the flocks and herds which had been held by them as army stores,
and then we set to work to give the Free State peace and peaceful laws. Our next
step was to march upon Harrismith, which was merely an armed promenade, for

the real work of the campaign had been completed when, on Victory Hill, near Slap Kranz, Commandant Prinsloo surrendered with all his forces, excepting the few who fled with De Wet and Olivier. Our flag is the symbol of victory in every village and town. May it always be the symbol of even-handed justice, for no power in all the world, unless backed by wise and pure laws, will hold Africa for twenty years.

I have never before attempted to express an opinion upon the future of Africa, yet now, when I have been nine months at the front, when I have marched through the Free State from border to border, noting carefully the demeanour of the people we have conquered, and the conduct of our troops towards those people, I may be allowed by the more tolerant of the British public to express an opinion. I do not see "white winged peace" brooding over this country. I see a people beaten, broken, out-generalled, and out-fought. I see a people who, even when whipped, maintain that the war has been an unholy war, brewed and bred by a few adventurers for sordid motives; and in my poor opinion there is little in front of us in South Africa but trouble and storm, unless someone with a cleaner soul than the ordinary politi-cian remains in Africa to represent our nation. Only one man seems to me to stand out as fitted by God and nature with the high qualities which the ruler of Africa should possess. He is a man who has the gift of leadership as few men--ancient or modern--ever possessed it, a man whose word is known to be unbreakable, whose hands are clean, whose record is stainless--the Field-Marshal, Lord Roberts. The man who is to rule South Africa must be a great soldier, not a tyrant, not a martinet, not a bundle of red tape tied up with a Downing Street bow and adorned with frills. The negro trouble is looming large on the African borders, and the negro chiefs know that in Lord Roberts they have their master. We must not pander to them to the injury of the Dutch, or how are we to weld Dutch and British into a national whole? Our generals have so conducted this campaign, especially this latter part of it, that not only does the Dutchman know that we can fight, but he knows that we can be generous with the splendid generosity of a truly great people. Our generals, with few exceptions, have left that record behind them, for which a nation's thanks are due; and few have done more than the commander of the Eighth Division, Sir Leslie Rundle, who can say that not only did he never lose an English gun, but that never did the enemy of his country succeed in breaking through his lines. Few men, placed as he was, week after week, month after month, would have been able to make so proud a boast.

These are possibly the last lines I shall ever write in connection with the Eighth Division. Their work is practically over here. My own is done, for my health is badly broken, and I shall follow this to England. But if I cannot march home with them, when they come back in triumph to receive from a grateful country the praise they have won, I can at least have the satisfaction of knowing that for many months I shared their vicissitudes, if not their glory.

CHARACTER SKETCHES IN CAMP.

THE CAMP LIAR.

In the days of my almost forgotten boyhood I remember reading in the Book of all books that the Wise Man, in a fit of blank despair, declared that there were several things under heaven which he could neither gauge nor understand, viz., "The way of a serpent upon a rock, and the way of a man with a maid," and I beg leave to doubt if Solomon, in all his wisdom, could understand the little ways of a camp liar in his frisky glory. Whence he cometh, whither he goeth, and why he was born, are conundrums which might tax the ingenuity of all the prophets, from Daniel downwards, to solve. I have sought him with peace offerings in each hand, hoping to beguile him from his sinful ways, and have located him not. I have risen in the chilly dawn, and laid wait for him with a gun, but have not feasted mine eyes upon him. I have lain awake through the still watches of the night planning divers surprises for him, but success has not come nigh unto me. I have cursed the camp liar with a fervour born of long suffering, and I have hired a Zulu mule-driver to curse him for me; but my efforts have come to nought, and now I am sore in my very bones when I think of him. All men whose fate it is to dwell under canvas know of his work, but no man hath yet laid hand or eye upon him. A man goeth to his blankets at night time feeling good towards all mankind, satisfied in his own soul that he has garnered in all the legitimate news that he is in any way entitled to handle for the public benefit; and lo! when he ariseth in the dawning he finds that the camp liar has neither slept nor slumbered, for the very air is full of stories concerning battles which have not been fought and victories which have not been won. From mouth to mouth, all along the lines, the stories run as fire runs along fuse, and no man born of woman can tell whence they came or where they will stop. Each soldier questioned swears the tale is true, because "'twas told to him by one who never lied." Yet, at evening, when the weary wretch who works for newspapers returns to his tent, with his boots worn through with fruitless search for the author of the "news," he learns that once again he has been the dupe of the "camp liar"; and he may well be forgiven if he then heaps a whole continent of curses on the invisible shape which, forming itself into a lie, is small enough to enter a man's mouth, and yet big enough to permeate a whole camp. What is a camp liar? It is not a man, neither is it a maid, neither is it dog nor devil. It is a nameless shadow, which flits through the minds of men, fashioned by the Father of Evil to be a curse and a scourge to war correspondents. A mining liar is an awful liar, but he takes tangible form, and one can grapple with him when he appears upon a prospectus. A political liar is a pitiful liar, and vengeance finds him out upon the hustings, and eggs and the produce of the kitchen garden are his reward. A legal liar is a loquacious liar, but he is bounded by his brief and the extent of his fees. But the camp liar has no bounds, and is equally at home in all languages, at one moment dealing with an army in full marching order, and the next battening festively upon one man in a mudhole. There is no height to which the camp liar dare not ascend, there is nothing too trivial for it to touch. It has neither sex nor shape; but, like a fallen angel ousted from Heaven, and not wanted in Hades, it flits through camp a mental microbe, spawning falsehoods in the souls of soldiers.

The camp liar concocts a story of a fearful fight, and fills the air with the groans of the dying, and makes a weird picture out of the grisly, grinning silence of the ghastly dead. Kopjes are stained a rich ripe red with the blood of heroes, and arms, and legs, and skulls, and shattered jaw bones hurtle through the air midst the sound of bursting shells, like straws in a stable-yard when the wind blows high. The very poetry of lying is touched with a master hand when charging squadrons sweep across the veldt and the sunlight kisses the soldier's steel. Then comes the pathos dear to the liar's soul--the farewells of the dying, sobbed just seven seconds before sunset into comrades' ears; the faltering voice, the tear-dimmed eyes, the death rattle in the throat, the last hand clasps, the last deep-drawn breath, in which--mother--Mary--and Heaven are always mingled; and then the moonlight and the moaning of the midnight wind!----The war correspondent leaps from the tent, springs into his saddle with his note-book in his mouth and an indelible lead pencil in each hand,

and rides over kopje and veldt ten dreary miles to gaze upon the scene of that awful battle, and finds--one dead mule, and a nigger driver, dead drunk. Then, if he has had a religious education, he climbs out of the saddle, sinks on his knees, and prays for the peace of the camp liar's immortal soul. But if, as is often the case, he has had a secular upbringing, he spits on the dead mule, kicks the nigger, slinks back to camp by a roundabout route, and swears to everyone that he has been forty miles in another direction in a railway truck.

Four or five days later, just at that hour in the morning when a man clings most fondly to his blankets, another rumour breaks the early morning's limpid silence, a rumour of a battle of great import raging eighteen miles away, just within easy riding distance for a smart correspondent. But the man of ink and hardships chuckles this time. He has been fooled so often by the imp of camp rumours; so murmurs just loud enough to be heard in heaven, "That infernal camp liar again," and rustles his blankets round his ears and drops cosily back into dreamland; but when, later on, he learns that an important battle has been fought, and he has missed it all because he did not want to be fooled by the camp liar, then what he mutters is muttered loud enough to be heard in a different place, and the folk there don't need ear trumpets to catch what he says either.

CHARACTER SKETCHES IN CAMP.

THE NIGGER SERVANT.

It is raining outside my tent. It has rained for three days and nights, and looks quite capable of raining for three days more; everything is simply sodden. You try to look around you at the men's camps. At every step your boots go up to the ankle, squelch, in the black mud. You slip as you walk, and go down on your hands and knees in the slimy filth; that brings out all the poetry in your nature. If you have had a Christian training in your youth, you think of David dodging Saul, and your sympathies go out towards the stupid king. The mud is everywhere; the horses have trodden it to slime in many places, in others the feet of the soldiers have transformed it to batter. Everything is cold, dreary, dismal; even the tobacco is damp, and leaves a taste in a man's mouth like the receipt of bad news from home. I look at the soldiers hanging around like sheep round a blocked-up shed in a snowstorm, and I feel sympathetic. Their puttees are wet, and there is a suggestion of future rheumatism in every fold that encircles their calves; I can't see much more of them except their weather-beaten faces. They wear their helmets and their blue-black overcoats, but both are wet. They don't look happy, and the cause is not hard to find: they have slept out for three nights without tents. Their blankets are like sponges that have been left in a tub. Each blanket seems to hold about three gallons of water.

I arrived at this computation by watching the men wringing their bedding. Two men got hold of a blanket, one at each end; they twist it different ways, and the water runs out in a stream. The soldiers relapse into language. Most of their adjectives have a decidedly pink tinge, and I shouldn't wonder if they became scarlet if this sort of weather continued.

My nigger slops along through the slush and tells me that my lunch is ready. He is not a happy-looking nigger by any means. A white man looks bad enough in the mud and cold, but a nigger presents a pitiful spectacle. His face goes whitish green, with an undercurrent of slatey grey running through it. The brilliancy leaves the coal-black eyes, and they become as lifeless and limp as a professional politician at a prayer meeting. The mouth goes agape, the thick lips become flabby, and fall away from the teeth. The mouth does not seem to fit the face, but hangs on to it like a second-hand suit on a backyard fence. My nigger is no better, and no worse, than the rest of them. He looks like a chapter in Lamentations, and is about as much at home in the sodden camp as a bar of wet soap in a sand heap. Just now he is good for nothing except to sing doleful hymns in a key sad enough to frighten a transit mule away from a bag of mealies. When he is not singing sadly he is quoting Scripture and thinking about his immortal soul. When the sun comes out to-morrow and the day after, he will be dancing a most unholy dance or be making love to "Dinah," filling in the intervals by cursing in three different languages stray horses that steal our fodder.

It is really astonishing what a difference the weather makes to the morals of the South African nigger. Give him plenty of sunshine, and he forgets he ever had a soul, and throws slabs of blasphemy, picked up from the Tommies around him, with painful liberality. When he gets tired of English oaths, he drops into Cape Dutch, and some of the curses contained in that language are solid enough to hurt anything they hit. Later on he drifts into his native tongue, raises his voice a couple of oc-taves, and streaks the atmosphere with multi-coloured oaths, until you imagine you are listening to a vocal rainbow. But take away the sunshine, give him a wet hide and a wet floor to camp on, and he straightway becomes all penitence and prayer. His face, peering out dismally between the upturned collar of his weather-stained coat and the down-drawn brim of his battered hat, looks like a soiled sermon, and he is altogether woeful.

When the weather is warm he decks himself out in any piece of gaudy finery he can lay hands upon. He loves to wear a glaring yellow roll of silk or cloth around his hat, a blue or green 'kerchief about his throat, and a crimson girdle encircled about his loins. Then he thinks he is a midsummer sunset, and swaggers round like a peacock in full plumage, looking for something to "mash." He has no sense of the eternal law of averages. It does not trouble him if the whole seat of his most important garment is represented by a hole big enough to put a baby in, if he only has the artistic decorations I have mentioned above. Nor does he see anything out of the way in the fact that one of his feet is encased in an officer's top boot and the other in a remnant of a Boer farmer's cast-off veldtschoon. His soul yearns towards feathers. He will pluck a grand white plume from the tail of an ostrich if he gets a favourable opportunity, and place it triumphantly in his torn and soiled slouch hat, or he will pick up a discarded bonnet from a dust pile and rob it of feathers placed there by feminine hands, in order that he may look a black Beau Brummell.

His manners, like his morals, change with the weather. When the barometer registers "fine and clear," you may expect a saucy answer if you rate him for a late breakast; when it registers "warm, and likely to be warmer," you may consider yourself lucky if you get a morning meal at all. But when it indicates "hot," and the mercury still rising, you know that the time has arrived for you to climb out of your coat and commence cooking for yourself, unless you feel equal to the task of spreading a saucy nigger in sections around the adjacent allotments. It is not always healthy to adopt the latter plan, especially if your "boy" happens to be a Basuto or a Zulu. Should he belong to either of those tribes, threaten him as much as you like, but don't hurry to put your threats into practice; or the nigger may do the scattering, and you may do the penitent part of the business. You may bully him as much as you like when the barometer is falling, for then the life is all out of him, and he has not sufficient spirit left in him to resent any sort of insult.

Even "Tommy" knows this, and on a cold day will call a big Zulu servant by a name which implies that the Zulu's father and mother were never legally married. The Zulu will only smile dismally, and tell "Tommy" that he will pray for the salvation of his soul. Three days later, when the air is dancing in the heat-rays, if Mr. Atkins, emboldened by former success, repeats the speech, the Zulu will rise and confront him with blazing eyes, showing at the same time a wide range of beautiful white teeth, set in a savage snarl, and give Mr. Atkins a choice of titles which it would be hard to improve upon even in a Dublin dockyard, and he will not be slow to back his mouth with his hands should the argument become pressing, as more than one of her Majesty's lieges have found out to their deep and lasting humiliation.

When a combination of rain and religion has depressed him the nigger servant is one of the most abject-looking mortals that ever wore clothes, and makes as sad a spectacle as a farmyard fowl on a front fence in a thunderstorm. But he must not be judged altogether by his appearance on such occasions. He can be loyal to his "boss," and when fit and well he will fight when roused as a devil might fight for the soul of a deacon. He loves to ride or drive a horse, but he is not fond of horses, as I understand the term. He has no idea of making a pet of his charge. A horse is to him merely something to get about upon, and he cannot understand our fondness for our equine friends. I have noticed the same trait in the Boer character. To a Boer a horse is usually merely a means of transit from spot to spot; not a comrade, not a companion. I was not astonished to find this feeling amongst the niggers, because I have noticed it among the natives in every colony in Australia, and even amongst such inveterate horsemen as the Sioux Indians of America and the Maories of New Zealand; but I was surprised to note how little sympathy existed between the Boer and his equine helper.

The nigger servant is a sporting sort of party, and never loses an opportunity to indulge his tastes in this direction. I had an excellent chance the other day to note how fond he is of a bit of hunting. We had camped before sundown in a rather picturesque position, and I was watching the effect of the declining sun on the gloomy kopjes, when I noticed a commotion in all the camps, in front, at the rear, and on both flanks. In ten seconds every nigger in the whole camp had deserted his work and was frantically dashing out on to the veldt. They uttered shrill cries as they ran, and every man had some sort of weapon in his hand, either a tomahawk, a billet of wood, or a rock. With marvellous celerity they formed a huge circle, though what they were after was a puzzle to me. I fancied for awhile that one of their number must have run "amuck," and the rest meant to send him to slumber. Quickly they narrowed the circle, the whole body of them moving as if linked together and propelled by unseen mechanism. When the circle got about the third the size of an ordinary cricket ground I saw what they were after. A brace of hares had caught their eyes, and this was their method of capturing the fleet-footed, but stupid, "racers of the veldt." First one nigger and then another detached himself from the circle, and, darting in, had a shy at the quarry with whatever missile he had with him. If he missed--and a good many of them missed--the speedy little bit of fur, he returned crestfallen to the circle again, amidst jeers and laughter from the rest. The hares darted hither and thither in that ever narrowing circle of foes, until a couple of well-aimed shots, one with a rock as big as a cricket ball, and one with a tomahawk, laid them out, and they became the prize of the successful marksmen. The nigger "boy" has to be paid one pound a week and his "scoff," and, taking him all in all, in spite of his faults, which are many, I verily think he earns it.

CHARACTER SKETCHES IN CAMP.

THE SOLDIER PREACHER.

(Written at Enslin Battlefield.)

He was standing at eventide facing the rough and rugged heights of Enslin. The crimson-tinted clouds that emblazoned the sky cast a ruddy radiance round his head and face, making him appear like one of those ancient martyrs one is apt to see on stained-glass windows in old-world churches in Rome or Venice. His feet were firmly planted close to the graves of the British soldiers and sailors who had fallen when we beat the Boers and drove them back upon Modder River.

In one hand he held a little, well-worn Bible; his other hand was raised high above his close-cropped head, whilst his voice rang out on the sultry, storm-laden air like the clang of steel on steel:

"Prepare ter meet yer God!"

No one who looked at the neat, strong figure arrayed in the plain khaki uniform of a private soldier, at the clean-shaven, square-jawed face, at the fearless grey-blue eyes, could doubt either his honesty or earnestness. Courage was imprinted by Nature's never-erring hand on every lineament of his Saxon features. So might one of Cromwell's stern-browed warriors have stood on the eve of Marston Moor.

"Prepare ter meet yer God!"

To the right of him the long lines of the tents spread upwards towards the kopje; to the left the veldt, with its wealth of grey-green grass, sown by the bounteous hand of the Great Harvester; all around him, excepting where the graves raised their red-brown furrows, rows of soldiers lounged, listing to the old, old story of man's weakness and eternal shame, and Christ's love and everlasting pity. On the soldier preacher's breast a long row of decorations gleamed, telling of honourable service to Queen and country. Before a man could wear those ribbons he must have faced death as brave men face it on many a battlefield. He must have known the agonies of thirst, the dull dead pain of sleepless nights and midnight marches, the tireless watching at the sentry's post, and the onward rush of armed men up heights almost unscalable. On Egypt's sun-scorched plains he must have faced the mad onslaughts of the Dervish hosts, and rallied with the men who held the lines at Abu Klea Wells, where gallant Burnaby was slain. The hills of Afghanistan must have re-echoed to his tread, else why the green and crimson ribbon that mingled with the rest? His eyes had flashed along the advancing lines of charging impi, led by Zulu chiefs. Yet never had they flashed with braver light than now, when, facing that half-mocking, half-reckless crowd, he cried:

"Prepare ter meet yer God!"

Rough as the thrust of a broken bayonet was his speech, unskilled in rhetoric his tongue, his periods unrounded as flying fragments of shrapnel shell; yet all who listened knew that every word came from the speaker's soul, from the magazine of truth. Some London slum had been his cradle, the gutters of the great city the only University his feet had known, the costers' dialect was native to his tongue; yet no smug Churchman crowned with the laurels of the schools could so have stirred the blood of those wild lads, fresh from the boundless bush and lawless mining camps beneath Australian suns.

"Prepare ter meet yer God!"

And even as he spoke we, who listened, plainly heard the rolling thunder of our guns as they spoke in sterner tones to the nation's foes from Modder River. It was no new figure that the soldier preacher placed before us. It was the same indignant Christ that swept the rabble from the Temple; the same great Christ who calmly faced the seething mob in Pilate's judgment hall; the same sweet Christ who took the babes upon His knee; the same Divine Christ who, with hyssop and gall, and mingled blood and tears, passed death's dread portals on the dark brow of Calvary. The same grand figure, but quaintly dressed in words that savoured of the London slums and of the soldier's camp, and yet so hedged around with earnest love and childlike faith that all its grossest trappings fell away and left us nothing but the ideal Christ.

Once more we heard the distant batteries speak to those whose hands had rudely grasped the Empire's flag, and every rock, and hill, and crag, and stony height took up the echo, like a lion's roar, until the whispering wind was tremulous with sound. Then all was hushed except the preacher's voice.

"Prepare ter meet yer God! I've come ter tell yer all abart a General whose armies hold ther City of Eternal Life. If you are wounded, throw yer rifles down, 'nd 'e will send the ambulance of 'is love, with Red Cross angels, and 'is adjutant, whose name is Mercy, to dress yer wounds. Throw down yer rifles 'nd surrender. No rebels can enter the City of Eternal Life. You can't storm ther walls, Or take ther gates at ther point of ther baynit, for ther ramparts are guarded 'nd ther sentries never sleep. When ther bugles sound ther larst reville you will ever 'ear, 'nd ther colonel, whose name is Death, gives the order ter march, you'll have nothink to fear abart, if yer bandoliers are full o' faith 'nd yer rifles are sighted with good works. Yer uniforms may be ragged, and you may not even have a corporal's stripe to show; but if yer can pass ther sentries fearlessly, you'll find a general's commission waitin' for yer just inside ther gate. But yer earn't fool with my General. Remember this: ther password is, 'Repentance,' 'nd nothink else will do. The sentry on duty will see you comin' and will challenge you. 'Who goes there?' 'Friend!' 'Advance, friend, 'nd give ther counter-sign!' If you say, 'Good works,' you'll find 'is baynit up against yer chest. If yer say you forgot to get it, you'll be in ther clink in 'ell in ther twinklin' of an eye; but if yer say, loud 'nd clear, 'Repentance,' 'e will lower 'is baynit 'nd say, 'Pass, friend. All's well!'"

PRESIDENT STEYN.

Out on the veldt, far from the wife and home he loves so well, he stands, our country's bold, unyielding foe. And even as he stands he knows that the finger of Fate has written his own and his country's doom in letters large and deep on the walls of time. Yet, with unblenching brow, he waits the falling of the thunderbolt, a calm, grand figure, fit to live in history's pages when every memory of meaner men has passed into oblivion, M.T. Steyn, President of the shattered Free State of South Africa. Around this man the human jackals howl to try with lying lips to foul his memory. Yet, as a rock, age after age, throws back with contemptuous strength the waves that break against its base, so every action of his manly life gives the lie to tales which cowards tell.

He is our foe, no stabber in the dark, moving with stealthy steps amidst professions of pretended peace, but in the open, where the gaze of God and man can rest upon him, he stands, defiant, though undone. He staked his country's freedom, his earthly happiness, and his high position in the great game of war; staked all that mortal man holds dear; staked it for what? For love of gain! May he who spawned that lie to stir our people's hearts to boundless wrath against this falling man live to repent in sackcloth and in tears the evil deed so done. . . . Staked it for what? To feed his own ambition! I tell you no; the undercurrent which brought forth the deed sprang from a nobler and a higher source. His country stood pledged in time of peace to help in time of war a sister State, and when the bond fell due he honoured it, though none knew better than this noble man that when he loosed the dogs of war he crossed a lion's path.

Now he is tottering to his fall, amidst the ruins of a crumbling State, forsaken by the Powers that egged him on with covert promises of armed support, abandoned to the tender mercies of his foes by those on whose behalf he drew the sword. Yet, even now, the dauntless spirit of the man rises above the wreckage of disaster. A little band of heroes ring him round. Though every man in all that fearless few is England's foe, yet we, who boast the Vikings' blood in every vein, can we not honour them? So did our forefathers stand round Harold when Norman William trod with armed heel on English soil. So stood our fathers when Blucher's laggard step hung back from Waterloo. Are we not great enough to look with pride upon a gallant foe? Or has our nation fallen from its high estate, has chivalry departed from our blood, and left us nothing but the dregs which go to make a nation of hucksters? If so, then let us leave the battlefields to better men, and train our children solely for the market-place. But these are idle words, born of the spleen which such a thought engenders. Full well I know the temper of our people, terrible in their wrath, but swift to see the nobleness in those who face them boldly.

And these be noble men, my masters. They rally round their chief, as you and yours would rally round a British leader if foreign hordes swept with resistless might over England's historic soil. All that they loved they've lost, and nothing now remains to them but honour and a patriot's grave; and in the grim game of war it is our stern task to give them what they seek--a soldier's death beneath the doomed flag which, in their stubborn pride, they will never forsake. But even whilst we hem them round with bristling bayonets, ready for the last dread act in this red drama, let us pay them the tribute due to all brave men; for he who gives his life to guard a cause he holds most dear is worthy of our admiration, though he be ten thousand times our foe. What should we think of men who, left to guard the Kentish fields, threw down their arms and sued for peace to any leader of an invading host because our cause seemed lost? Should we not curse them as a craven crowd, and teach our lisping babes to mock their memory? Would any fair-faced girl in all the British Isles wed any man who would not fight until the sinews slackened with slaying in defence of the homeland? If so, they are not fashioned of the metal of which their granddames were made.

And what we honour as the prince of virtues in a Briton shall we condemn as vice in this little band of Free State Boers and their leader, loyal to a lost cause? No, England, no! It is not you that shriek anathemas to the weeping skies because the foe dies hard. The gutter gamin and the brutal lout who never owned a soul fit to rise above the level of the kettle singing on the hearth may brand the name of

Steyn and his stout burghers with infamy; but the clean-souled people of the Motherland, the people from whose ranks our greatest fighters and thinkers spring, will not endorse that cry. No, not though every slanderous throat shall shriek until they cannot wail an octave higher.

It is not from such great men as Roberts that we hear these pitiful tales concerning those who give us battle. He who has been a man of war from childhood to old age would never stoop to soil his manly lips to woo the fleeting favours of a mob, and he has proved himself as wise in council as upon the death-strewn fields of war. So wise, so brave, so loyal to his word, that even those whom he, at his country's call, has had to crush, lift their hats reverently at the mention of his name, because he wears upon his hero soul the white flower of a blameless life. Would Kitchener, whose dread name strikes terror to the heart of every burgher, would he befoul his foeman's fame? I tell you no, though whilst a foe remains in arms he strikes with all a giant's force and spares not; but when the blow has fallen, he of all men would preserve his enemies' fair fame intact. So it should be whilst those who stand in arms against our country and our country's flag refuse the terms we offer. We should make war so terrible that every enemy should dread the sound of British bugles as they would dread the trump of doom. When once the country's voice has called for war, then war should sweep with resistless might over land and sea, until sweet peace should seem a boon to be desired above all earthly things by those who stand in arms against us. If Steyn and those who with heroic hearts hedge him round refuse to bow to destiny and the God of Battles, then he and they must fall before the bayonets of our soldiery as growing corn falls before the sickle of the reaper. But even in their fall they can claim as their heaven-born heritage our nation's deepest admiration for their dauntless devotion to their love of country, home, and kindred. And we will but add laurels to the renown our soldiers have won if we, with unsparing hand, mete out to them the praises due to manly foes. Ours be the task to slay them where they stand; not ours the task to rob them of the glory they have won.

LOUIS BOTHA, COMMANDANT-GENERAL OF THE BOER ARMY.

Louis Botha, who has cut so deep a mark in the pages of history, is only a young man yet, being about seven-and-thirty years of age. He is a "fine figure of a man," standing in the neighbourhood of six feet in his boots. His face is handsome, intellectual, and determined; his expression kindly and compassionate. The razor never touches his face, but his brown beard is always neatly trimmed, for the young Commandant-General is particular in regard to his personal appearance in a manly way, though in no respect foppish. He is now, and always has been, an excellent athlete, a good rifle shot, and a first-class horseman; not given at any time to indoor pastimes over much, though fond of a quiet game of whist. He was born in Natal, of Dutch parents, and married to Miss Emmett, a relative of Robert Emmett, the Irish Revolutionist. Young Botha was educated at Greytown, and though a good, sound commercial scholar, he gave no evidence in his schoolboy days of what was in him. No one who knew him then would have dreamed that before he was forty years of age he would be the foremost soldier of his country. His folk were moderately well off, but the adventurous spirit of the future general sent him inland from Natal when a large number of Natal and Free State Boers enlisted under the flag of General Lucas Meyer, who was bent upon making war upon a powerful negro tribe in the neighbourhood of Vryheid. During the fighting young Botha was his general's right-hand man, displaying even at that early age a cool, level head and a stout heart. When the Boers were firmly settled upon the land Vryheid was declared a Republic, and Lucas Meyer was elected first President. But the new Republic lasted only about three years, and was then, by mutual consent, merged into Transvaal territory, and both Lucas Meyer and Louis Botha were elected members of the Volksraad. Louis Botha retained his seat right up to the time hostilities broke out between Great Britain and the Republics under Mr. Kruger and Mr. Steyn.

During the many stormy scenes which preceded the actual declaration of war Louis Botha proved that he possessed the coolest and most level head in the Volksraad. He opposed the war, and, with prophetic eye, foresaw the awful devastation of his country which would follow in the footsteps of the British army. But when the time came, and his country was irretrievably pledged to war, he was not the man to hang back. He was one of those who had much to lose and little indeed to gain by taking up arms against us, for, by honest industry, he had become a wealthy farmer and stockbreeder. At the first call to arms he threw aside his senatorial duties, and took up his rifle, rejoining his old commando at Vryheid as commandant under General Lucas Meyer. It is said that at the battle of Dundee General Meyer, feeling convinced that the God of Battles had decided against him and his forces, decided to surrender to the British, but Louis Botha fiercely combated his general's decision, and point-blank refused to throw down his arms or counsel his men to do so. What followed all the world knows, and Botha went up very high in the estimation of the better class of fighting burghers. At the Tugela, before the first big battle took place, General Meyer was taken ill, and had to retire to Pretoria, and Louis Botha was then elected assistant-general, and the planning of the battle was left entirely to him.

It was a terribly responsible position to place so young a man in, for he was face to face with the then Commander-in-Chief of the British army, Sir Redvers Buller, a general of dauntless determination and undoubted ability. Experience, men, and all the munitions of war were in favour of the British general; but the awful nature of the country was upon the side of the newly fledged Boer leader, and he made terrible use of it. The day of Colenso, when Sir Redvers Buller received his first decisive check, will not soon be forgotten in the annals of our Army. A man of weaker fibre than the British leader would have been daunted by the disasters of that day, for there he lost ten guns and a large number of men. But Buller carried in his blood all the old grit of our race, and the heavier the check the more his soul was set upon ultimate victory. I have been over that battle ground, and have looked at the positions taken up by Louis Botha. They were chosen with consummate skill, born of a thorough knowledge of the nature of the country and inherent generalship.

I have looked at the country Sir Redvers Buller had to pass through to get at his wise and skilful adversary. The man who dared make the attempt that Buller made must have had nerves of steel, and a soul that would not blench if ordered to storm the very gates of Hades. The worst fighting ground that I saw in all the Free State was but a mockery of war compared to the ground around Colenso, and I have seen some terrible places in the Free State. But a man has to see the ground Buller fought in to realise the magnitude of the task the Empire set him at the beginning of the war. Great as Lord Roberts is, I doubt if he would have done more than Buller did under the same circumstances.

That battle of Colenso made young Louis Botha famous, and from that hour the eyes of the burghers were turned towards him as the one man fit to lead them. At Spion Kop, when the Boer leader, Schalk Burger, vacated the splendid position he had been ordered to take up, Louis Botha's genius grasped the mighty import of the situation, and he at once realised that Schalk Burger had blundered terribly, and it was he who retook those positions with such disastrous consequences to our forces. His fame spread far and near, and his name became a thing to conjure with. When the Commandant-General of the Boer Army, General Joubert, lay dying, he was asked who was the best man to fill his place. And he, the grey veteran, did not hesitate for a second, but with his dying breath gasped out the name of Louis Botha. The Boer Government promptly appointed him to the position, and from that day to this he has been the paramount military power in the Boer lines. He is not the only one of his line fighting under the Transvaal flag. There are four other brothers in the field, one of whom, Christian Botha, is now a general, and a good fighter. As a soldier Louis Botha has proved himself a foeman worthy the steel of any of our generals; as a man his worst enemy can say nothing derogatory concerning him, for in all his actions he has borne himself like a gentleman. He is generous and courteous in the hour of victory, stout-hearted and self-reliant in the time of disaster--just the type of soldier that a great nation like ours knows how to esteem, even though he is an enemy in arms against us.

WHITE FLAG TREACHERY.

Few things have astonished me more during the progress of this war than the number of charges levelled against our foes in reference to the treacherous use of the white flag. Almost every newspaper that came my way contained some such account; yet, though constantly at the front for nine months, I cannot recall one solitary instance of such treachery which I could vouch for. I have heard of dozens of cases, and have taken the trouble to investigate a good many, but never once managed to obtain sufficient proof to satisfy me that the charge was genuine. On one occasion I was following close on the heels of our advancing troops, and had for a comrade a rather excitable correspondent. When within about fourteen hundred yards of the kopjes we were advancing to attack, the Boers opened a heavy rifle fire; and, though we could not see a solitary enemy, our fellows began to drop. It was very evident that the enemy were secreted in the rocks not far from a substantial farmhouse, from the roof of which floated a large white flag (it turned out later to be a tablecloth braced to a broom handle).

"There's another case of d---- white flag treachery," shouted my companion. "I wonder the general don't turn the guns on that farm and blow it to Hades."

"What for?" I asked.

"What for! Why, they are flying the white flag, and shooting from the farmhouse. Isn't that enough?"

"Quite enough, if true," I replied. "But how the devil do you know they are shooting from the farmhouse?"

"They must be shooting from the farmhouse," he yelled. "Why, I've been scouring all the rocks around with my glasses, and can't see a blessed Boer in any of 'em. No, sir, you can bet your soul they are skulking in that farm. They know we won't loose a shell on the white flag---the cowards!"

I did not think it worth while to argue with a man of that stamp, but kept my glasses on that farm very closely during the fight that followed. Right up to the time when our men rushed the kopjes and surrounded the farmhouse I did not see a man enter or leave the house, and when I rode up I found that two women and three children were in possession. Furthermore, on examination, I soon discovered that, as the doors and windows faced the wrong way, it would have been impossible for a Boer to do much shooting at our men, unless the walls at the gable end were loop-holed, which they were not, I know, for I examined them minutely. Fortunately for the credit of the British Army, most of our generals are coolheaded men who do not allow the irresponsible chatter of the army to influence them. Otherwise our guns would have been trained upon many a homestead on charges quite as flimsy and groundless as the one quoted above.

I suppose that cases of treachery have really occurred during the war. In a mixed crowd like that which composes the burgher army, there are sure to be some mortals fit to do any mean trick, just as sure as there are men fit to do or say anything in the British Army, But I cannot, and I will not, believe that the great bulk of these men are such paltry cowards as to make the "white flag" act a common one. It may be news to British readers to know that the burghers complain of the behaviour of our troops as bitterly as we complain of theirs; and I think, from personal observation, that their charges are as groundless as are some charges made by the same class of hysterical individuals, though of different nationality. Their pet hatred, when I was a prisoner in their hands, was the Lancers. They used to swear that the Lancers never spared a wounded man, but ran him through as they galloped past him. I was told this fifty times, and each time told my informant flatly that I declined to believe the assertion, and should continue to disbelieve it until I had undeniable proof, for it would take a good deal to convince me that a British soldier would strike a fallen foe even in the heat and stress of battle. One day they asked me to come and look at the dead body of one of their field cornets, whom they alleged to have been done to death whilst wounded by our Lancers. I went and saw the man, and at a glance saw that the wounds were not lance wounds at all, but ripping bullet wounds. He had been sniped by some Australian riflemen from a high kopje whilst in a valley. I tried to explain this to the excited burghers, but they only sneered at me for my trouble, until one of their own doctors coming along had a look at the corpse, and promptly verified my statements. That calmed them considerably, and they looked at the thing in cooler blood, and soon saw that it was really absurd to put the blame of the man's death on the shoulders of the Lancers, though they stoutly maintained that our cavalry were at times guilty of such monstrous conduct. I have often heard them solemnly swear never to give a Lancer a chance to surrender if they once got him within rifle range.

Personally, I could never see just what the Boers would gain by the white flag business. As a rule, our troops did not want coaxing into rifle range; they marched within hitting distance readily enough, and did not require a white flag to lure them into a tight place, so that the object to be gained by the enemy by such disgraceful tactics never seemed to me to be too apparent. If they had ever by such means been able to entrap an army, or to bring about the wholesale slaughter of our men, I could understand things a bit better; but they had little to gain and an awful lot to lose by such tactics. There is no slight risk attached to the act of firing on an advancing army treacherously under cover of the white flag. Such a deed rouses all the slumbering devil in the men, and the foe found guilty of such a deed would get more bayonet than he would find conducive to his health when it came to his turn to be beaten.

THE BATTLE OF MAGERSFONTEIN.

MAGERSFONTEIN.

The Australians, after relieving Belmont from the Boer commando, suddenly received orders to march upon Enslin, as the Boers had attacked that place, which was held by two companies of the Northamptonshires under Captain Godley; the latter had no artillery, whilst the enemy, who were over 1,000 strong, had one 12-pounder gun with them, but the sequel proved that the Boer is a poor fighter in the open country. He is hard to beat in hilly and rocky ground when acting on the defensive, but he is not over dangerous as an attacking power. Let him choose his ground, and fight according to his own traditions, and the best soldiers in the world will find it no sinecure to oust him. As soon as the Boers put in an appearance at Enslin, Lieutenant Brierly, of the Northumberland Fusiliers, who is attached to the Northamptons, made his way to a kopje, which had formerly been held by Boer forces, and a mere handful of men fairly held the enemy in check at that point for over seven hours. The enemy made frantic efforts to dislodge this gallant little band, but failed dismally, and they had not the heart to try to take the kopje by storm, though there were enough of them around the hill to have eaten the little band of Britishers. In the meantime Captain Godley and his men held the township. Again and again the enemy threatened to rush the place, but their valour melted before the determined front of the besieged, and they drew off, taking their gun with them, their scouts having warned them that the Australians, with a section of the Royal Horse Artillery and two guns, were coming upon them from the direction of Belmont, whilst a body of the 12th Lancers and a battery of artillery were dashing down from Modder River. The Australians, who are now 720 strong, the New South Wales Company of 125 men having joined Colonel

Head's forces, remained at Enslin, and entrenched there in order to keep open the line of communication between General Methuen's army and Orange River; a section of Royal Horse Artillery and two guns is with them. On half a dozen occasions the Boers have threatened to sweep down upon them from the hilly country adjacent, but up to the time of writing nothing serious has occurred.

On Sunday last we heard the sound of heavy firing coming from the direction of Modder River; scouts coming in informed us that an engagement between General Methuen's force and the enemy, under the astute General Cronje, had commenced. Seeing that Australia was liable to remain idle for the time being, I determined to push on with my assistant, Mr. E. Monger, of Coolgardie, West Australia. When we arrived at Modder River we found the fight raging at a spot about four and a half miles beyond Modder River bridge. Our forces were in possession of the river and the plain beyond; but General Cronje had entrenched himself in a line of ranges stretching for several miles across the veldt. So well had the Boer general chosen his ground, and such good use had he made of the natural advantages of his position, that the British found themselves face to face with an African Gibraltar. The frowning rocks were bristling with rifles, which commanded the plain below, trenches seamed the hillsides in all directions, and in those trenches lay concealed the picked marksmen of the veldt--men who, though they know but little of soldiering from a European point of view, yet had been familiar with the rifle from earliest boyhood; rough and uncouth in appearance, dressed in farmers' garb, still under those conditions, fighting under a general they knew and trusted, amidst surroundings familiar to them from infancy, they were foemen worthy of the respect of the veteran troops of any nation under heaven.

At every post of vantage Cronje, with consummate generalship, had posted his artillery so that it would be almost impossible for our guns to silence them, whilst at the same time he could sweep the plains below should our infantry attempt to storm the heights at the point of the bayonet. At the bottom of the kopjes, right under the muzzle of his guns, he had excavated trenches deep enough to hide his riflemen, but he had thrown up no earthworks, so that our guns could not locate the exact spot where his rifle trenches lay. All the earth from the trenches had been very carefully removed, and the low blue bush which covers these plains completely screened his trenches from view. In front of the trenches, and extending some considerable distance out in front of the veldt, the clever Boer leader had placed an immense amount of barbed wire entanglement, so fashioned that no cavalry could live amongst it, whilst even the very flower of our infantry would find it hard work to charge over it, even in daylight. The Boer forces are variously estimated at from 12,000 to 15,000 men. The number and nature of their guns can only be guessed at, but that the enemy's men are well supplied in that respect there can be no question. Our forces I estimate at about 11,000 men of all arms, including the never-to-be-forgotten section of the Naval Brigade, to whom England owes a debt of gratitude too deep for words to portray; for their steadiness, valour, and accuracy of shooting saved England from disaster on this the blackest day that Scotland has known since the Crimea.

Our troops extended over many miles of country. Every move had to be made in full view of the enemy upon a level plain where a collie dog could not have moved unperceived by those foemen hidden so securely behind impregnable ramparts. During the whole of Sunday our gunners played havoc with the enemy, the shooting of the Naval Brigade being of such a nature that even thus early in the fight the big gun of the bluejackets, with its 42-pound lyddite shell, struck terror into the hearts of the enemy. But the Boers were not idle. Whenever our infantry, in manoeuvring, came within range'of their rifles, our ranks began to thin out, and the blood of our gallant fellows dyed the sun-baked veldt in richest crimson.

During the night that followed it was considered expedient that the Highland Brigade, about 4,000 strong, under General Wauchope, should get close enough to the lines of the foe to make it possible to charge the heights. At midnight the gallant, but ill-fated, general moved cautiously through the darkness towards the kopje where the Boers were most strongly entrenched. They were led by a guide, who was supposed to know every inch of the country, out into the darkness of an African night. The brigade marched in line of quarter-column, each man stepping cautiously and slowly, for they knew that any sound meant death. Every order was given in a hoarse whisper, and in whispers it was passed along the ranks from man to man; nothing was heard as they moved towards the gloomy, steel-fronted heights but the brushing of their feet in the veldt grass and the deep-drawn breaths of the marching men.

So, onward, until three of the clock on the morning of Monday. Then out of the darkness a rifle rang, sharp and clear, a herald of disaster--a soldier had tripped in the dark over the hidden wires laid down by the enemy. In a second, in the twinkling of an eye, the searchlights of the Boers fell broad and clear as the noonday sun on the ranks of the doomed Highlanders, though it left the enemy concealed in the shadows of the frowning mass of hills behind them. For one brief moment the Scots seemed paralysed by the suddenness of their discovery, for they knew that they were huddled together like sheep within fifty yards of the trenches of the foe. Then, clear above the confusion, rolled the voice of the general--"Steady, men, steady!"--and, like an echo to the veterans, out came the crash of nearly a thousand rifles not fifty paces from them. The Highlanders reeled before the shock like trees before the tempest. Their best, their bravest, fell in that wild hail of lead. General Wauchope was down, riddled with bullets; yet, gasping, dying, bleeding from every vein, the Highland chieftain raised himself on his hands and knees, and cheered his men forward. Men and officers fell in heaps together.

The Black Watch charged, and the Gordons and the Seaforths, with a yell that stirred the British camp below, rushed onward--onward to death or disaster. The accursed wires caught them round the legs until they floundered, like trapped wolves, and all the time the rifles of the foe sang the song of death in their ears. Then they fell back, broken and beaten, leaving nearly 1,300 dead and wounded just where the broad breast of the grassy veldt melts into the embrace of the rugged African hills, and an hour later the dawning came of the dreariest day that Scotland has known for a generation-past. Of her officers, the flower of her chivalry, the pride of her breeding, but few remained to tell the tale--a sad tale truly, but one untainted with dishonour or smirched with disgrace, for up those heights under similar circumstances even a brigade of devils could scarce have hoped to pass. All that mortal men could do the Scots did; they tried, they failed, they fell. And there is nothing left us now but to mourn for them, and avenge them; and I am no prophet if the day is distant when the Highland bayonet will write the name of Wauchope large and deep in the best blood of the Boers.

All that fateful day our wounded men lay close to the Boer lines under a blazing sun; over their heads the shots of friends and foes passed without ceasing. Many a gallant deed was done by comrades helping comrades; men who were shot through the body lay without water, enduring all the agony of thirst engendered by their wounds and the blistering heat of the day; to them crawled Scots with shattered limbs, sharing the last drop of water in their bottles, and taking messages to be delivered to mourning women in the cottage home of far-off Scotland. Many a last farewell was whispered by pain-drawn lips in between the ringing of the rifles, many a rough soldier with tenderest care closed the eyes of a brother in arms amidst the tempest and the stir of battle; and above it all, Cronje, the Boer general, must have smiled grimly, for well he knew that where the Highland Brigade had failed all the world might falter. All day long the battle raged; scarcely could we see the foe-- all that met our eyes was the rocky heights that spoke with tongues of flame when- ever our troops drew near. We could not reach their lines; it was murder, grim and ghastly, to send the infantry forward to fight a foe they could not see and could not reach. Once our Guards made a brilliant dash at the trenches, and, like a torrent, their resistless valour bore all before them, and for a few brief moments they got within hitting distance of the foe. Well did they avenge the slaughter of the Scots; the bayonets, like tongues of flame, passed above or below the rifles' guard, and swept through brisket and breastbone. Out of their trenches the Guardsmen tossed the Boers, as men in English harvest fields toss the hay when the reapers' scythes have whitened the cornfields; and the human sheaves were plentiful where the British Guardsmen stood. Then they fell back, for the fire from the heights above them fell thick as the spume of the surf on an Australian rock-ribbed coast. But the Guards had proved to the Boers that, man to man, the Briton was his master.

In vain all that day Methuen tried by every rule he knew to draw the enemy; vainly, the Lancers rode recklessly to induce those human rock limpets to come out and cut them off. Cronje knew the mettle of our men, and an ironic laugh played round his iron mouth, and still he stayed within his native fastness; but Death sat ever at his elbow, for our gunners dropped the lyddite shells and the howling shrap- nel all along his lines, until the trenches ran blood, and many of his guns were silenced. In the valley behind his outer line of hills his dead lay piled in hundreds, and the slope of the hill was a charnel-house where the wounded all writhed amidst the masses of the dead; a ghastly tribute to British gunnery. For hours I stood within speaking distance of the great naval gun as it spoke to the enemy, and such a sight as their shooting the world has possibly never witnessed. Not a shell was wasted; cool as if on the decks of a pleasure yacht our tars moved through the fight, obeying orders with smiling alacrity. Whenever the signal came from the balloon above us that the enemy were moving behind their lines, the sailors sent a message from England into their midst, and the name of the messenger was Destruction; and when, at 1.30 p.m. of Tuesday, we drew off to Modder River to recuperate we left a ghastly pile of dead and wounded of grim old Cronje's men as a token that the lion of England had bared his teeth in earnest.

Three hundred yards to the rear of the little township of Modder River, just as the sun was sinking in a blaze of African splendour on the evening of Tuesday, the 13th of December, a long, shallow grave lay exposed in the breast of the veldt. To the westward, the broad river, fringed with trees, ran murmuringly, to the eastward, the heights still held by the enemy scowled menacingly, north and south, the veldt undulated peacefully; a few paces to the northward of that grave fifty dead Highlanders lay, dressed as they had fallen on the field of battle; they had followed their chief to the field, and they were to follow him to the grave. How grim and stern those dead men looked as they lay face upward to the sky, with great hands clenched in the last death agony, and brows still knitted with the stern lust of the strife in which they had fallen. The plaids dear to every Highland clan were represented there, and, as I looked, out of the distance came the sound of the pipes; it was the General coming to join his men. There, right under the eyes of the enemy, moved with slow and solemn tread all that remained of the Highland Brigade. In front of them walked the chaplain, with bared head, dressed in his robes of office, then came the pipers, with their pipes, sixteen in all, and behind them, with arms reversed, moved the Highlanders, dressed in all the regalia of their regiments, and in the midst the dead General, borne by four of his comrades. Out swelled the pipes to the strains of "The Flowers of the Forest," now ringing proud and high until the soldier's head went back in haughty defiance, and eyes flashed through tears like sunlight on steel; now sinking to a moaning wail, like a woman mourning for her first-born, until the proud heads dropped forward till they rested on heaving chests, and tears rolled down the wan and scarred faces, and the choking sobs broke through the solemn rhythm of the march of death. Right up to the grave they marched, then broke away in companies, until the General lay in the shallow grave with a Scottish square of armed men around him, only the dead man's son and a small remnant of his officers stood with the chaplain and the pipers whilst the solemn service of the Church was spoken.

Then once again the pipes pealed out, and "Lochaber No More" cut through the stillness like a cry of pain, until one could almost hear the widow in her Highland home moaning for the soldier she would welcome back no more. Then, as if touched by the magic of one thought, the soldiers turned their tear-damp eyes from the still form in the shallow grave towards the heights where Cronje, the "lion of Africa," and his soldiers stood. Then every cheek flushed crimson, and the strong jaws set like steel, and the veins on the hands that clasped the rifle barrels swelled almost to bursting with the fervour of the grip, and that look from those silent, armed men spoke more eloquently than ever spoke the tongues of orators. For on each frowning face the spirit of vengeance sat, and each sparkling eye asked silently for blood. God help the Boers when next the Highland pibroch sounds! God rest the Boers' souls when the Highland bayonets charge, for neither death, nor hell, nor things above, nor things below, will hold the Scots back from their blood feud. At the head of the grave, at the point nearest the enemy, the General was laid to sleep, his officers grouped around him, whilst in line behind him his soldiers were laid in a double row, wrapped in their blankets. No shots were fired over the dead men resting so peacefully, only the salute was given, and then the men marched campwards as the darkness of an African night rolled over the far-stretching breadth of the veldt. To the gentlewoman who bears their General's name the Highland Brigade sends its deepest sympathy. To the mothers and the wives, the sisters and the sweethearts, in cottage home by hillside and glen they send their love and good wishes--sad will their Christmas be, sadder the new year. Yet, enshrined in every womanly heart, from Queen Empress to cottage girl, let their memory lie, the memory of the men of the Highland Brigade who died at Magersfontein.

SCOUTS AND SCOUTING.
DRISCOLL, KING OF SCOUTS.

ORANGE RIVER COLONY.

I have a weakness for scouts. Good scouts seem to me to be of more importance to an army in the field than all the tape-tied intelligence officers out of Hades. They don't get on well with the regular officers as a rule, because scouts are like poets--they are born, not manufactured. They are people who do not feel as if God had forsaken them for ever if they don't get a shave and a clean shirt every morning, they are just a trifle rough in their appearance and manners; but they ride as straight as they talk, and shoot straighter than they ride. They have to be built for the business. All the training in the world won't make a scout unless nature has commenced the job; mere pluck is not worth a dog's bark in this line of life, though without pluck no scout is worth a wanton woman's smile. A good scout wants any amount of courage; he wants a level head--a head of ice, and a heart of fire. He wants to know by instinct when to rush onward and chance his life to the heels of his horse and the goodness of God, and he wants to know with unfailing certainty when to crawl into cover and hide. He must understand how to ride with no other guide than the lay of the country, the course of the sun, or the position of the stars. He must have eyes that note every broken hill, every little hollow, every footprint of man or horse on the veldt.

He must be an excellent judge of distance, of time, of numbers. He must be able to tell at a glance whether a cloud of dust is caused by moving troops or by the action of the elements. Above all, he must be truthful, not given to exaggeration of his friends' strength or his enemy's weakness. When he makes his report it should need no corroboration. If a scout is worth his salt, his advice should be accepted and acted upon promptly.

I often go out with the scouts; they are the eyes of the army. A man who knocks around with scouting parties knows more, sees more, hears more of the real state of affairs than nine-tenths of the staff officers ever know, hear, or see. Men fresh from the Old Country seldom make good scouts. Take the Yeomanry, for instance. They are plucky enough, but not one in a hundred of them has the making of a scout in him. All his fathers and his grandfather's and his great-grandfather's breeding trends in other directions, and there is an awful lot more in the breeding of men than most folk imagine. The American makes a good scout. If he knows nothing of the life, he soon picks it up. So does the Australian, and the Canadian, and the Colonial-born South African. Something in the life appeals to them. They get the "hang" of it with very little trouble. There are some English-born men, however, who develop into rattling great scouts. These men are mostly adventurous fellows, who have roamed about the world, and had the corners knocked off them. I have two of them in my mind's eye just at present. One of them is an Irishman named Driscoll, Captain of the Scouts who are the eyes and ears of Rundle's army. The other is an Englishman named Davies, a captain in the same gallant little band. The first lieutenant is a Cape colonial of English extraction, named Brabant, a gallant son of a gallant general. Captain Driscoll is a typical Irishman, just such a man as the soul of Charles Lever would have revelled in, a man of dauntless daring, with a heart of iron, and a face to match. Strangely enough, the captain does not pride himself a bit on his pluck, but he thinks a deuce of a lot of his beauty. As a matter of fact, he has the courage of ten ordinary men, but he would not take a prize in a first-class beauty show. (Lord send I may be far from the reach of his revolver when this reaches his eye.) He has that dash of vanity in his composition which I have found in all good Irishmen, and he prides himself far more on the execution his eyes have done amidst the Dutch girls than of the work his deadly rifle has wrought in the ranks of the Dutch mea Yet, if you want to know if Driscoll can shoot, just go to Burmah, where for ten years he held the position of captain in the Upper Burmah Volunteer Rifles. That was where I heard of him first, as the most deadly rifle and revolver shot in all the East.

The Boers know him now as the prince of rifle shots and the king of scouts. He is standing in the wintry sunlight just in front of my tent as I am writing, one hand on the bridle of his horse, rapping out Dutch oaths with a strong Cork accent to a nigger who has not groomed his pet animal properly. The nigger is very meek, for past experience has told him that Irish blood is hot, and an Irishman's boot quick and heavy. He is a picturesque figure, this Celtic scout leader, just such a picture as Phil May could bring to life on a sheet of paper with a few strokes of his master hand. He is about eleven stone in weight, and, roughly, five feet eight, clean cut and strong, with a face which tells you he was born in Cork, and had knocked about a lot in tropic lands; eight-and-thirty if he is a day, though he swears at night around the camp fire that the pretty Dutch girls have guessed his age as twenty-seven. He wears a slouch hat, around which a green puggaree coils lovingly. In his right hand his rifle rests as if it felt at home there. His coat is worn and shabby, khaki in colour; riding pants of roughest yellow cords, patched in places unspeakable, leggings around his sinewy calves, and feet planted in neat boots make up the whole man. He is clean shaven except for a moustache, dark brown in colour, which sprouts from his upper lip.

In his softer moments Driscoll tells us that it used to "cur-r-r-l" before he had the "faver" in Burmah, and on such occasions we assure him that it "cur-r-rls" even yet. It is more polite to agree with him than to cross him--and a lot safer. He is as full of anecdote as heaven is of angels, and I mean to use him in the sweet days of peace, unless some stay-at-home journalist niches him from me in the meantime. Driscoll and Davies are fast friends. The Englishman is not such a picturesque figure as the Irishman. Englishmen seldom are, somehow; but he is a man, a real white man, all over. He is rather a good-looking, well set-up young fellow, who always looks as if he had just had a bath; not a dude by any manner of means, but a fellow with a soft eye for a pretty ankle, and a hard fist for a foe--one of those quiet chaps a man always likes to find close beside him in a row. Driscoll almost weeps over him to me sometimes. "He's the devil's own at close quarters," says the Irishman. "Never want a better chum when it comes to bashing the enemy. If he could only shoot a bit 'straighther and talk a bit sweether to the colleens he'd be perfect." All the same, I have, and hold, my own opinion concerning the "talking." Many a smile which the gallant Celt appropriated to himself as we rode out of a conquered town seemed to me to belong of right to the rosy-faced Welsh lad on the off-side. To hear these two men chatter over a glass of hot rum in my tent at night one would think they had never faced danger. Yet never a day goes by but one or the other of them has to run the gauntlet of Boer rifles; whilst Jack Brabant, who is death on cigars or anything else that will emit smoke, and who curls up and says little, has been near death so often that it will be no stranger to him when it comes in all its finality.

Driscoll was in Burmah when the news came of the first disaster to the Irish troops in South Africa. He threw up his business as lightly as a coquette throws up a midsummer lover, and started for the war. At Bombay he was stopped by a yard or two of red tape, and had to go back to Calcutta, where he used his Irish tongue to such purpose that he got a permit to leave India, and made his way to the scene of trouble. He first joined General Gatacre as orderly officer. Later he was attached to the Border Mounted Rifles as captain, and did splendid service at the battles of Dordrecht and Labuschagne's Nek In the latter place he was the first man to gallop into the Boer laager before the fight had ceased. Captain, then Lieutenant, Davies was as close to his side as a shadow to a serpent, and they only had fourteen men with them at the time. After this Driscoll, whose skill as a scout had been remarked on all sides, was ordered to form a body of fifty scouts to act as the very eyes of the rapidly moving Colonial Division under General Brabant. This was promptly done, most of the men picked being Colonial-born Britishers. Soon after the formation of his band, Driscoll, with fifty men, attacked Rouxville from four sides at once. Dashing in, he demanded surrender of the place, as if he had an army at his back to enforce his demands, a piece of Irish impudent valour that would have cost every man amongst the little band his life had the Boers known that he was unbacked. But they did not know it, and consequently surrendered, and he hoisted the British flag and disarmed the residents--a really brilliant piece of work, for which Driscoll's Scouts have up to date received no public credit.

The Scout and his men took a warm part in the, very warm fight at Wepener, where many a good Briton fell. He had lost a good few fellows in the many fights, but Driscoll's name soon charmed others to his little band. At Jammersberg Drift the Scouts were so badly mauled that over a fourth of their number were counted out, but the places of the fallen men were soon filled, and to-day the number is almost complete. Driscoll has one especially good quality. He never speaks slightingly of his enemy unless he well deserves it. Few men have had so many hand-to-hand encounters with the burghers as he has; few men have held their lives by virtue of their steady hand on a rifle as frequently as this wild, good-natured, merry Irish-man has done. Yet of the Boer as a fighter he speaks most highly. "He don't like cold steel, and shmall blame to'm," says Driscoll, "but for the clever tactics he's a devil of a chap, 'nd the men who run him down are mostly the men who run away from him. They're not all heroes, any more than all women are angels. Some of 'em are fit only for a dog's death, but most of 'em are good men; and if I wasn't an Irishman I wouldn't mind being a Boer, for they've no call to hang their heads and blush when this war is over."

I asked him if he had ever of his own knowledge come into contact with any-thing savouring of white flag treachery. "Once I did," said the great scout, and for a while his eyes were filled with a sombre fire which spoke of the volcano under the genial human crust. "Onct," and he lapsed into the brogue as he spoke; "only onct, and there's a debt owin' on it yet which has got to be paid. It was at Karronna Ridge. I was out wid me scouts, 'nd I saw a farmhouse flying the white flag--a great flag it was, too, as big as a bed sheet. I'm not sure that it was not wan, too. I rode towards it, thinking the people wanted to surrender, and sent two of me men, two young lads they were--good boys, eager for duty. I sent 'em forward to ask what was the matther inside; and when they got within fifteen paces of the house the Boers inside opened fire from twenty rifles, and blew 'em out of the saddle. I had to ride with me little troop for dear life then, for the rocks all around us were alive with rifles. That house still stands; but if Driscoll's name is Driscoll it's going to burn, and the cur who flew the white flag in it, if I can get him, for the sake of the dead boys out on the veldt there. That's the only dirty trick I knew them play, and they must have been a lot of wasters, not like the general run of their fighters."

Three nights ago Driscoll, Davies, Brabant, and twenty men camped in a farm-house a long way from the British lines, for these men scour the country for many miles in all directions. The night was cold and rough, a bleak wind whistling amidst the kopjes half a mile away. Just as the scouts were sitting down to supper, the farm-er's wife rushed in, and said to Driscoll, in a voice between a sob and a scream, "Do you know, sir, that our burghers are in the kopjes, and are watching the farm?" and as she spoke she wrung her hands wildly. The Irish scout rose from the table and bowed, as only an Irish scout can bow, for the "vrow" was about thirty years of age, and pleasing to the eye beyond the lot of most women. "I am awfully glad to hear it, madam," he said in his execrable Dutch. "I've been looking for that commando for a week past. As they have doubtless sent a message by you, please send this back for me. Tell their officers, if they will accept an offer to come and dine with Driscoll's Scouts here to-night, they shall be made welcome to the best we have in the way of kindness. For it must be cold waiting outside in the wind. Tell them they shall go as they come, unmolested and unwatched, and in the morning we'll come out and give 'em all the fight they want in this world." Then, sweeping the floor with a graceful wave of his green puggareed soft slouch hat, Driscoll bowed the astonished dame out of the dining-room, whilst his officers and men nearly choked themselves with their hot soup, as they noticed him surreptitiously drawing a pocket mirror from his breeches pocket. For well they knew that the dare-devil leader was thinking far more of the effect his looks had had on the Dutch housewife than of the effect of his message on the enemy. Yet, at the first promise of dawn, he unrolled himself from his blanket on the hard floor, and was the foremost man to show in the open, where the enemy's rifles might reach him. But no rifles sounded, for the Boers had declined the invitation both to supper and breakfast.

HUNTING AND HUNTED.

ORANGE RIVER COLONY.

There is a funny side to pretty nearly every kind of tragedy if one only has the humorous edge of his nature sufficiently well developed to see it. Not that the humour is always apparent at the time--that comes later. I am led to these reflections as I watch Lieutenant "Jack" Brabant, of the Scouts, dancing a wild war dance round our little camp fire. He is a picturesque figure in the firelight, this thirty-year-old son of the renowned General Brabant, ten stone weight I should say, all whipcord and fencing wire, rather a hard-faced man; no feather-bed frontiersman this, but a tough, hard-grained bit of humanity, who has fought niggers and hunted for big game at an age when most young fellows are thinking more of poetry and pretty faces than of hard knocks and harder sport. I know him for a rattling good shot at either man or beast, a fine bushman, and a dandy horseman. He is a rather quiet fellow, as a rule, but all the quietness is out of him to-night, and he only wants to be stripped of his tight yellow jacket, cord breeches, leather gaiters, soft slouch hat with green puggaree, and then, given a coat of black paint, he would pass well for some warrior chief doing a death dance in the smoke. He is boiling with passion, his left fist, clenched hard as the head of an axe, moves up and down, in and out, like the legs of a kicking mule midst a crowd of cart-horses. In his right he swings his Mauser carbine, and a man don't need to be a descendant of a race of prophets to know that something has gone gravely wrong with the lieutenant, otherwise he would not be making a circus of himself in this fantastic fashion.

I lay my pencil aside for a minute or two to catch what he is saying, and when I have got the hang of the story I don't wonder he feels as mad as a wooden-legged man on a wet mud-bank. He had been out all day since the very break of dawn with a couple of scouts, searching the kopjes for a notorious Boer spy, whose cleverness and audacity had made him a thorn in our side. If there was a man in the British lines capable of running the "slim" Boer to earth, that man was Lieutenant Jack Brabant. It had been a grim hunt, for the spy was worthy of his reputation, and the pursuers had to move with their fingers on their triggers, and a rash move would have meant death. All the forenoon he dodged them, in and out of the kopjes, along the sluits, up and down the dongas; sometimes they pelted him at long range with flying bullets, sometimes he sent them a reminder of the same sort. And so the day wore on; but at last, towards evening, they fixed him so that he had to make a dash out across the veldt. He was splendidly mounted, and when the time came for a dash he did not waste any time making poetry. Neither did Brabant and his two men; they galloped at full speed after the fleetly flying figure, and when they saw that a broad and deep donga ran right across his track, cutting him off from the long line of kopjes for which he was making, they counted him as theirs. He only had one chance, to gallop into the donga, jump out of the saddle and fire at them as they closed in on him; and, as they rode far apart, it was a million to one on missing in his hurry in the fading light. But the gods had decided otherwise, for the whiplike crack of rifles suddenly cut the air, and the bullets fell so thick around the pursuers that the three men could almost breathe lead. Half a mile away, on the far side of the donga, appeared a squad of Yeomanry, blazing away like veritable seraphs at Brabant and his men, whilst they let the flying Boer go free. Brabant whipped out his handkerchief, and waved it frantically; but the lead only whistled the faster, and he had only one chance for his life, and that was to wheel and ride at full speed for the nearest cover, where he and his men hid until the Yeomen rode up. Then Brabant hailed them, and asked them what the devil they meant by trying to blow him and his men out of the saddle.

There was a pause in the ranks of the Yeomen, then a voice lisped through the gathering gloom, "Are you fellahs British?"

"Yes, d--n you; did you think we were springbok?"

"No, by Jove, but we thought you were beastly Booahs. Awfully sorry if we've caused you any inconvenience. What were you chasing the other fellah foah, eh?"

"Oh!" howled the disgusted backwoodsman with a snort of wrath, "we only wanted to know if he'd cut his eye tooth yet."

"Bah Jove," quoth the Yeoman, "you fellahs are awfully sporting, don't yer know."

"Yes," snarled the angry South African, "and the next time you Johnnies mistake me for a Booah and plug at me, I'll just take cover and send you back a bit of lead to teach you to look before you tighten your finger on a trigger."

Talking of the Yeomen brings back a good yarn that is going round the camps at their expense. They are notorious for two things--their pluck and their awful bad bushcraft. They would ride up to the mouth of a foeman's guns coolly and gamely enough, but they can't find their way home on the veldt after dark to save their souls, and so fall into Boer traps with a regularity that is becoming monotonous. Recently a British officer who had business in a Boer laager asked a commander why they set the Yeomen free when they made them prisoners. "Oh!" quoth the Boer, with a merry twinkle in his eye, "those poor Yeomen of yours, we can always capture them when we want them." This is not a good story to tell if you want an **encore**, if you happen to be sitting round a Yeoman table or camp fire.

But it is time I got back to the subject which lay in my mind when I sat down to write this epistle. The lieutenant's war dance took me off the track for a while, but I thought his story would come in nicely under the heading of "Hunting and Hunted." Camp life gets dull at times, so does camp food, the eternal round of fried flour cakes and mutton makes a man long for something which will remind him that he has still a palate, so when one of the scouts came in and told me that he had seen three herds of vildebeestes, numbering over a hundred each, and dozens of little mobs of springbok and blesbok, within ten miles of camp, away towards Doornberg, I made up my mind to ride out next day, and have a shot for luck. My friend Driscoll, captain of the Scouts, rammed a lot of sage advice into me concerning Boers known to be in force at Doornberg. I assured him that I had no intention of allowing myself to drift within range of any of the veldtsmen, so taking a sporting Martini I mounted my horse and set forth, intending to have a real good time among the "buck." At a Kaffir kraal I picked up a half-caste "boy," who assured me that he knew just where to pick up the "spoor" of the vildebeeste, and he was as good as his boast, for within a couple of hours he brought me within sight of a mob of about fifty of the animals, calmly grazing. I worked my way towards them as well as I could, leaving the "boy" to hold my horse; but, though I was careful according to my lights, I was not sufficiently good as a veldtsman to get within shooting distance before they saw me or scented me. Suddenly I saw a fine-looking fellow, about as big as a year-and-a-half-old steer, trot out from the herd. He came about twenty yards in my direction, and I had a grand chance to watch him through my strong military glasses. He looked for all the world like a miniature buffalo bull, the same ungainly head and fore-quarters, big, heavy shoulders, neat legs, shapely barrel, light loin, and hindquarters, the same proppy, ungainly gait. I unslung my rifle to have a shot at him, when he wheeled and blundered back to the herd, and the lot streamed off at a pace which the best hunter in England would have found trying, in spite of the clumsiness of their movements. The half-caste grinned as he came towards me with the horses, grinned with such a glorious breadth of mouth that I could see far enough down his black and tan throat to tell pretty well what he had for breakfast. This annoyed me. I like an open countenance in a servant, but I detest a mouth that looks like a mere burial ground for cold chicken. We rode on for a mile or two, and then saw a pretty little herd of springbok about eighteen hundred yards away on the left. Slipping down into a donga, I left the horse and crawled forward, getting within nice, easy range. I dropped one of the pretty little beauties. I tried a flying shot at the others as they raced away like magic things through the grass, which climbed half-way up their flanks, but it was lead wasted that time.

My coffee-coloured retainer gathered up the spoil, and paid me a compliment concerning my shooting, though well I knew he had sized me up as a "wastrel" with a rifle, for his shy eyes gave the lie to his oily tongue. We hunted round for awhile, and then from the top of a little kopje I saw a beautiful herd of vildebeestes one hundred and sixteen in number, lumbering slowly towards where we stood. The wind blew straight from them towards us, so that I had no fear on the score of scent. Climbing swiftly down until almost level with the veldt, I lay cosily coiled up behind a rock, and waited for the quarry. They came at last, Indian file, about a yard and a half separating one from the other, not a hundred and twenty yards from where I lay. I had plenty of time to pick and choose, and plenty of time to take aim, so did not hurry myself. Sighting for a spot just behind the shoulder, I sent a bit of lead fair through a fine beast, and expected to see him drop, but he did nothing of the kind. For one brief second the animal stood as if paralysed; then, with a leap and a lurch, he dashed on with his fellows. I fired again, straight into the shoulder this time, and brought him down; but he took a third bullet before he cried *peccavi*. I had a good time for pretty near the whole of that day, and was lamenting that I had not brought a Cape cart and pair of horses with me to bring home the spoil, when, happening to look into the face of my brown guide, I saw that his complexion had turned the colour of blighted sandalwood. He did not speak, but swift as thought ripped out his knife, and cut the thongs which bound the springbok and other trophies of the day's sport to his saddle, letting everything fall in an undignified heap on to the veldt. Then, without a word of farewell, or any other kind of word for that matter, he drove his one spur into the flank of his wretched nag, and fled round the bend of a kopje, which, thank Providence, was close handy, and as he went I saw something splash against a rock a dozen yards behind him. I had glanced hurriedly over the veldt the moment I caught that queer expression on the saffron face of my assistant, but as far as the eye could reach I could see nothing. Now, however, looking backwards, I saw three or four men riding out of a donga two thousand five hundred yards away.

Twenty-five seconds later I had caught and passed my fleeing servant, who was heading for some kopjes, which lay right in front, about a mile and a half away. As I passed him he yelled, "Booers, baas, Booers! Ride hard, baas, ride hard; there are three hundred in the donga." When I heard that item of news I just sat down and attended strictly to business, and I am free to wager that never since the day he was foaled had that horse covered so much ground in so short a space of time as he did by the time he reached the kopjes. My servant had adroitly dodged into a sluit which hid him from view, and I knew that he could work his way out far better than I could. Besides, if they captured him, the worst he would get would be a cut across the neck with a sjambok for acting as hunting-guide to a detested Rooitbaaitje; whilst as for me, they would in all probability discredit my tale concerning the hunting trip, and give me a free, but rapid, pass to that land which we all hope to see eventually, but none of us are anxious to start for; because a correspondent has no right to carry a rifle during war time, a thing I never do unless I am out hunting. I gave my tired horse a spell, whilst I searched the veldt with my glasses, then slipping through a gully I made my way out on to the veldt, got in touch with a donga that ran the way I wanted to travel, got into its bed, gave my horse a drink, and rode on until dark; then I made my way into camp, and religiously held my peace concerning the doings of that day, because I did not want the life chaffed out of me. A few days later I happened to call at the Colonial camp, and was asked to dine by one of the officers.

"Like venison?" he asked cheerily.

"Yes, when it comes my way," I replied.

"Got some to-day," he said. "It's nicely hung, too; not fresh from the gun."

"Shoot it yourself, eh?"

"Well, no, not exactly; was out on patrol on Monday, and saw a couple of lousy Dutchmen. They didn't think we were round, so were enjoying themselves shooting buck. We nearly got one of 'em with a long shot."

"Didn't they show fight?" I asked innocently.

"Fight?" he said, with scorn unutterable in his accent. "Not a bit of it. They dropped their game, and cleared as if a thousand devils were after them. I never saw men ride so fast."

"Positive they were Dutchmen?" I ventured.

"Yes," he laughed; "why, I'd know one of those ugly devils five miles off."

That settled me, and I said no more.

WITH THE BASUTOS.

When the Eighth Division was skirting the borders of Basutoland I thought it would not be a waste of time to cross the border, and if possible interview one of the chiefs. My opportunity came at last. Our general decided to give his weary men a few days' rest, so getting into the saddle at Willow Grange I rode to Ficksburg, and there crossed the River Caledon, whose yellow waters, like an orange ribbon, divide Basutoland from the Free State. At this point the river runs between steep banks, and when I crossed it was about deep enough to kiss my horse's girths, though I could well believe that in the flood season it becomes a most formidable torrent. An artificial cutting has been made on both sides to facilitate the passage of traders, black and white, but even there the ford is so constituted that the Boers on the one side and the blacks on the other could successfully dispute the passage of an invading army with a mere handful of men.

Once across the river one soon felt the influence of Jonathan, the "black prince." The niggers, naked except for the loin cloth, swaggered along with arms in their hands, and grinned with insolent familiarity into our faces. They may have an intense respect and an unbounded love for the British--I have read scores of times that they have--but I beg leave to doubt it. Physically speaking they are a superb race of men, these sable subjects of our Queen. Their heads sit upon their necks with a bold, defiant poise, their throats are full, round, and muscular, their chests magnificent, broad and deep, tapering swiftly towards the waist. Their arms and legs are beautifully fashioned for strong, swift deeds. Strip an ordinary white man and put him amongst those black warriors, and he would look like a human clothes rack. They walk with a quick, springy step, and gave me the impression that they could march at the double for a week without tiring. But they are at their best on horseback. To see them barebacked dash down the side of a sheer cliff, plunge into the river, swim their horses over, and then climb the opposite bank when the face of the bank is like the face of a wall is a sight worth travelling far to see.

There are many things in this world that I know nothing at all about, but I do know a horseman when I see him, for I was bred in a land where nine-tenths of the boys can ride. But nowhere have I seen a whole male population ride as these Basuto warriors ride, and the best use England can make of them is to turn them into mounted infantry. Give them six months' drill, and they will be fit to face any troops in Europe. I never saw them do any fighting, but they carry the fighting brand on every lineament--the bold, keen eye, the prominent cheek-bone, the hard-set mouth, the massive jaw, the quivering nostril, the swing and spring of every movement, all speak the fighting race.

And their women; what of them? From the back of the head to the back of the heel you could place a lance shaft, so straight are they in their carriage. Their dress is a bunch of feathers and the third of a silk pocket handkerchief, with a copper ring around the ankle and another around the wrist. They do most of the daily toil, such as it is, though I know of no peasant population in any other part of the world who get a living as easily as these folk. The men allow the women to do most of the field labour, but when the grain is bagged the males place it in single bags across the back of a pony, and so take it to market. They walk beside the tiny little ponies and balance the grain slung crosswise on the animal's back, and when the grain has been sold or bartered they bound on to their ponies and career madly homewards, each one trying to outdo his neighbour in deeds of recklessness in the hope of winning favour in the eyes of the dusky maidens. They are mean in regard to money or gifts, and know the intrinsic value of things just as well as any pedlar in all England. Judging the "nigger" merely as a human being, irrespective of sentiment, colour, and so forth, I can only say that in my estimation he and his are far better off in every respect than the average white labourer and his family in England. These folk have plenty to eat, little to do, and are very jolly. They would be perfectly happy if they only had a sufficient number of rifles and a large enough supply of ammunition to enable them to drive every white man clean away from their borders.

When I arrived at Jonathan's village that warrior was away with a band of his young men, so that I could not see him, though I saw his son at a wedding which was being held when I reached the scene. I was taken through rows of naked, grinning savages, of both sexes, to be introduced to the bride and bridegroom, whom I found to be a pair of mission converts. When I saw the pair the shock nearly shook my boots off. The bride, a full-blooded young negress, was dressed in a beautiful white satin dress, which fitted her as if it had been fired at her out of a gun. It would not meet in front by about three inches, and the bodice was laced up by narrow bands of red silk, like a foot-baller's jersey. In her short, woolly hair she had pinned a wreath of artificial orange blossoms, which looked like a diadem of snow on a mid-winter mudheap. Down her broad back there hung a great gauzy lace veil, big enough to make a fly-net for a cow camel in summer. It was not fixed on to her dress, nor to her wreath, but was tied on to two little kinky curls at each side of her head by bright green ribbons, after the fashion of a prize filly of the draught order at a country fair. Her hands were encased in a pair of white kid gloves, man's size, and a pretty big man at that, for she had a gentle little fist that would have scared John L. Sullivan in his palmiest days.

When I was introduced to the newly shackled matron she put one of those gloved hands into mine with a simpering air of coyness that made me feel cold all over, for that hand in the kid glove reminded me of the day I took my first lesson from Laurence Foley, Australia's champion boxer, and he had an eight-ounce glove on (thank Heaven!) on that occasion. In her right hand the bride carried a fan of splendid ostrich feathers, with which she brushed the flies off the groom. It was vast enough to have brushed away a toy terrier, to say nothing of flies, but it looked a toy in that giant fist.

The groom hung on to his bride's arm like a fly to a sugar-stick. He was a tall young man, dressed in a black frock coat, light trousers, braced up to show that he wore socks, shoes, white gloves, and a high-crowned hat. He carried his bride's white silk gingham in one hand, and an enormous bunch of flowers in the other. He tried to look meek, but only succeeded in looking sly, hypocritical, and awfully uncomfortable. At times he would look at his new spouse, and then a most unsaintly expression would cross his foxy face; he would push out his great thick lips until they threw a shadow all round him; open his dazzling white teeth and let his great blood-red tongue loll out until the chasm in his face looked like a rent in a black velvet gown with a Cardinal's red hat stuffed in the centre. He may have been full of saving grace--full up, and running over--but it was not the brand of Christianity that I should care to invest my money in. When he caught my gaze riveted upon him, he tried to look like a brand plucked from the burning; he rolled his great velvet-black eyes skyward, screwed up the sluit which ran across his face, and which he called a mouth, until it looked like a crumpled doormat, folded his hands meekly over his breast, and comported himself generally like a fraudulent advertisement for a London mission society.

From him I glanced to his "Pa," who had given him away, and seemed mighty glad to get rid of him. "Pa" was dressed in pure black from head to heel--just the same old suit that he had worn when he struck this planet, only more of it. He was guiltless of anything and everything in the shape of dress except for a large ring of horn which he wore on top of his head. He did not carry any parasols, or fans, or geegaws of any kind in his great muscular fists. One hand grasped an iron-shod assegai, and the other lovingly fondled a battle-axe, and both weapons looked at home where they rested. He was not just the sort of father-in-law I should have hankered for if I had been out on a matrimonial venture; but I would rather have had one limb of that old heathen than the whole body of his "civilised" son, for with all his faults he looked a man. A chum of mine who knew the ways of these people had advised me to purchase a horn of snuff before being presented to the bride and groom, and I had acted accordingly.

When the ceremony of introduction was over, and I had managed to turn my blushing face away from "Ma" and the bevy of damsels, as airily clothed as herself, I offered the snuff box to the happy pair. The groom took a tiny pinch and smiled sadly, as though committing some deadly sin. The bride, however, poured a little heap in the palm of her hand about as big as a hen's egg, regardless of her nice white kid gloves. This she proceeded to snuff up her capacious nostrils with savage delight, until the tears streamed down her cheeks like rain down a coal heap. Then she threw back her head, spread her hands out palm downwards, like a mammoth duck treading water, and sneezed. I never heard a human sneeze like that before; it was like the effort of a horse after a two-mile gallop through a dust storm. And each time she sneezed something connected with her wedding gear ripped or gave way, until I began to be afraid for her. But the wreck was not quite so awful as I had anticipated, and when she had done sneezing she laughed. All the crowd except the groom laughed, and the sound of their laughter was like the sound of the sea on a cliff-crowned coast.

A little later one of the bridesmaids, whose toilet consisted of a dainty necklace of beads and a copper ring around one ankle, invited me to drink a draught of native beer. The beer was in a large calabash, and I felt constrained to drink some of it. These natives know how to make love, and they know how to make war, but, as my soul liveth, they don't know how to make beer. The stuff they gave me to drink was about as thick as boardinghouse cocoa; in colour it was like unto milk that a very dirty maid of all work had been stirring round in a soiled soup dish with an unwashed forefinger. It had neither body nor soul in it, and was as insipid as a policeman at a prayer meeting. Some of the niggers got gloriously merry on it, and sang songs and danced weird, unholy dances under its influence. But it did not appeal to me in that way, possibly I was not educated up to its niceties. All I know is that I became possessed of a strange yearning to get rid of what had been given me--and get rid of it early.

The wedding joys were of a peculiar nature. Bride and bridegroom, linked arm in arm, marched up and down on a pad about twenty yards in length, a nude minstrel marched in front, and drew unearthly music from a kind of mouth organ. Girls squatting in the dust *en route* clapped their hands and chanted a chorus. The groom hopped first on one leg and then on the other, and tried to look gorgeously happy; the bride kicked her satin skirts out behind, pranced along the track as gracefully as a lady camel in the mating season; behind the principal actors in the drama came a regiment of youths and girls, and the antics they cut were worthy of the occasion. Now and again some dusky Don Juan would dig his thumb into the ribs of a daughter of Ham. The lady would promptly squeal, and try to look coy. It is not easy to look coy when you have not got enough clothes on your whole body to make a patch to cover a black eye; but still they tried it, for the sex seem to me to be much alike on the inside, whether they dress in a coat of paint or a coat of sealskin.

By-and-by the groom took his bride by the arm, and made an effort to induce her to leave her maids of honour and "trek" towards the cabin which henceforth was to be her home. The lady pouted, and shook his hand off her arm; whilst the maidens laughed and clapped their hands, dancing in the dust-strewn sunlight with such high kicking action as would win fame for any ballet dancer in Europe. The young men jeered the groom, and incited him to take charge of his own. He hung down his ebony head and looked sillily sullen, and the bride continued to "pout." Have you ever seen a savage nigger wench pout, my masters? Verily it is a sight worth travelling far to see. First of all she wraps her mouth in a simper, and her lips look like a fold in a badly doubled blanket. Then slowly, she draws the corners towards, the centre, just as the universe will be crumpled up on the Day of Judgment. It is a beautiful sight. The mouth, which, when she smiled, looked like a sword wound on the flank of a horse, now, when the "pout" is complete, looks like a crumpled concertina. The groom again timidly advanced his hand towards the satin-covered arm of his spouse, and the "pout" became more pronounced than ever. The white of one eye was slyly turned towards the bridesmaids, the other rolled with infinite subtlety in the direction of him who was to be her lord and master; and the "pout" grew larger and larger, until I was constrained to push my way amidst the maids to get a look behind the bride, for I fancied the back of her neck must surely have got somehow into the front of her face. When I got to the front again the "pout" was still growing, the rich red lips in their midnight setting looking like some giant rose in full bloom that an elephant's hoof had trodden upon. So the show proceeded. At last one of the bridesmaids stepped from amidst her sisters, and playfully pushed the bride in the direction of her home. Then the "pout" gave way to a smile, the white teeth gleaming in the gap like tombstones in a Highland churchyard. I had been a bit scared of her "pout," but when she smiled I looked round anxiously for my horse. After a little manoeuvring, the blissful pair marched cabinwards, with the whole group of naked men and maids circling round them, stamping their bare feet, kicking up clouds of dust like a mob of travelling cattle. The men yelled some barbarous melody, flourished their arms, smote upon their breasts, and anon gripping a damsel by the waist circled afar like goats on a green grass hill slope. The maids twisted and turned in fantastic figures, swaying their nobly fashioned bodies hither and thither, whilst they kept up a continuous wailing, sing-song cry. So they passed from my sight into the regions of the honeymoon, and the clubbings and general hidings which follow it.

I only stayed a few days amongst these savages, but, short as my stay was, I arrived at the conclusion that the sooner they are disarmed the better. There are hundreds of white women living upon isolated farms within easy riding distance of the

Basuto villages, and as we are disarming the husbands and brothers of these women it is our solemn duty to see that the savage warriors have not the means within their reach to injure or outrage those whom we have left practically defenceless. It is true that these women are the wives, daughters, and sisters of our enemy, but surely in all England there does not breathe a man so poor in spirit as to wish to place them at the mercy of a horde of barbarians. Ours is a grave responsibility in regard to this matter. Just at present the native warriors are quiet in their kraals, but a day will surely dawn when the younger and more turbulent fighting men will lust for the excitement of war. They look upon the Boer farmers who dwell near their borders as so many interlopers, whose title deeds were signed by the rifle, and they long for the time to come when they can sweep them backwards with the strong arm. They never speak of the land close to their border as the Free State. They call it with deadly significance the "conquered territory," and the idea of reconquest is strong in their minds. Of old time the Boer farmers stood ever ready to defend what they had conquered with the rifle, and the nigger had learned to dread the Dutch rifle as he dreads few things in this world. To-day he knows that the Boer is helpless, and is unsparing in his insolence to his old-time foe. Later on friction between the white man and the black is certain to ensue, and if he has the upper hand the black man will not stop at mere insolence.

I don't know how the Imperial Parliament may feel about it, but I do know that if there is wrong done the Boers by the blacks, the South African farmers of British blood will rise like one man to defend the men and women of their own colour. They will never permit the black man to dominate the white, and that will cause friction between the Colonists and the Imperial Government. There is more in this than may meet the eye at the first glance, for if the Colonists rise to battle with the blacks the Imperial troops will have to assist them whether the Government of the day likes or dislikes it, or else we shall see the Colonists of our own blood clamouring for the withdrawal of British rule in South Africa, and we shall hear again the cry for a South African Republic. Not a "Dutch" South African Republic next time, but a blended nationality, and Colonial Britons and Colonial Dutchmen will be found fighting side by side under one flag, for one common cause.

Surely, if it is not wise to allow the whites to carry arms, it is not wise or right to allow sixty thousand fierce fighting men to remain fully equipped and mounted.

To me it seems that now, whilst we have two hundred and fifty thousand fighting men in Africa to overawe and intimidate the warriors, we should take from them, by force if necessary, everything in the shape of warlike weapons. White men are not permitted in any of our Colonies to ride or strut about the country armed to the teeth. Therefore, I ask, why should these negroes be privileged to do what Australians or Canadians are forbidden to do? They have no valid excuse for being in possession of weapons of war. They have now no enemies capable of attacking them upon their borders. There is no animal life of a savage or dangerous character near them, and their armament is a menace to the public safety. If their young men will not settle down to the peaceful calling of husbandmen, tillers of the soil, and breeders of stock, let them be drafted into our Army for service abroad. If there is not enough for the more elderly men to do in the farming line, let them turn their energies towards the development of the diamond mines and gold mines that lie within their borders--mines which at present they will not work themselves nor allow any white man to work.

I have spent a good many years of my life exploring new mineral territory, and have seen much of the best auriferous country known to modern times; but that Basuto country, presided over and held by a mere gang of black barbarians, ought, in my estimation, to be one of the richest gems in the British diadem. That good payable gold-bearing rock exists there I know beyond question. I also know beyond all doubt that diamonds are to be easily won from the soil, and I am thoroughly cognisant of the fact that at least one, and I believe many, quicksilver mines can be located there. Others who know the country well have told me of coal and tin and silver mines, and samples have been shown to me which made my mouth water. Yet, all this wealth, which nature's generous hand has scattered so liberally for the use of mankind, is jealously locked away year by year by men who, in their savage state, have no use for it themselves, yet will not, upon any consideration whatever, grant a mining concession to a white man, no matter what that white man's nationality may be. Verily, the heathen badly want educating, and we have now 250,000 of the right kind of schoolmasters within handy reach of them.

MAGERSFONTEIN AVENGED.

THABA NCHU.

When, a few months ago, I stood upon the veldt almost within the shadow of the frowning brow of Magersfontein's surly heights, and looked upon the cold, stern faces of Scotland's dead, and listened to the weird wailing of the bagpipes, whilst Cronje gazed triumphantly down from his inaccessible mountain stronghold upon his handiwork, I knew in my soul that a day would dawn when Scotland would demand an eye for an eye, blood for blood. I read it written on the faces of the men who strode with martial tread around the last sad resting-place Of him they loved--their chief, the dauntless General Wauchope. Vengeance spoke in the sombre fire that blazed in every Scotsman's eye. Retribution was carved large and deep on every hard-set Scottish face; it spoke in silent eloquence in the grip of each hard, browned hand on rifle barrels; it found a mute echo in each knitted brow, and leapt to life in every deep-drawn breath; it sparkled in each tear that rolled unheeded and unchecked down war-scarred cheeks, and thundered in the echo of the men's tread across the veldt, right up to Cronje's lines, as they marched campwards. The Highland Brigade had gazed upon its dead; and neither time, nor change, nor thought of home, or wife, or lisping babe, would wipe the memory of that sight away until the bayonet's ruthless thrust gave Scotland quittance in the rich, red blood of those who did that deed.

That hour has come. The men who sleep in soldiers' graves beside the willow-clad banks of the Modder River have been avenged. Or, if the debt has not been paid in full, the interest owing on that bond of blood has at least now been handed in. It was not paid by our Colonial sons; not from Australian or Canadian hands did the stubborn Boers receive the debt we owed. They were not Irish hearts that cleared old Scotland's legacy of hate on that May Day amidst the African hills; it was not England's yeoman sons who did that deed. But men whose feet were native to the heather, men on whose tongues the Scottish burr clung lovingly--the bare-legged kilted "boys" whom the lasses in the Highlands love, the gallant Gordons.

Let the tale be told in Edinburgh Town; let it ring along the Border; let the lass, as she braids the widow's hair, whisper the story with love-kissed breath; let the lads, as they come from their daily toil, throw out their chests for the sake of their breeding; let the pessimist turn up the faded page of history, written when the world was young, and find, if he can, a grander deed done by the sons of men since the morning stars sang together.

So to my tale. It was the 1st of May. We had the Boers hard pressed in Thaba Nchu in a run of kopjes that reached in almost unbroken sequence farther than a man's eye might reach. The flying French was with us, chafing like a leashed grey-hound because he could not sweep all before him with one impetuous rush. Rundle, too, was here, with his haughty, handsome face, as keen as French, but with a better grip on his feelings. Six thousand of the foe, under Louis Botha, cool, crafty, long-headed, resourceful, have held the kopjes. Again and again we manoeuvred to trap them, but no wolf in winter is more wary than Botha, no weasels more watchful than the men he commanded. When we advanced they fell back, when we fell back they advanced, until the merest tyro in the art of war could see that a frontal at-tack, unless made in almost hopeless positions, was impossible. So Hamilton swept round their right flank, ten miles north of Thaba Nchu, and gave them a taste of his skill and daring, whilst Rundle held their main body here at Thaba Nchu. Rundle made a feint on their centre in strong force, and they closed in from both flanks to resist him. Then he drew off, as if fearing the issue. This drew the Boers in, and they pounded our camp with shells until one wondered whether the German-made rub-bish they used would last them much longer. Then we threatened their left flank quickly and sharply, giving Hamilton time to strike on their right; and he struck without erring, whipping the enemy at every point he touched, driving them out of their positions, and holding them firmly himself, so threatening their rear and the immense herds of sheep and oxen they have with them, making a footing for the British to move on and cut Botha off from his base at Kroonstad.

Whether he will now stand his ground and fight or make a break for the main army of the Boers is hard to calculate, for the Boer generally does just what no one expects he will attempt to do. It was during Hamilton's flanking effort that the Gordons vindicated their character for courage. Captain Towse, a brave, courteous soldier and gentleman, whom I had had the pleasure of meeting at Graspan, and whose guest I had been on several occasions, was the hero of the hour. He is a fine figure of a man, well set up, good-looking, strong, active. He was, I think, about the only soldier I have seen who could wear an eye-glass and not lose by it. In age he looked about forty. I remember snapping a "photo" of him as he was "tidying up" the grave of gallant young Huddart, an Australian "middy," who lay buried on the veldt; but the Boers collected that portrait from me later on, worse luck. On this fateful day Captain Towse, with about fifty of the Gordons, got isolated from the main body of British troops, and the Boers, with that marvellous dexterity for which they are fast becoming famous, sized up the position, and determined upon a capture. They little dreamt of the nature of the lion they had snared in their toils. With fully two hundred and fifty men they closed in on the little band of kilted men, and in triumphant tones called upon them to throw down their arms and surrender. It was a picture to warm an artist's heart. On all sides rose the bleak, black kopjes, ridge on ridge, as inhospitable as a watch-dog's growl. On one hand the little band of Highlanders, the picturesque colours of their clan showing in kilt and stocking, perfect in all their appointments, but nowhere so absolutely flawless as in their leadership. Under such leaders as he who held them there so calm and steady their forbears had hurled back the chivalry of France, and had tamed the Muscovite pride, and they were soon to prove themselves men worthy of their captain.

On the other side rose the superior numbers of the Boers. A wild and motley crew they looked compared with the gem of Britain's army. Boys stood side by side with old men, lads braced themselves shoulder to shoulder with men in their manhood's prime, ragged beards fell on still more ragged shirt fronts. But there were manly hearts behind those ragged garments, hearts that beat high with love of home and country, hearts that seldom quailed in the hour of peril. Their rifles lay in hands steady and strong. The Boer was face to face with the Briton; the numbers lay on the side of the Boer, but the bayonet was with the Briton.

"Throw up your hands and surrender." The language was English, but the accent was Dutch; a moment, an awful second of time, the rifle barrels gleamed coldly towards that little group of men, who stood their ground as pine trees stand on their mountain sides in bonny Scotland. Then out on the African air there rang a voice, proud, clear, and high as clarion note: "Fix bayonets, Gordons!" Like lightning the strong hands gripped the ready steel; the bayonets went home to the barrel as the lips of lover to lover. Rifles spoke from the Boer lines, and men reeled a pace from the British and fell, and lay where they fell. Again that voice with the Scottish burr on every note: "Charge, Gordons! Charge!" and the dauntless Scotchman rushed on at the head of his fiery few. The Boer's heart is a brave heart, and he who calls them cowards lies; but never before had they faced so grim a charge, never before had they seen a torrent of steel advancing on their lines in front of a tornado of flesh and blood. On rushed the Scots, on over fallen comrades, on over rocks and clefts, on to the ranks of the foe, and onward through them, sweeping them down as I have seen wild horses sweep through a field of ripening corn. The bayonets hissed as they crashed through breastbone and backbone. Vainly the Boer clubbed his rifle and smote back. As well might the wild goat strike with puny hoofs when the tiger springs. Nothing could stay the fury of that desperate rush. Do you sneer at the Boers? Then sneer at half the armies of Europe, for never yet have Scotland's sons been driven back when once they reached a foe to smite.

How do they charge, these bare-legged sons of Scotia? Go ask the hills of Afghanistan, and if there be tongues within them they will tell you that they sweep like hosts from hell. Ask in sneering Paris, and the red records of Waterloo will give you answer. Ask in St. Petersburg, and from Sebastopol your answer will come. They thought of the dreary morning hours of Magersfontein, and they smote the steel downwards through the neck into the liver. They thought of the row of comrades in the graves beside the Modder, and they gave the Boers the "haymaker's lift," and tossed the dead body behind them. They thought of gallant Wauchope riddled with lead, and they sent the cold steel, with a horrible crash, through skull and brain, leaving the face a thing to make fiends shudder. They thought of Scotland, and they sent the wild slogan of their clan ringing along the line until the British troops, far off along the veldt, hearing it, turned to one another, saying: "God help the Boers this hour; our Jocks are into 'em with the bay'nit!"

But when they turned to gather up those who had fallen, then they found that he whose lion soul had pointed them the crimson path to duty was to lead them no more. The noble heart that beat so true to honour's highest notes was not stilled, but a bullet missing the brain had closed his eyes for ever to God's sunlight, leaving him to go through life in darkness; and they mourned for him as they had mourned for noble, white-souled Wauchope, whose prototype he was. They knew that many a long, long year would roll away before their eyes would rest upon his like again in camp or bloody field. But it gladdened their stern warrior hearts to know that the last sight he ever gazed upon was Scotland sweeping on her foes.

And when our noble Queen shall place upon his breast the cross which is the soldier's diadem, their hearts will throb in unison with his, for their strong hands on that May Day helped him to win what he is so fat to wear; and when our Sovereign honours him she honours them, and well they know it. And when the years have rolled away, and they are old and grey, and spent with wounds and toil, fit for nothing but to dandle little grand-babes on their knees, young men and maids will flock around, and pointing out the veteran to the curious stranger say, with honest pride, "He was with Towse the day he won the cross."

THE CONDUCT OF THE WAR.

ORANGE RIVER COLONY.

There are hundreds of men lying in unmarked graves in African soil to-day who ought to be alive and well, others who have been done to death by the crass ignorance, the appalling stupidity, the damnable conceit which will brook no teaching. I have seen men die like dogs, men who left comfortable homes in the old land to go forth to uphold the power and prestige of our nation's flag. I have seen them gasping out their lives like stricken sheep, just in the springtide of their manhood, when the glory and the lust of life should have been strong upon them I have watched the Irish lad with the down upon his brave boyish face pass with the last deep-drawn quivering sob over the border line of life, into the shadows of the unsearchable beyond, a wasted sacrifice upon the grim altar of incapacity. I have seen the kilted Scottish laddie lie, with hollow cheeks and sunken eyes, waiting for the whisper of the wings of the Angel of Death. I have seen the death damp gather on his unlined brow, and watched the grey pallor creep upwards from throat to temple; until my very soul, wrung with anguish unutterable, has risen in hot revolt against the crimes of the incapable.

I have knelt by England's fair-faced sons, the child of the cities, the boy from the fens, the youth from the farm, and watched the shadows creeping over eyes that mothers loved to look upon. I have seen the wasted fingers, grown clawlike, plucking aimlessly at the rude blankets as if weaving the woof of the winding-sheet, and have listened with aching heart to the aimless babbling of the dying, in which home and friends were blended, until the tired voice, grown aweary with the weight of utterance, died out like the crooning of a lisping child, as the soul slipped through the golden gateway that leads to the glory beyond the grave. I have watched them pile the earth above the last home of Cambria's sons, the gallant children of the old Welsh hills. I have seen them laid to sleep, as harvest hands will lay the sheaves in undulating rows when the summer shower has passed; and over every shallow grave I have sent a curse for those whose brutish folly caused the flower of Britain's army to wither in the pride of their peerless boyhood.

For the men who fall in battle we can flush our tears with pride, and though our hearts may ache for those we love, yet is there an undercurrent of hot joy to know they fell as soldiers love to fall, face forward to the foe. But for those who die, as more than half of Britain's dead have died in this last war, stricken by pestilence brought about by ignorance and indolence, we have only sorrow and tears and prayers, blended with hate and contempt for the triple-dyed dandies and dunces who robbed us of those who should have been alive to-day to be the bulwark of the Empire, the pride of the nation, and the joy of many homes.

Why did they die, these strong young soldiers of our Queen? Was it because their hearts failed them in the presence of hardship and danger? I tell you, No. The hardships of the campaign only roused them to greater exertions. Bravely and uncomplainingly they answered every call of duty, ready by night or day to go anywhere, or do anything, if only they were led by men worthy of our Queen's commission, worthy of the cloth they wore. Why did they die? Was it because of poisoned or polluted water, left in their path by the enemy whom they were fighting? Not so. No, not so. The Boers left no death-traps in our path. Why did they die? Was it because the country through which we marched lent itself climatically to the propagation and dissemination of fever germs? No, England, no! In all the world there is no finer climate than that in which our gallant soldiers died like rotting sheep. Wherever else the blame may lie, no truthful man can lay the blame of those untimely graves upon the climate or the country of our enemies.

I will tell you why they died, and tell you in language so plain that a wayfaring man, even though a fool, cannot misunderstand me, for the time has arrived when the whole Empire should know the truth in all its native hideousness. Those men were done to death by wanton carelessness upon the part of men sent out by the British War Office. They were done to death through criminal neglect of the most simple laws of sanitation. Men were huddled together in camp after camp; they were allowed to turn the surrounding veldt and adjacent kopjes into cesspools and excreta camps. In some camps no latrines were dug, no supervision was exercised. The so-called Medical Staff looked on, and puffed their cigarettes and talked under their eye-glasses--the fools, the idle, empty-headed noodles. And whilst they smoked and talked twaddle, the grim, gaunt Shadow of Death chuckled in the watches of the night, thinking of the harvest that was to follow.

Then the careless soldiers passed onward, leaving their camp vacant, and later came another batch of soldiers. Perhaps the men in charge would be men of higher mental calibre; they would order latrines to be dug, and all garbage to be burnt or buried. But by this time the germs of fever were in the air, the men would sicken and die, just as I have seen them sicken and die upon a score of mining fields away in the Australian bush; and all for the want of a little honest care and attention, all for the want of a few grains of good, wholesome, everyday common sense. Had proper care been taken in regard to these matters, four-fifths of those who now fill fever graves in South Africa would be with us, hale and hearty men, to-day.

But, England, you must not complain. "Tommy" is a cheap article; he only costs a few pence per day, and if he dies there are plenty more ready and willing to take his place. Don't think of him as a human being. Don't think of him as some woman's husband and breadwinner. Don't think of him as some grey-haired widow's son, whose support he has been. Don't think of him as some foolish girl's heart's idol. But think of him as a part of the country's revenue. Think of him as "One-and-fourpence a day."

What excuse can or will be made by the authorities for the wholesale murder of our men I know not. Possibly those high and haughty personages will sniff contemptuously and decline to give any explanation at all. And you, who hold the remedy in your own hands, what will you do? Will you at election times put a stern question to every candidate for the Commons, and demand a straight and unqualified answer to your questions. Remember this: You supply the men who do the fighting; the nation at a pinch can do without a Roberts, a Duller, or a Kitchener, but, as my soul liveth, it cannot do without "Tommy."

If you want Army reform, you must commence with the "Press gang"; you must stand in one solid mass firmly behind those war correspondents who have not feared to speak out plainly. You must send men to the Commons pledged to stand behind them also, men who will not flinch and allow themselves to be flouted by every scion of some ancient house; for if you do not support the war correspondents of the great newspapers, how are you ever to know the real truth concerning the doings of our armies in the field? I tell you that you have not heard one-millionth part of the truth concerning this South African enterprise, and now you never will know the truth. Had the abominable practice of censorship been abolished prior to this war, most of the abuses which have made our Army the laughing stock of Europe would have been set right by the correspondents, for they would have pointed out the evils to the public through the medium of their journals, and an indignant people would have clamoured for reform in a voice which would brook no denial. As things are at present, the military people during the progress of the war have their heel upon the necks of the journalists, and the public are robbed of what is their just right, the right of knowledge of passing events; only that which suits the censor being allowed to filter over the wires. Had it been otherwise, hundreds of young widows in Ireland, Scotland, England, and Wales would be proud and happy wives to-day.

But do not let me rouse your phlegmatic blood, my Britons; sit down, with your thumbs in your mouths, my masters, and allow a coterie to flout you at will, whilst the Frenchmen, the Germans, the Russians alternately laugh at and pity you. Pity you, the sons of the men who chased their fathers half over Europe at the point of the blood-red bayonet! Have you grown tame, have you waxed fat and foolish during these long years of peace? Is the spirit that swept the legions of France through the Pyrenees and carried the old flag up the heights of Inkerman in the teeth of Russian chivalry--is it dead, or only sleeping? If it but slumbers, let me cry, Sleeper, awake, for danger is at the gates! Not the danger due from foreign foes, but a greater danger--the danger of unjust government, for where evil is hidden injustice reigns.

Our military friends tell us that censorship of Press work is necessary for the welfare of the Army. They urge that if we correspondents had a free hand the enemy might gain valuable information regarding the movements of our troops. To us who for the greater portion of a year have been at the front there is grim irony in that assertion. Fancy the Boer scouts wanting information from us which might filter through London newspapers! That flimsy, paltry excuse can be dismissed with a contemptuous laugh. That is not why the military people want our work censored. The real reason is that their awful blunders, their farcical mistakes, and their criminal negligence may not reach the British public. Just try for one brief moment to remember some of the "censored" cables that have been sent home to you during the war, and then compare it with such a cable as this, which would have come if the Press men had a free hand:

"Kruger's Valley, Jan. 12.

"The ---- Division, under General ----, arrived at
Kruger's Valley four days ago. No latrines have been
dug ... weather terribly hot, with rain threatening.
This Division moves out in about a week. Its place will
be taken by troops just arrived at Durban from England.
Should we have rain in the meantime half the new draft
will be down with enteric fever before they are here a
week, and the death rate will be simply awful. General ----
and staff will be responsible for those deaths."

The military folk would, doubtless, designate such a telegram "a piece of d----d impudence."

But the latrines would be dug, the camp would be kept free from foulness, and the new draft would not die untimely deaths, but would live to fight the enemies of their country.

Why the camps in South Africa were not models of cleanliness passes my comprehension. There was no need to harass "Tommy" by setting him to do the work. Every Division was accompanied by swarms of niggers, who drew from Government L4 10s. per month and their food. These niggers had a gentleman's life. They waxed fat, lazy, and cheeky. Four-fifths of them rode all day on transport wagons, and never earned a fourth of the wages they drew from a sweetly paternal Government. Why could not those men have been used in every camp to make things safe and comparatively comfortable for "Tommy," who had to march all day, with his fighting kit upon his back march and fight, and not only march and fight, but go on picket and sentry duty as well? Those niggers ought to have, been turned out to dig and fill in latrines for our soldiers, they ought to have been compelled to do all the menial work of the camps; but they never did anything of the sort "Tommy" was treated for the most part like a Kaffir dog, whilst the saucy niggers led the lives of fightingcocks, and to-day any ordinary Army Service nigger thinks himself a better man than "Tommy," and doesn't hesitate to tell you so. It would be instructive to know the name of the genius who fixed the scale of nigger wage at L 4 10s. per month, with rations. Fully half that sum could with ease have been saved the British taxpayer, and the nigger would have taken it with delight, and jumped at the chance of getting it. As a matter of fact, the nigger has had a huge picnic, and has been well paid for attending it. He has never been kept short of food. He has never had to march until his feet were almost falling off him. He has not had to fight for the country that fed and clothed him. Poor "Tommy!"

HOME AGAIN.

I stood where Nelson's Column stands--a stranger, and alone. Alone amidst a mighty multitude of men and maids. I saw a people drunk with joy. I looked from face to face, and in each flashing eye, and on each quivering lip, a nation's heart lay bared to all the world, for England's capital was but the throbbing pulse of England's Empire. Our nation spoke to the nations that dwell where the sea foam flies, and woe to them who do not heed the tale that the city told. There was no sun, the city lay enveloped in silvery shadows, like some grey lioness that knows her might and is not quickly stirred to wrath or joy, like meaner things. I looked above, and saw the monument of him whose peerless genius gave us empire on the seas. I looked below, and saw, far as my eyes could range, a seething mass of men, as good, as gallant, and as great of heart as those who fought and fell beneath his flag, and in my blood I felt the pride of empire stirring, and knew how great a thing it is to call one's self a Briton.

I looked along that swaying mass of human flesh and blood, and saw the best that England owns waiting to welcome, with heart-stirring cheers, the gallant lads whose lion hearts had carried London's name and fame along the rough-hewn tracks of war. I saw the cream of Britain's chivalry and Britain's beauty there. Men and women from the countryside, from Ireland and from Scotland, all eager to pay tribute to the London lads who had so proudly proved to all the world that it was not for a soldier's pay, not for the love of gain, but for a nation's glory that they had risked limb and life beneath an African sun. Then, as I looked, I caught a distant hum of voices--a far-off sound, such as I have heard amid Pacific isles when wind and waves were beating upon coral crags, and foam-topped rollers thrashed the surf into the magic music of the storm-tossed sea. It was the roar of London's multitudes welcoming home her own; and what a sound it was! I have heard the music of the guns when our nation spoke in the stern tones of battle to a nation in arms; I have heard the crash of tempests on Southern coasts when ships were reeling in the breath of the blast, and souls to their God were going; I have crouched low in my saddle when the tornado has swept trees from the forest as a boy brushes flowers with his footsteps. But never had I heard a sound like that. It was the voice of millions, it was the great heart-beats of a mighty nation, it was a welcome and a warning--a welcome to the descendants of the 'prentice lads of Old London, a warning to the world. I caught the echoes in my hands, I hugged them to my heart, I let them pour into my brain, and this is the tale they told: "Sluggish we are, ye people, slow to wake, strong in the strength of conscious might. Jibe at us, jeer at us, flout us and threaten us; but beware the day we turn in our strength. We have sent forth a few of our children, but they were but as a drop in the ocean. All Britain sent two hundred and fifty thousand strong men to Africa; London, if need be, can send five hundred thousand more to the uttermost parts of the earth. Aye, and when they have died, as these would have died if need be, we can open our hearts and send five hundred thousand more, and yet be strong for our home fighting." It was a nation speaking to the nations, and that is the tale it told. Let the nations take heed and beware, for the language was the language of truth.

I listened; and lo! through the storm of cheering, through the cries of women and the strong shouting of men in their prime, I caught another sound, a sound I knew and loved--the sound of marching men. Music hath charms to stir the blood and make men mad, but there is no music in all the earth like the trained tread of men who have marched to battle. I knew the rhythm of that tread; I knew that the "boys" of Old London were coming, and my nostrils seemed filled with the fumes of fighting. I looked again, and, saw them, hard faced, clean limbed, close set, as soldiers should be who have faced the storm and stress of war, as proud a band as Britain ever had, soldier and citizen both in one, fit to be a nation's bulwark and a nation's trust; and in the crowd around them there were a thousand thousand men as good, as game, as gritty, as they, for they were the children of the people, the men of the shop-counter, the men of the city office, the men of every artisan craft, the very vitals of London. They had sprung from the womb of the city, and the city could give birth to a million more if need be.

I saw them pass amidst a storm of cheers, and I, who had seen them out on the

African veldt under the foeman's guns, lifted up my voice to cheer them onward, for well I knew that there was nothing in the gift of England that they were not worthy of, those children of the "flat caps," those offspring of the 'prentice lads of London. I knew how they had starved; I knew how they had suffered through the freezing cold of the African winter; I knew how gallantly, how uncomplainingly, they had marched with empty bellies and aching limbs, ready to go anywhere, to do anything, ready to fight, and, if it were the will of the great God of Battles, ready to lay down their young lives and die. I knew those things, and, knowing them, gave them a cheer for the sake of Australia, for the sake of the kinship which binds us as no bonds of steel could bind us and them. I heard a voice at my knee whimpering, the voice of a gutter kid, who had dodged in there out of the way of the police. I looked at his ragged clothes, looked at his grimy face, looked at his hands, which looked as if they had never looked at soap, and I said: "What are you yelping for, kiddie?" And he, looking up at me through his tears, fired a voice at me through his sobs, and said: "I'm yelping, mister, because I'm only a little 'un, and can't see me mates come home from the war." Then I laughed, and tossing him up on my shoulder let him jamb his dirty fist on the only silk hat I possess, whilst he looked at his "mates" march home; for they were his mates--he was a child of London, and some day--who knows?--he may be a general.

The Codes Of Hammurabi And Moses
W. W. Davies

QTY

The discovery of the Hammurabi Code is one of the greatest achievements of archaeology, and is of paramount interest, not only to the student of the Bible, but also to all those interested in ancient history...

Religion   **ISBN:** *1-59462-338-4*   **Pages:132**
MSRP $12.95

The Theory of Moral Sentiments
Adam Smith

QTY

This work from 1749. contains original theories of conscience amd moral judgment and it is the foundation for systemof morals.

Philosophy   **ISBN:** *1-59462-777-0*   **Pages:536**
MSRP $19.95

Jessica's First Prayer
Hesba Stretton

QTY

In a screened and secluded corner of one of the many railway-bridges which span the streets of London there could be seen a few years ago, from five o'clock every morning until half past eight, a tidily set-out coffee-stall, consisting of a trestle and board, upon which stood two large tin cans, with a small fire of charcoal burning under each so as to keep the coffee boiling during the early hours of the morning when the work-people were thronging into the city on their way to their daily toil...

Pages:84

Childrens   **ISBN:** *1-59462-373-2*   **MSRP $9.95**

My Life and Work
Henry Ford

QTY

Henry Ford revolutionized the world with his implementation of mass production for the Model T automobile. Gain valuable business insight into his life and work with his own auto-biography... "We have only started on our development of our country we have not as yet, with all our talk of wonderful progress, done more than scratch the surface. The progress has been wonderful enough but..."

Pages:300

Biographies/   **ISBN:** *1-59462-198-5*   **MSRP $21.95**

The Art of Cross-Examination
Francis Wellman

QTY

I presume it is the experience of every author, after his first book is published upon an important subject, to be almost overwhelmed with a wealth of ideas and illustrations which could readily have been included in his book, and which to his own mind, at least, seem to make a second edition inevitable. Such certainly was the case with me; and when the first edition had reached its sixth impression in five months, I rejoiced to learn that it seemed to my publishers that the book had met with a sufficiently favorable reception to justify a second and considerably enlarged edition. ..

Pages:412

Reference   ISBN: *1-59462-647-2*   *MSRP $19.95*

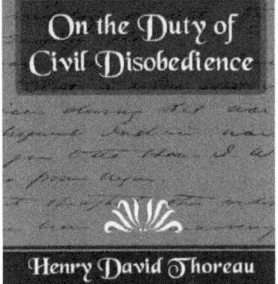

On the Duty of Civil Disobedience
Henry David Thoreau

QTY

Thoreau wrote his famous essay, On the Duty of Civil Disobedience, as a protest against an unjust but popular war and the immoral but popular institution of slave-owning. He did more than write—he declined to pay his taxes, and was hauled off to gaol in consequence. Who can say how much this refusal of his hastened the end of the war and of slavery ?

Law   ISBN: *1-59462-747-9*   **Pages:48**

MSRP $7.45

Dream Psychology Psychoanalysis for Beginners
Sigmund Freud

QTY

Sigmund Freud, born Sigismund Schlomo Freud (May 6, 1856 - September 23, 1939), was a Jewish-Austrian neurologist and psychiatrist who co-founded the psychoanalytic school of psychology. Freud is best known for his theories of the unconscious mind, especially involving the mechanism of repression; his redefinition of sexual desire as mobile and directed towards a wide variety of objects; and his therapeutic techniques, especially his understanding of transference in the therapeutic relationship and the presumed value of dreams as sources of insight into unconscious desires.

Pages:196

Psychology   ISBN: *1-59462-905-6*   *MSRP $15.45*

The Miracle of Right Thought
Orison Swett Marden

QTY

Believe with all of your heart that you will do what you were made to do. When the mind has once formed the habit of holding cheerful, happy, prosperous pictures, it will not be easy to form the opposite habit. It does not matter how improbable or how far away this realization may see, or how dark the prospects may be, if we visualize them as best we can, as vividly as possible, hold tenaciously to them and vigorously struggle to attain them, they will gradually become actualized, realized in the life. But a desire, a longing without endeavor, a yearning abandoned or held indifferently will vanish without realization.

Pages:360

Self Help   ISBN: *1-59462-644-8*   *MSRP $25.45*

www.bookjungle.com *email: sales@bookjungle.com fax: 630-214-0564 mail: Book Jungle PO Box 2226 Champaign, IL 61825*

QTY

The Rosicrucian Cosmo-Conception Mystic Christianity *by Max Heindel* ISBN: *1-59462-188-8* $38.95
The Rosicrucian Cosmo-conception is not dogmatic, neither does it appeal to any other authority than the reason of the student. It is; not controversial, but is; sent forth in the, hope that it may help to clear... New Age/Religion Pages 646

Abandonment To Divine Providence *by Jean-Pierre de Caussade* ISBN: *1-59462-228-0* $25.95
"The Rev. Jean Pierre de Caussade was one of the most remarkable spiritual writers of the Society of Jesus in France in the 18th Century. His death took place at Toulouse in 1751. His works have gone through many editions and have been republished... Inspirational/Religion Pages 400

Mental Chemistry *by Charles Haanel* ISBN: *1-59462-192-6* $23.95
Mental Chemistry allows the change of material conditions by combining and appropriately utilizing the power of the mind. Much like applied chemistry creates something new and unique out of careful combinations of chemicals the mastery of mental chemistry... New Age Pages 354

The Letters of Robert Browning and Elizabeth Barret Barrett 1845-1846 vol II ISBN: *1-59462-193-4* $35.95
by Robert Browning and Elizabeth Barrett Biographies Pages 596

Gleanings In Genesis (volume I) *by Arthur W. Pink* ISBN: *1-59462-130-6* $27.45
Appropriately has Genesis been termed "the seed plot of the Bible" for in it we have, in germ form, almost all of the great doctrines which are afterwards fully developed in the books of Scripture which follow... Religion/Inspirational Pages 420

The Master Key *by L. W. de Laurence* ISBN: *1-59462-001-6* $30.95
In no branch of human knowledge has there been a more lively increase of the spirit of research during the past few years than in the study of Psychology, Concentration and Mental Discipline. The requests for authentic lessons in Thought Control, Mental Discipline and... New Age/Business Pages 422

The Lesser Key Of Solomon Goetia *by L. W. de Laurence* ISBN: *1-59462-092-X* $9.95
This translation of the first book of the "Lernegton" which is now for the first time made accessible to students of Talismanic Magic was done, after careful collation and edition, from numerous Ancient Manuscripts in Hebrew, Latin, and French... New Age/Occult Pages 92

Rubaiyat Of Omar Khayyam *by Edward Fitzgerald* ISBN:*1-59462-332-5* $13.95
Edward Fitzgerald, whom the world has already learned, in spite of his own efforts to remain within the shadow of anonymity, to look upon as one of the rarest poets of the century, was born at Bredfield, in Suffolk, on the 31st of March, 1809. He was the third son of John Purcell... Music Pages 172

Ancient Law *by Henry Maine* ISBN: *1-59462-128-4* $29.95
The chief object of the following pages is to indicate some of the earliest ideas of mankind, as they are reflected in Ancient Law, and to point out the relation of those ideas to modern thought. Religion/History Pages 452

Far-Away Stories *by William J. Locke* ISBN: *1-59462-129-2* $19.45
"Good wine needs no bush, but a collection of mixed vintages does. And this book is just such a collection. Some of the stories I do not want to remain buried for ever in the museum files of dead magazine-numbers an author's not unpardonable vanity..." Fiction Pages 272

Life of David Crockett *by David Crockett* ISBN: *1-59462-250-7* $27.45
"Colonel David Crockett was one of the most remarkable men of the times in which he lived. Born in humble life, but gifted with a strong will, indomitable courage, and unremitting perseverance... Biographies/New Age Pages 424

Lip-Reading *by Edward Nitchie* ISBN: *1-59462-206-X* $25.95
Edward B. Nitchie, founder of the New York School for the Hard of Hearing, now the Nitchie School of Lip-Reading, Inc, wrote "LIP-READING Principles and Practice". The development and perfecting of this meritorious work on lip-reading was an undertaking... How-to Pages 400

A Handbook of Suggestive Therapeutics, Applied Hypnotism, Psychic Science ISBN: *1-59462-214-0* $24.95
by Henry Munro Health/New Age/Health/Self-help Pages 376

A Doll's House: and Two Other Plays *by Henrik Ibsen* ISBN: *1-59462-112-8* $19.95
Henrik Ibsen created this classic when in revolutionary 1848 Rome. Introducing some striking concepts in playwriting for the realist genre, this play has been studied the world over. Fiction/Classics/Plays 308

The Light of Asia *by sir Edwin Arnold* ISBN: *1-59462-204-3* $13.95
In this poetic masterpiece, Edwin Arnold describes the life and teachings of Buddha. The man who was to become known as Buddha to the world was born as Prince Gautama of India but he rejected the worldly riches and abandoned the reigns of power when... Religion/History/Biographies Pages 170

The Complete Works of Guy de Maupassant *by Guy de Maupassant* ISBN: *1-59462-157-8* $16.95
"For days and days, nights and nights, I had dreamed of that first kiss which was to consecrate our engagement, and I knew not on what spot I should put my lips..." Fiction/Classics Pages 240

The Art of Cross-Examination *by Francis L. Wellman* ISBN: *1-59462-309-0* $26.95
Written by a renowned trial lawyer, Wellman imparts his experience and uses case studies to explain how to use psychology to extract desired information through questioning. How-to/Science/Reference Pages 408

Answered or Unanswered? *by Louisa Vaughan* ISBN: *1-59462-248-5* $10.95
Miracles of Faith in China Religion Pages 112

The Edinburgh Lectures on Mental Science (1909) *by Thomas* ISBN: *1-59462-008-3* $11.95
This book contains the substance of a course of lectures recently given by the writer in the Queen Street Hall, Edinburgh. Its purpose is to indicate the Natural Principles governing the relation between Mental Action and Material Conditions... New Age/Psychology Pages 148

Ayesha *by H. Rider Haggard* ISBN: *1-59462-301-5* $24.95
Verily and indeed it is the unexpected that happens! Probably if there was one person upon the earth from whom the Editor of this, and of a certain previous history, did not expect to hear again... Classics Pages 380

Ayala's Angel *by Anthony Trollope* ISBN: *1-59462-352-X* $29.95
The two girls were both pretty, but Lucy who was twenty-one who supposed to be simple and comparatively unattractive, whereas Ayala was credited, as her Bombwhat romantic name might show, with poetic charm and a taste for romance. Ayala when her father died was nineteen... Fiction Pages 484

The American Commonwealth *by James Bryce* ISBN: *1-59462-286-8* $34.45
An interpretation of American democratic political theory. It examines political mechanics and society from the perspective of Scotsman James Bryce Politics Pages 572

Stories of the Pilgrims *by Margaret P. Pumphrey* ISBN: *1-59462-116-0* $17.95
This book explores pilgrims religious oppression in England as well as their escape to Holland and eventual crossing to America on the Mayflower, and their early days in New England... History Pages 268

QTY

The Fasting Cure *by Sinclair Upton*   ISBN: *1-59462-222-1*   **$13.95**
In the Cosmopolitan Magazine for May, 1910, and in the Contemporary Review (London) for April, 1910, I published an article dealing with my experiences in fasting. I have written a great many magazine articles, but never one which attracted so much attention... New Age/Self Help/Health Pages 164

Hebrew Astrology *by Sepharial*   ISBN: *1-59462-308-2*   **$13.45**
In these days of advanced thinking it is a matter of common observation that we have left many of the old landmarks behind and that we are now pressing forward to greater heights and to a wider horizon than that which represented the mind-content of our progenitors...   Astrology Pages 144

Thought Vibration or The Law of Attraction in the Thought World   ISBN: *1-59462-127-6*   **$12.95**
by William Walker Atkinson   *Psychology/Religion Pages 144*

Optimism *by Helen Keller*   ISBN: *1-59462-108-X*   **$15.95**
Helen Keller was blind, deaf, and mute since 19 months old, yet famously learned how to overcome these handicaps, communicate with the world, and spread her lectures promoting optimism. An inspiring read for everyone...   Biographies/Inspirational Pages 84

Sara Crewe *by Frances Burnett*   ISBN: *1-59462-360-0*   **$9.45**
In the first place, Miss Minchin lived in London. Her home was a large, dull, tall one, in a large, dull square, where all the houses were alike, and all the sparrows were alike, and where all the door-knockers made the same heavy sound...   Childrens/Classic Pages 88

The Autobiography of Benjamin Franklin *by Benjamin Franklin*   ISBN: *1-59462-135-7*   **$24.95**
The Autobiography of Benjamin Franklin has probably been more extensively read than any other American historical work, and no other book of its kind has had such ups and downs of fortune. Franklin lived for many years in England, where he was agent...   Biographies/History Pages 332

Name	
Email	
Telephone	
Address	
City, State ZIP	

☐ **Credit Card**   ☐ **Check / Money Order**

Credit Card Number	
Expiration Date	
Signature	

Please Mail to: Book Jungle
PO Box 2226
Champaign, IL 61825
or Fax to: 630-214-0564

ORDERING INFORMATION

web: *www.bookjungle.com*
email: *sales@bookjungle.com*
fax: *630-214-0564*
mail: *Book Jungle PO Box 2226 Champaign, IL 61825*
or PayPal *to sales@bookjungle.com*

Please contact us for bulk discounts

DIRECT-ORDER TERMS

**20% Discount if You Order
Two or More Books**
Free Domestic Shipping!
Accepted: Master Card, Visa,
Discover, American Express

www.ingramcontent.com/pod-product-compliance
Lightning Source LLC
Chambersburg PA
CBHW080730020726
47503CB00010B/2861